WITHIN

EACH

MAN

NOLAN CORDOVANO

1832

One

Within each man there lies a monster.

Words Lloyd Reed had never heard. Words to be snubbed were he to hear them, his body ravaged by lice and stinking of rotten fish. He'd slept the afternoon amongst their entrails; steaming mounds of viscera piled high and covered in flies. They sat along the waterfront in various stages of decay like glistening effigies offered up in payment to the sea and growing by the day as the fishmongers gutted their catches and discarded the remnants to packs of wild dogs who feasted and quarreled in endless barbarity along the bloodsoaked coast. From the piles rose a stench so foul not even the mosquitoes hunted there, and there Lloyd Reed rested his head.

Under moonlight he woke. On young legs eager to continue in heathenry he entered the taverns of Montague Street, the fetor of putrefaction all about him. It clung to the rags which were his clothing, rubbed onto the Creoles through whom he pushed and jostled. It permeated the coinpurse he drew from his pocket and remained there when he tucked it away again. The liquor cast down his throat and spilled on his person could not overtake the stench, which spread like a plague into the alehouses, the roadhouses, the public houses and the gambling alleys, and gave the harlot cause to turn her head away for stolen breaths while he quivered into her like a rutting animal.

What money he had was gone by morning. He ran his fingers through the seams of the coinpurse in hopes of some overlooked pocket and found none.

To the shore he returned. Dogs scurried from his path. He plopped into the sand and sprawled his limbs over piles of fish innards and stared drunkenly at the dawning sky, yet he found no rest. The dogs returned. They sniffed at his rags and growled when he shooed them away. He flipped to his side, to his belly, onto his back again, but sleep remained out of reach.

A rising sun lifted a cloud of must from the seaboard thick enough to choke on, thick enough to raise Lloyd up and send him staggering down the beach with no aim other than a lungful of breath. He lurched from his bedding place like a drowning man come up for air; gasping and squinting, a trail of stumbling footprints left in his wake as testament to his condition.

His boots harassed him. One of the outsoles had come loose from the toebox and flapped with each footfall. Enough to catch an ounce of beach and toss it upward. Granules sprayed against his face. Particles worked their way into his sock, ground against his skin. He shortened the stride of one foot to redirect the sand forward, which resulted in a limp that, from a distance, resembled a hobbled old man roaming destitute along the wharf.

The tide had turned. Boats had reached their buoys, nets stretched across their decks. Those unfit for fishing sat in solace on dryland. Busted vessels, whitehalls. An old slaver whose keel had rotted away and served as home to half the mongrels on the beach.

At sea or at land, all but one; a seven-meter-long dory caught up on a sandbank with the tide receding. The boatman stood waist-deep in the swell with a shoulder against the stern, an arm stretched over the gunwale, cursing.

Lloyd stopped his hobbling and spun around the way he'd come. The boot sole doubled up and he tripped forward with his arms flailing out like a crane taking flight. Without grace he landed. The sound of his name came barking across the water and he righted himself and turned to it.

"Lloyd, Goddamnit," the boatman's free arm gesticulated an order.

Up the shoreline from where Lloyd had come was nothing. A dog with mange, fish carcasses in the distance, nothing more. He looked at the dog and the steaming heaps of innards and swallowed.

"Lloyd!"

To the sea he turned. The shoreline faded behind him. Water filled his boots, lapped against his thighs. It rose above his waist and dropped again as he slogged eyes-down past the boatman and came abreast of the dory. He pressed his hands against the hull. Beneath his feet the sandbank shifted. It gave way in pieces under the force of his legs.

From the seagull's view they were but two specks in the ocean; the skinny one in front laboring with his back arched, muffled grunts, the stutter of the boat inching forward on each swell, while behind him Gordon Blackwood cursed the heavens, cursed Lloyd, equated his predicament in some incoherent fashion with the whores of Montague Street, and fell entirely underwater when the dory at last wriggled free of its bondage and pitched forward.

Lloyd pulled himself dripping over the gunwale and seated himself with his back wedged in the bow while Gordon fought to haul his girth from the water. An ungainly exertion that, when finished, left the two staring at each other from bow to stern with the empty hull between them.

"Well get to the bloody oars then," Gordon said finally. "I'm of half a mind to take one up and crush your dratted skull in. You've got any excuse for yourself?"

Lloyd crawled to the center thwart. He took an oar in each hand and pulled at them with his eyes on his captain who sat in the stern and glowered back. The oars rattled in the oarlocks. A thunking sound slapped over the water with each pull.

Still a distance from the buoys, Gordon started up again. "Nothing," he paused to wipe something stringy from his nostril. "Just show up when the fancy strikes you. Drunk still-- is that the idea? It's written on you like a goddamn mountebank. God knows who gave you the money. I told you this was an everyday job, not a come-as-you-please affair."

"I ain't drug you off that sandbank so's you can curse me," said Lloyd.

"It's me that pays your wage, remember that."

"You ain't paid me."

"Pull starboard, you're drifting."

"I said you ain't paid me nothing. I been at it a month."

"Starboard is that way," Gordon motioned past Lloyd's ear. "Is this what you'd like to get paid for? Port, starboard," he jabbed at the sides of the boat accordingly. "I get paid on the fish I catch, and there are no fish when you disappear for three days and row in circles. I've given you a simple job; pull the bloody oars."

Lloyd pulled. The oars rattled in the locks. Swells broke dull and hollow against the bow.

The boatman wiped his nose again. "I know when a month is,

you needn't remind me. You'll get your pay. I don't need your complaints-- I don't give you mine. Not four days ago I was robbed of my coinpurse. Took my jacket off and when I put it on again the pocket was empty. That's the problem with gutting fish on the beach; it's not only the dogs that are mongrels, it's the refuse of this town. Thieves and whores is all it is, the whole damn city. All of New Orleans. I find the delinquent and I'll gut him same as the fish, God help me."

The buoys securing the net were two seetonnens stolen from the Georgia coast. They bobbed like giant pine cones; massive conical barrels banded with fourteen iron hoops and anchored with stone blocks through which wrought iron chains ran up to the mooring rings. Across their oaken tops were carved their owner's insignias.

As the dory drew closer Lloyd raised the oars over the gunwales and dropped them onto the bottom boards. Under Gordon's frown he stumbled to the bow and bent his waist over the breasthook where he waited with arms outstretched for the boat to reach the netting. He stared at the insignias as he had done on each trip to the nets, though Gordon's blade had long since rendered them undecipherable. Still, he eyed them.

"Pull the bloody net over," Gordon's bellowing brought him out of his fixation, "and quit your dawdling."

Lloyd obeyed. The net came over the gunwales to pin the dory between the buoys. Gordon leaned from the stern with an arm extended. He grabbed the netting and pulled it until it stretched across the width of the boat. Fish hung suspended by the gills. They fell onto the bottom boards with violent shakes of the men's wrists. As they pulled the dory athwart between the buoys its interior filled with red snapper and grouper, wet and glistening and writhing about in the hopelessness of fish out of water, their eyes unblinking under the sun.

Halfway between the seetonnens they pulled another yard of netting from the water and revealed a two-foot section torn away. Gordon ground his teeth. His face reddened and he looked across the net to where Lloyd sat as though he'd found a likely culprit.

Lloyd said nothing. Several fish remained caught up by the gills and he set to work releasing them until the boatman quit his glaring and turned to rummage under the sternsheets.

"All the fish in the sea and it wouldn't do," Gordon labored to speak while dragging the repair box over the boards. "Holes in the nets, fresh tar on the buoys. The oarlocks need greasing. That fool docker wants his cut for standing about, and in a moment of carelessness a man's pockets will be turned out. You see that?"

Lloyd looked up from his work. Gordon pointed a finger at the shoreline.

"The slaver?"

"Aye. It held men's fortunes between its hulls-- in its time."

"It's only the keel gone bad," said Lloyd. "Patch it and I reckon it'd float. I been inside, I seen its chains is still hanging."

"Doesn't matter if it floats," Gordon popped the latch. He swung open the lid. "Hasn't mattered for a quarter of a century. You can thank Jefferson for that, and all the rest of the sons of bitches in Washington. Hold this."

Lloyd took the twine in his hands. "Who's Jefferson?"

"Thomas Jefferson."

"Who's that?"

Gordon took his eyes from the repair box and cast them on his bowman. "You've never heard of Thomas Jefferson?"

"I don't reckon."

"How old are you?"

"I can't say exactly."

"How does a man not know his own bloody age?"

"I never been told it."

"You must at least be twenty."

"I could be twenty-one or I could be twenty-two. That's how I figure it."

"And in all that time you've never heard of Thomas Jefferson."

Lloyd only held the twine and waited, his eyes red-rimmed from drink.

"It doesn't matter. Hold these," Gordon extended net needles and a seine float and gave them an impatient shake until Lloyd took them. Next came a rusted blade and this too was added to Lloyd's holdings. "Jefferson is the swine who made the trade illegal. Took the future from my father's hands and led me to this misery," he waved his knuckles at the sea. "The Blackwood family name: synonymous with ruin. But there's still a way."

"Slaving?"

"If you're smart about it-- if you grease the right palms. It's happening all around us: in the Caribbean, Cuba. It's happening in South America. It's happening right here in the bloody marshes if a man knows where to look, and by God I know where to look. Here now, cut me a length."

Lloyd pinched the seine in his armpit and shoved the needles in a trouser pocket. With his hands unburdened he cut an arm's length of twine and passed it to Gordon.

"Stretch the net out for me."

Lloyd dropped the blade into his pocket, forced the twine in after, and took hold of the net with the seine still clamped under his arm. Gordon bent his head to his work. Lloyd studied the top of it; the thinning hair, sunburned ears poking out amongst the grey.

"Needles."

Lloyd pulled the twine from his pocket. The rest came tumbling out with it-- the blade, the needles and, lastly, the coinpurse, which landed on the dying grouper like a monogramed bonnet to crown their heads.

From opposite sides of the net they stared at it, bowman and boatman, the swell clunking against the dory. Gordon made a sound, something that was not speech yet conveyed intent. It came with spittle and a red face. The scleras of his eyes bulged white and he stood, glowered across the net like a bull across a fence gate, then attempted to pull an oar from its rusted lock.

Lloyd scurried back past the forward thwart, up against the breasthook. Beyond that sloshed the sea. His body jerked when Gordon ripped the oar free. The oarlock came with it, rusted screws and shards of wood popping as it broke away from the gunwale. Only the net stretching tight across the dory separated the two men. Gordon pushed against it. Lloyd leaned back, pressed his back into the point of the bow, a whisper out of reach of the oar that came swinging over the net.

Another wheeze of fury sputtered from the boatman's lips. More spittle. He repositioned his hold on the oar handle and this time took a highstep into the net, his swing coming overhead like a hammer throw. It cracked when it hit the thwart plank. Another tenuous step forward into the net and Gordon's boots broke through, squished against the confusion of fish underfoot. He set his feet firmly on the bottom boards, drew the oar back across his shoulder.

Lloyd leaned further back and watched Gordon wind his torso

around. Seven feet of wood came whistling through the air and Lloyd dumped himself over the gunwale like a seal returning to water. He surfaced several seconds later, an arm's length from the oar that Gordon smacked upon the sea.

The boatman fell against the hull with his fat belly hanging over the edge and attempted another swing, but Lloyd was floating with the current, away from the dory, away from Gordon Blackwood.

"Goddamn you Lloyd," Gordon raised a fist. "Run back to where you came from. Go back to your wilderness, for if I find you I'll gut you open and bleed you dead."

But his words were absorbed by ocean, and Lloyd floated like a seetonnen unshackled from its moorings, dipping and rising with the movement of the water until the dory was hidden by the swells that carried him shoreward. The churn of the sea forced its way down his throat. He flailed, closed his mouth uselessly against it. Long before he reached dryland his stomach purged a hot stream of bile into the saltwater. When he crawled at last onto the beach, dragging behind him wilted tendrils of green and brown and malodorous seaweed, it was like some ancient creature slithering out of viking lore, some aberration of the sea; a reptilian man that bowed his head and convulsed in violent retches until he collapsed to his back with his face to the sun and bits of vomit clinging to his lips.

No one was there to see him. Boats were out to sea, the fishmongers waited upshore. A pack of dogs ignored him, they'd cornered a bitch and took no interest in his wretchedness. He came to his feet finally and trampled through the sand with his boot sole flapping all the way to the muck-covered bricks of Montague Street where pigs wallowed in mud puddles and the feces of all manner of hoofed animals sat like banquets for the swarming flies. He avoided the filth much the same as the passerby steered their paths clear of him. Food consumed his thoughts. The hangover had left him, his newly emptied stomach grumbled.

In back of a tavern he came upon an inebriated man who had fallen unconscious behind a mule cart. Between the man's fingers was a crust of bread. At Lloyd's approach he woke. He flung his arms out and cursed, his free hand brandishing a knife, and Lloyd turned from the man's rantings and ran until his legs tired. He found no food that day. When night came he laid his head on a section of wooden planking beneath a bridge and closed his eyes but found no rest. Each footfall over the bridge was the boatman's step. Passing voices seemed to hold inflections of Gordon's speech. When at last he convinced himself of the safety of his refuge the storm came; a pent up drizzle that built to a shower. Water careened over the planking and he rose, cold and dripping, and wandered the unlit streets of New Orleans in the slapping rain.

His memory guided him to the harlot's window and he called up to her. For some time there came no answer. Only darkness in the window. He called again.

At last the shutters opened and she peered down at him standing on the paving stones while rainwater whipped about him.

"Qu'est-ce? Qu'est-ce que tu veux?"

"Hey," he said. "Let me come up. Remember me?"

"No."

"I saw you last night."

"You have money?"

Lloyd shook his head in the darkness. "No."

She made to close the shutters and he shouted up again. She paused, leaned out. *"Va-t-en. Tu pues."*

"Hey what's that mean? I don't speak that."

"You smell," she said. "Go away." She swung closed the shutters.

In the alleyways where he slept that night and the next, mosquitos swarmed in clouds of black, yet he stayed away from the beach. He scratched the bites and, on the second morning with a stolen chicken tucked under his arm, fled to the marshes where he wrung its neck and cooked it over a fire of palmetto wood. At night he returned to the city to wander the narrow streets where women stood with bare shoulders and painted faces. He had no money for them, nor for the taverns where his beggary was answered with threats of violence. At last he drifted back to the planking beneath the bridge and slept with his knees drawn into his chest though the night was not cold.

Before morning he was grabbed by the arms and heaved to his feet. The officers wore nothing to denote their legitimacy other than vigilante badges pinned to their shirt fronts. They spoke little English.

He was registered under his full name, Lloyd Raymond Reed, in the Third Municipality Jail and, after the officers and jailor convened in French, was placed in a cell filled with equally destitute-looking men. They kept their distance; the smell of his person had grown pungent. He stood with his back against a wall and studied the cell for signs of food.

Time passed. Twice he saw black slaves led down the corridor between the cells. He heard them first, the metallic clink of chains, and each time they passed he raised his head and watched them walk with iron shackles heavy on their ankles and rubbing raw the skin at their wrists. When the jailor came for him he was standing against the wall with his hands in his trouser pockets.

"Come," the accent was French, the mouth that spoke it

hidden under a long mustache.

Lloyd walked in front. The jailor instructed him to walk straight, turn, go through the door. On the other side was a table and two chairs. In one of them sat Gordon Blackwood.

"Sit," said the jailor.

Lloyd spun on his flopping boot sole but the jailor had closed the door and stood before it with his arms folded over his chest.

"I don't want nothing to do with him," said Lloyd.

"Monsieur Blackwood has paid your release."

"Give him his money back. I'll go back to the cell."

"Ce n'est pas possible."

"Let me go."

"Sit down, Lloyd," Gordon ordered.

"No."

Gordon came out of the chair onto his feet. Lloyd raised his palms.

"Sit down, goddamnit."

Lloyd sat.

"You want to go back to the cell? Because that's an option. You've seen these niggers parading around-- you'll be chained up with them and put on the public works. I'm here to give you a second option."

"You ain't here to help me."

"If you want out of this hole, you'll take what's offered."

Lloyd crossed his arms.

"I'll come for you tomorrow," said Gordon, "in the evening. All I need is for you to pull the oars and keep your mouth shut."

"Row for you?"

"And keep your mouth shut."

"This ain't working the nets."

"No it's not working the bloody nets," Gordon's face reddened and spittle had formed on his lips the way it did when his patience began to wane. "When a man sees a way forward he takes it. I've kept my eyes open, I've seen the world. And now it's opened itself belly-up to me. I need a man to handle the oars tomorrow night and you're that man. This is your way forward, Lloyd. That, or Monsieur De la Rue puts you on the public works. Doesn't matter if you're colored or white, he'll be paid."

Lloyd turned his head to the jailor. The man's face showed no expression, the mustache hadn't moved.

"What then?" Lloyd said. "After I row you."

"You go your own way."

"You gonna pay me?"

Gordon shot from the chair. In two strides he reached Lloyd. He curled his sea knuckles into a fist and smashed them into Lloyd's face and Lloyd fell, grunted when Gordon's boot caught him in the ribs, and only escaped another when De la Rue left his post to wrap his arms around Gordon Blackwood and pull at him like a man yanks a terrier off a rat.

Blood ran from Lloyd's mouth. It twisted along his jaw toward his ears and dried there like two rivers of burnt crimson that was not washed off but instead crusted over, reducing his face to some crude caricature of wretchedness that De la Rue found brooding in the shadows of the cell the following evening. The jailor pulled him out, no words spoken, nothing logged into the register, and tossed him into the street where Gordon waited with his big hands foreshadowing violence.

The dory was not moored at the wharf. It floated over a mile away, just outside the marshes where cypress branches bent like spider legs over the water. The bow line had been tethered around a makeshift piling of driftwood and when they reached it the moon had long since replaced the sun. By its hue shimmering over the still waters Lloyd unmoored it. He coiled the line and threw it over the side and climbed in. Gordon sat in the stern. The oarlock had been repaired. The netting was absent, the seines and hooks gone, the bottom boards cleared and emptied. Only Gordon, watching from the sternsheet, and Lloyd with his spine outlined against his shirt as he dipped the oars into the moonlit water.

He rowed for a quarter of an hour until they were deep in the swamplands and hidden from the world. At Gordon's direction he steered the dory further inland past tupelo trees and cypress covered in spanish moss, the limbs reaching out from the moonlight like fingers poised to pluck them from the dark. Along the banks came the sounds of bullfrogs and owls and the dry croaking calls of egrets that hushed at their approach and resumed at the dory's retreat.

Over an hour he rowed until, in a spot Lloyd found no different than any other, Gordon bent under the sternsheet and drew a lantern and blanket and crawled past him up to the bow with the boat rocking side to side. The lantern, once lit, revealed nothing. The yellow glow it cast forth was swallowed by the marshlands and blocked completely when Gordon draped it with the blanket. It shined again, was covered, the signal repeated twice more, and an order was barked in a whisper to stop rowing. They floated through the night sounds with the smell of decaying vegetation rising gaseous out of the bog.

Lloyd twisted his head around. Gordon leaned over the bow.

From the banks beyond him a second lantern blinked three times and vanished.

"Stay by the boat," Gordon whispered. "Don't tie it. Turn it around with the stern aground so we can load them easy. Keep your mouth shut and your eyes open."

Lloyd began a question but was hushed. The dory stuttered when its bow rode up a mudbank. Gordon climbed out and pushed at the breasthook, then turned and walked off with the lantern flinging light against the trees.

The dory drifted. Lloyd turned it with an oar and gave a backwards pull and the stern came to a stop again against the mud. He climbed out, still clenching the bow line, and stood in the trees a fair distance from the reach of the two lanterns. The slave broker held one at his side. Gordon held his own out before him. From its glow Lloyd saw a row of dark bodies sitting in the mud with the light dancing in muted reflection over their irons. Five men and a woman.

"Tell them to stand," said Gordon.

"Get up," said the broker. He raised his lantern and the chains jangled in response.

Gordon stepped closer. His face wrinkled in the flickering orange. "What is this?" he said.

"It's six. What we agreed upon."

"They were supposed to be fresh."

"They're alive and obedient."

"They're old and broken is what they are. They'll fetch no more price than what I'm paying."

"Nonsense. It's the light. Take a look at the girl there, her breasts haven't fallen, she's got good teeth."

"Show me."

Lloyd set the bow line in the mud and stepped closer. The six were linked together by chains strung through fetters at their hands and ankles. By the paltry glow of the lanterns he saw only shadows of their faces, but even in that light he could see there was no fight in them. They were nearly naked, rags of canvas cloth covered their genitals. The girl in question wore nothing above the waist. She was young. Her breasts firm. On her face a vacant look, except her eyes, wet with fear as the broker brought his hand to her mouth and pulled open her lips.

"You see that?" said the broker. "Good teeth, good gums. Someone'll want her, if not for the labor then for something soft to poke in the night." He laughed, showing the glint of his own teeth.

"Not if she's clapped up she won't," said Gordon. "I know the tricks."

"Look for yourself," the broker set the lantern in the mud. With both hands he wrenched down the girl's leggings, exposing her nakedness to the open air. He grabbed her ankles and spread them as far as the fetters would allow and waved Gordon in to inspect her genitals.

From where Lloyd stood she could not see him. He watched her turn her head away. She stared out into the cypress as if something in all that rotting swampland might free her from such crude examination, but there was only the croaking of the frogs that came forth, the smell of decay, and Gordon kneeling before her, lantern raised like a man inspecting livestock at auction.

"See?" said the broker. "She'll fetch a price."

"Maybe. Not these old men though."

"There's plenty of labor left in them. Come, look. This one speaks English," the broker stopped at a short man with heavy cheekbones protruding beneath his eyes. "Tell him you speak it."

The negro turned his eyes from one white man to the other. "I speak."

The broker drew from his belt a polished club and swung it into the negro's midsection. The man crumpled, bringing those on either side of him to the ground. The broker grabbed him immediately by the elbow and pulled him up. "There's one thing that'll never change-- their disobedience. You give them a word of praise and they respond with mockery," he placed the ball of the club under the man's chin and lifted it an inch. "Now tell Mister Blackwood here all about your good English."

"Dat right," the man's voice carried across the mudbank in wavering bass notes. It reached Lloyd clearly, yet he stepped forward to better hear it, still beyond the lantern's reach. "In adder time long 'go, I am linguister. Speak many lingo: Vai, Yaruba, Igbo, Hausa. Man speak lingo you no sabee, I make de parlay, one lingo to de adder. Dat anadder time, anadder worl', but I no lose nutting."

"You see that?" said the broker.

"That's pidgin. You said he spoke English."

"He makes himself understood-- it's all that matters. A man that can make sense out of those negro languages is worth twice any other."

They continued down the line, the two men with their lanterns before them, shining the light over the men's bodies, inspecting. Gordon paused to ask questions, to feel a man's neck, prod here or there in search of signs of ill health. He appraised their teeth and gums, their ears, necks, hands and genitals, down to the soles of their feet. When they reached the girl they stopped.

"You have the keys?" said Gordon.

"Of course," the broker produced them from his person. Two

keys on a brass ring.

Gordon nodded. He stood only an arm's length from the slave broker. With his free hand he reached into his vest and drew out a Deringer and fired it into the broker's neck. The reverberation clapped over the water, dissolved into silence. No bats or frogs or egrets, not even fireflies glistened in the wake of the report.

The broker stumbled back. He put a hand to his throat. Blood spewed from between his fingers. He fell to the mud, dropped the lantern. The flame hissed and went out.

"Lloyd!" shouted Gordon. Then again, "Lloyd! Help me find those keys. The fool's gone and flung them into the mud."

Lloyd's legs shook, he could not run. He felt a beating in his ears and he caught the eyes of the slaves staring frightened into the night from where he emerged like a spirit hidden away until called forth by the boatman who was bent over the ground like some crazed hunchback, scraping his feet over the muck and swinging the lantern to and fro.

Lloyd knelt at the far edge of its light. His breath came heavy. The drumming in his ears would not slow. He set his hands into the mud more to balance himself than anything else, and when the cold brass ring sunk into his palm he flinched. He clasped it, stood, turned to Gordon. The man was still bent, still scouring. Behind him the slave broker had risen, one hand still clamped against his throat. In the other, the club. He raised it, stepped out of the darkness in clumsy lurches and swung it into the base of Gordon's skull. The sound it made when it broke through the bone was a wet crunch like a foot breaking through thin ice. Gordon's body pitched forward. His limbs fell limp and doll-like with him. The broker flogged Gordon's head once more, though the first blow had thoroughly crushed it, and there on his knees the broker studied his handiwork in the last moments of his own life before finally sagging into the mud with blood still gurgling from his neck and percolating into the spilled brains of Gordon Blackwood.

For a long time Lloyd remained motionless. Long enough for the night sounds to fill the silence. The second lantern had extinguished where it had fallen. By the moonlight filtering through the cypresses Lloyd rose and walked to the boat. He cut wide around the two fallen men where they lay like lovers side by side. When he reached the dory he stopped and pivoted and waded back through the marshlands, back to the dead men, and turned out their pockets.

The Deringer was neither in Gordon's waistband nor his vest. Lloyd searched the mudbank up to where the water lapped, but it was lost. He returned to the bodies and opened their coats. Blood pooled beside them. Oily craters in the moonlight. It leaked over Lloyd's torn outsole and ran into his footprints.

He became aware again of the slaves only by the jangle of their chains as they came forward. He swung around. The linguist walked in front with his shackled wrists held high. His face made an expression common to all men when approaching danger. The palms of his hands were pink.

"Dem mens dead," said the linguist.

"I know it," said Lloyd. "I'm hunting his gun."

"Mebbe we help."

"I don't need your help."

"What you need?"

Lloyd looked at the short man and the five pairs of eyes lined up behind him. He'd not let go of the brass ring. He glanced down at it and back at the linguist and held it out. "This what you want?"

The man nodded.

"Here," Lloyd tossed it. "Now get out of here, I don't want nothing to do with you. This here's already enough problems."

The linguist retrieved the ring from the mud and slid the keyheads into the locks. A murmuring rose from the other five, a singsong pattern of syllables more foreign to Lloyd than what they spoke in the city. The linguist passed the keys down the line. Lloyd watched the fetters fall into the mud. He watched the slaves rub their wrists. Free of their chains, they remained in their places, chattering, miming exaggerated motions that made Lloyd forget the pistol and bend his head to watch. Different sounds came from different men, the linguist interjecting often, his throat reproducing the timbers of the others.

In unison they quieted and turned to Lloyd.

"You de boatman?" asked the linguist.

"That's the boatman," Lloyd motioned at Gordon. "I just row."

"But you got de boat."

"I do now."

"So you de boatman."

"I reckon."

"Mebbe you take us."

"Take you where?"

"Away," the linguist gestured to the darkness.

"I ain't taking you nowhere. Don't y'all have your own boat?"

"No."

"How'd you get here?"

"De boat bring us, but de boat no here no more. De time no right, de man leave. Two day here we wait for to come de slave man, dat man der," he pointed at Gordon. "Now he dead, you de boatman."

"Well I can't take you. Just go. Go that way," Lloyd pointed off in no particular direction.

"Dis aylaan. No way for to leave."

"I said I can't," Lloyd squinted through the cypresses to where the dory floated. Dawn was close to breaking.

"Only way on de boat."

Lloyd did not respond. He left the deadmen where they lay and splashed through the bogwater to the boat. The negroes followed behind. When he stopped they stopped in turn.

"None of y'all is going with me so there's no reason to follow."

"Why give us de key if you no tink to take us on de boat? Der allagedder in de wader."

"Ain't no alligators," Lloyd went on until he reached the dory. He climbed over the stern and drew an oar from the oarlock and put its end into the mudbank and pushed. The dory made a grating sound and became buoyant suddenly in the water.

The slaves stood at the edge of the bog. The sky was yielding to morning. Lloyd could see the umber of their skin like polished onyx against the cypresses. They broke into noise, an argument of sorts. Lloyd took a seat on the center thwart and heard the oars chunk as they hit the water.

"Wait!" The linguist splashed a few steps off the embankment and stopped knee-deep. His eyes were pried wide open and his cheekbones shone beneath his skin. "You help us, we help you."

"I already helped you," Lloyd took a pull at the oars. "And you ain't got nothing for me."

"We tell you where de gol' at."

Lloyd dropped the oar blades into the water. The dory stopped moving. "Tell me what?"

"Where de gol' at."

"Gold?"

"Kru man sabee," the linguist pointed at the tallest among them, a man with white hair and a white beard, his face wide and thick and silent.

"What's he know?"

"Long time 'go, his massa take him cross de river. Far. Where de rain no come. Long time he der, many year, see many ting. Dey fight de Spanish, de Indan. Dey fine de gol' der."

"How much?"

The linguist put the question to the Kru man who uttered something guttural in return.

"Lotta gol'," said the linguist.

The Kru man spoke again. The linguist leaned in. When the man finished the linguist gave his interpretation. "He say massa go wit whiteman sodger, fight de Spanish sodger in Spanish lan'. Dey take de wimmen, take de gol'. Take everting. But dey come back tru de lan' where de rain no fall, der altagedder diffren' sodger. Too many. So dey 'ide de gol'."

"How does he know where they hid it?" Lloyd rowed the dory closer.

"He know-- he de one who 'ide it. Den de Spanish sodger kill de whiteman sodger. Kru man go back to slave, dis time Spanish slave."

"Why doesn't he go back for it?"

"He tink he go back someday. Dat why he keep de stoory, no tell adder person. But he no go back. Too many buckra whiteman see him. What negro man wan wit gol'? Negro man no wan gol', negro man wan no be slave."

"He say all that?"

"Dis man Kru people, hard to unnerstan'. I say what he tink--

dat linguister job."

Lloyd leaned on the oars. He looked from the linguist to the Kru man and back again. "He gonna say where he hid it?"

"You take us in de boat."

Lloyd pressed his palms into the oar handles. The breaking of dawn had dulled the croaking of the swamplife, and by the eastern light cutting through the tupelos he regarded the woebegone figures, nearly naked, mist rising from the water like gaseous wraiths between the six of them and himself. "I can't take you nowhere," he said. "Anyone finds out I helped you and they'll kill me."

"It a lotta gol'."

Lloyd looked at his knee bones poking up beneath the trouser legs. The stink of the marsh seeped up his nose and stung his head. He looked at the Kru man again. "Just tell me where it is."

An exchange of sound volleyed between the linguist and the Kru man. Hand signals, a rise and fall of pitches. The linguist nodded at its finale. "He put it in de place where de Spanish sodger pray. De mishin. Everbody tink he bury de gol', but de Kru man smart, he no bury. He put it up 'aigh."

"What do you mean up high?"

"In de roof."

"Which mission?"

"Kru man no sabee dat."

"He doesn't know what mission?"

The linguist shrugged.

"He don't know the name of it or nothing?"

Another shrug.

Lloyd bent over the oar handles and waited, but nothing more followed. "Well that ain't worth nothing," he said. "That ain't worth nothing at all. You know how many missions there are?"

The linguist didn't answer. He swallowed and looked out over his cheekbones at Lloyd.

"That ain't worth nothing to me-- gold in some mission somewhere. Don't do me no good if you don't know which one."

"Der no more to tell. Now we go."

"Like hell."

"But we trap 'ere."

Lloyd shook his head.

"Take us," begged the linguist.

"Take you where?"

"To de shore."

"Then what, just let you go?"

The linguist nodded.

"There's daylight coming on-- I can't."

"But we die 'ere."

"You know what happens to a man who gets caught helping runaways? He gets hanged. That or shot."

"Please."

"Someone'll see us. They'll find Gordon dead in the swamp. They'll put me on the public works, work me till I'm near dead, then string me up by the neck."

"Help us."

"I got no reason to."

"We tell you 'bout de gol'."

"That story ain't worth nothing without the name of the mission," Lloyd rubbed his thumbs over the smooth wood of the oars. "I can't do nothing for you."

"But der nowhere to go. We die 'ere."

Lloyd took a position on the oars. The smell of decay rose from the water more profoundly than the stench in which Lloyd was wrapped. It floated on the air thick and humid, filled his lungs. His stomach turned.

He bent forward, the blades swung back.

"Dis a aylaan," the linguist called out. "Der allagedder 'ere, we trap 'ere."

The oars chunked the water, the boat pulled away.

The slaves stood watching him in the same formation as when the chains had bound them. Black bodies covered in rags. The Kru man stood tallest over them. At the end of the line was the girl, bare-breasted. She stood with her hands crossed over her pelvis. When the bark of a whooping crane sounded close by she only hunched her shoulders.

Lloyd didn't look up. He took a hard pull at the oars and kept on pulling until the six figures disappeared behind the cypress branches.

The dory glided through low-hung beams of sunlight sifting through the rising gas. Noise encircled him. Reptiles and amphibians and small fluttering birds concealed within the brush. He craned his neck around to stare and puzzle at the myriad canals running in a maze through sandbanks and clumps of trees, and with only the sun to guide him back he took one fork then took another.

When his arms tired he stopped and lowered the oars. He coughed and spat into the water. The blades disappeared beneath the surface. He rested his chin over his chest and closed his eyes.

For a long while he sat there while the swamplife croaked around him. His head ached. Lice molested him. The vertebrae of his neck pointed up at the morning sky.

He straightened finally, slowly, and pulled one oar free of the water. With the other he turned the boat in a slow half circle. When the bow pointed back the way he'd come he dipped both oars in and pulled.

In all that time the slaves had not moved. They stood where he'd last laid eyes on them, strung out in a line along the bank. Lloyd brought the dory close. The linguist took a step into the water, tentative, and when Lloyd said nothing the rest followed. They waded into the water until the algae touched their thighs, grabbed the stern when it came within reach. They climbed over the transom and huddled together on the bottom boards and did not raise their heads above the gunwales even once in all the hours it took Lloyd to find his way clear of the swamp and back to the coastline.

A mile from the docks he brought the boat to a stop behind a stand of tupelo trunks and stared out at the beach. His eyes stretched open so wide they dried and itched and he brought a knuckle up to rub them. He saw no one, still he waited. No one spoke. He ran his eyes up the coastline, squinted against the glare of the sun, and with his leg twitching in a nervous tick he finally plunged the oars into the water and rowed them ashore.

The beach was empty, the tide had washed the sand smooth. The negroes set their feet into it and when they'd vanished into a thicket of silverbells, the Kru man's head disappearing last, Lloyd pushed off with an oar blade and rowed another hundred yards upshore. He did not moor it. He simply vaulted the bow and landed with a splash in the water, and when his feet touched dry land he paused to watch the dory bob directionless in the surf, then turned and cut through swatches of washed-up seaweed and was gone.

———

By noon he reached the harlot's window. He called up to her in the plain light of day but there came no answer. He stood with his neck bent back and waited. Mud dried on his clothing in stiff crusted sheets that broke and flaked and fell to the ground in thin brown shards. Bog algae dried to his skin and clung there. It itched, he scratched at it. A dog stopped to sniff him. It continued on. The shutters on the window remained closed and no light shone behind them.

Further up the street he found a tavern that allowed him entry. He ordered rum and paid with a coin and was left alone. He drank in the shadows. A dulling of the senses came over him but he did not welcome it. Monsieur De la Rue occupied his thoughts as much as the girl, more so perhaps, and woven into those thoughts were memories of the cell, the public works gangs, Gordon's body with his head caved in. He pushed the rum away and waited for evening while his stomach growled. Keeping his hands beneath the table he counted out the coins he'd fished from the deadmen's pockets. Enough for the girl, no more.

It was evening. Again he stood in the street and called up to her, and again there came no answer. He waited against the wall several yards from her door and rubbed his toes against one another. The mud had not completely dried. It embraced his skin, dank and gritty. Only once the vigilante police came through. He bowed his head and kept still with his breath held, toes coming to rest in his shabby boots.

When she appeared he nearly overlooked her. She wore a large grey coat and a bonnet; she was dressed for errands. He came out from the wall and startled her.

"It's me," he said. "Let me up."

"I do not work tonight."

"Look," he showed her the coins.

She looked from his hands to his face, then along both directions of the darkening alley. "Come," she said, and led him in.

Without the drink to dull his senses, his passion was quickly sated. She rose when it was finished and lit a candle and cleaned herself by its light. The room was small, the light filled it.

Lloyd watched her from the mattress.

"Tu dois partir," she motioned to the door.

"I gotta leave?"

"Oui."

"I got nowhere to go."

"You cannot be here."

"I can't be out there neither. They're looking for me."

She stood, naked, a cloth against her skin. He wondered if she'd understood. When she still said nothing he rose from the mattress and fished through the rags on the floor that were his clothing and drew from them the last of the coins. He held them out to her. "Let me stay the night."

"All the night?"

"Till morning."

She counted the coins in his hand, considered something in the privacy of her own mind, then wet another rag. "You wash first."

He wiped himself down while she tucked the coins in a drawer. Then he tossed the rag back from where she'd drawn it and climbed into bed beside her. The mattress was narrow. The straw scratched at him through the sheet. He turned several times, listened to the girl's breath. When he leaned against her she pushed him away.

From the street came noises, men's voices. They rose through the shutters and reached Lloyd's ears and he stared into nothing, waiting, listening, until the itching and the voices and the waiting pulled him to his feet. He opened the shutter a crack and peered out.

Below on the paving stones a man's cart had become lodged in a hole. He pushed at it from behind but he was old, the cart was heavy. Another man stepped between the shafts in place of the missing donkey and took hold of each side and the two pushed and fought at it with the wheel clunking in the hole against the stones and their voices ringing hollow in the night.

"What are you doing?" the girl had woken. She sat upright on the mattress.

"Thought I heard someone."

"There is always someone."

He closed the shutter and came back to the bed and sat.

"Who looks for you?"

"Huh?"

"You said they look for you."

Lloyd shrugged. He could feel the girl's eyes on him through the darkness. More questions were coming, he could feel those also.

"Why are you here?" she said.

"Where-- here?"

"You have no place to go?"

"I reckon not."

"You are not from here. *Tu ne parle pas français.*"

He looked at her but her face was hidden in shadow.

"Where are you from?"

"You got a lot of questions all the sudden."

"You do not answer."

"Why do you want to know?"

"You give me money, you say please, let me stay the night, you don't sleep. Someone looks for you. You no speak French. I do not understand." She moved and the straw crinkled beneath them. "You are from Texas?"

"Further out."

"Further?"

"Past Texas. North, west, where there's mountains."

"But there is nobody there."

"That's why I come here."

"Why?"

"Thought maybe there'd be something for me here. Where there's people and such."

"There is much here."

"Ain't nothing here. Ain't no decent work. I ain't found a way yet."

"So you go back?"

"There ain't nothing where I come from but trapping. That ain't no life."

"You have no people? No family?"

Lloyd shook his head.

She held his eyes a moment then lied back down. The straw rustled. He waited for more questions but none came, and after a while her breath became deep and rhythmic again. Outside the street was silent. The men had unstuck the cart, only dogs moved now, roving in packs with their paws tapping the stones.

"Hey," Lloyd nudged the girl. She made a noise. "You know if there's any missions close by?"

"What?"

"You know the missions the Spanish made. Like churches. Is there any close by? Over Texas way?"

"I do not know what you are talking about." She shifted,

tugged at the sheet, then lay still.

When her breath recovered its cadence, Lloyd rose. He pulled on his soiled trousers, tucked the patchwork of cloth that was his shirt into his waistline, and drew it tight by a strip of rawhide lashing. He took his boots in one hand and, with the other extended, placed one bare foot before the other until he stood alongside the dresser. The wood was rough. He ran a hand down to the second drawer and pulled it open in slow measures, wary of its squeak. At the back he found the coins. They rubbed in small metallic clinks between his fingers. There in the dark he judged their value by both size and shape, then separated out a single quarter eagle and placed it in his pocket. The rest he returned to the dresser drawer. He pushed it closed, crept across the floorboards, then stole a glance at the girl-- though he could not see her in the darkness-- and left through the door.

Two

Men crossed the Sabine into Texas each day by the dozen. They paid their way in myriad currency and loaded all manner of contraptions aboard the flat top ferry, from crates of rum to sheep and pigs, several with slaves at their side like porters in waiting. They carried rifles, some more than one, and spat tobacco over the deck while the ferryman pulled at the cross-rope. Lloyd paid the man his quarter eagle, the same it had cost him some months back when he'd crossed in the other direction, and studied his fellow passengers. When they returned equal inspection he averted his eyes and instead watched the water roll past.

On the western bank were a trading post and a windowless hut that served drink. He had no money for either when he first passed through and he had no money for them now, yet he entered the hut and stood a moment along its wall and watched the men smoke Mexican cigarrillos and drop the finished nubs into the dirt. The smell of something dead hung in the room. It mixed with the smoke, thick and heavy.

From the haze came forth a man with a pelt wrapped about his head. Sweat beaded along his brow-- the hut was hot. He stopped before Lloyd and leaned closer to see him in the poor light. "You've no money or you'd be spending it," he said in humid breath.

"I reckon," said Lloyd.

"What's your trade?"

"Whatever needs doing."

"That's fine." He stood too close, Lloyd could see bits of tobacco caught in his beard. "There's them complaining all that comes across the river is drunkards and idlers and dirt-poor debtors and they ain't fit to settle Texas. But that's who does the fighting. Not the empresarios that run like sorry beggars to Mexico and promise to give away everything that might be had."

"What fighting?"

"Karankawa. And all the rest of 'em. Ain't no end to it. You got fight in you?"

Lloyd shook his head and shied away from the man's breath.

"There's money in it. Land to be had. Bodeman will give you two meals a day and a rifle, and whatever you scare off a dead indian is yours to keep. He'll take any man breathing."

"I ain't interested," said Lloyd.

"Ain't gonna find nothing better."

"I ain't come to fight indians."

"What you come for then?"

Lloyd turned his head away from the man's stale exhales. He stole a breath of clean air and brought himself around again. "I'm looking for a mission. One of them Spanish ones."

"You ain't gonna find no money in preaching. Jesus don't live on this side of the river."

"Still," said Lloyd.

"Hell," the man adjusted the pelt, then drew his hand across his mouth. "There's three, four of 'em, just west of here.

Bodeman'll stop at one, let you pray for their souls," he laughed drunkenly at this, his breath like bogwater swirling over rotted teeth.

Lloyd ducked out the hut and left the man deriding him from the doorway.

Along the banks of the Sabine grew leatherleaf mahonia amongst which drunkards would squat and shit and retch into the river and stagger back to the hut to drink up what remained of their money. So frequent were their trips they'd worn a path through the vegetation. Lloyd walked it until he saw where it led. From underneath a shrub there appeared suddenly an old man lying supine in the dirt with his pants loose about his hips. He smiled and beckoned Lloyd forward with a long bony finger, and Lloyd turned and cut through the mahonia and left the river crossing behind.

He walked westward under the sun and at night slept under a studded firmament that curved and melted into far horizons. On the third evening storm clouds appeared. At nightfall they split open and drummed the land in silence until everything in it was wet and wilted and hung listlessly from where it was rooted. Rain pelted Lloyd in endless baptism. Wherever he sat was pool or puddles. It leaked through the open boot sole, turned his feet to pale shriveled nubs. In the morning he dried them in the sun, then ripped a fistful of ryegrass from the earth and separated the strands into one long line which he twisted from the middle down to the ends. He tied the finished cord around his boot and, that evening, in such miserable vestiture, reached the walls of the mission that had sat all afternoon out of reach like a parapet on the skyline.

In its shadows a pair of bedraggled indians bent over the threshing floor. They stilled their flails at Lloyd's approach. They offered no greeting. Their eyes remained fixed on him, he felt them on his backside, and when he crossed under the belltower into the courtyard he was met with countless more; opaque and uninspired and rimmed in mucus, their bodies huddled against the walls. Long-faced children sat among them. Flies swarmed over the tallow stoves.

An indian rose on seeing Lloyd, crossed the courtyard and ducked under an arched walkway to a door that sat crooked in its frame. He rapped on the wood and a moment later the door opened and the padre emerged. He shuffled out cloaked in a gray habit and when he walked he seemed to struggle under its weight. A tuft of hair grew from the widow's peak of his otherwise bald crown. He brushed it delicately aside while his neck twisted in direction of the indian's outstretched finger. When he saw Lloyd he tilted his head. His mouth tightened into the imitation of a smile.

"Joven," his voice wispy across the courtyard. *"Bienvenido. Ven, pasa, pasa."*

"I don't speak that," said Lloyd.

"You speak English."

"That's right."

"Come," he invited Lloyd forward with a motion of his arm. *"Ven."* His accent poured thickly, the words held wetness in them. When Lloyd reached him he saw where saliva had collected along the padre's lips.

"This a mission?"

"Sí."

"One of them Spanish ones?"

"All the children of god are welcome in his house. Even the indian."

"These ones don't look so good."

The padre's arms were crossed and hidden under the tunic

sleeves. He leaned back and regarded Lloyd with his neck still bent. "There are many mouths and little food. The whites make war on the Karankawa, take their land, take everyone's land. They bring sickness."

"I ain't come to take no land."

"That is good."

"You got water?"

The padre turned on his heel. "Come."

They entered through the open door into the padre's quarters where a flask of wine sat on a table beside a cup. Two chairs waited. The padre pulled one out for Lloyd and took another cup from the shelving and sat himself in the other.

"It is rare to have guests," said the padre. He poured the wine and set the glass before Lloyd.

"There ain't no water?"

"The wine is *sagrado*. Sacred. The blood of Christ."

Lloyd sniffed it. He put it to his lips. He drank, then set it on the table. "Y'all don't got no horses here?"

"No."

"I got need for one."

"The needs of men are many."

"Yeah, well, that's the one I got. That and food. You know where I can get either?"

"There are other missions; four under protection of the presidio. They will have horses."

"The presidio?"

"Sí, el presidio," the padre reached across the table with his hand turned up. "You are not drinking. Drink, drink," he motioned with his hand.

"I was hoping for water," Lloyd turned the cup. He stared into it, then drank. The room's furnishings were sparse. He studied them while the padre slurped at his wine. "You been here long?"

"Many years I am here."

"You ever see American soldiers come through? Had slaves with 'em?"

"Slaves?"

"One, anyway."

"There are many soldiers, many slaves. You seek someone?"

"No."

"There is always war," the padre filled his cup again. He reached to fill Lloyd's, but the cup was still full. "Drink."

"I'm looking for a mission where there was a battle outside. American soldiers, Spanish soldiers. There was a slave with 'em, the Spanish won. They killed the Americans, took the slaves with 'em. I guess the Americans were coming out of Mexico or something."

The padre drank while he listened, his eyes slipping over the rim of the cup. When Lloyd finished, the padre put down the wine and licked his already wet lips. "What visions have you seen?"

"I ain't seen no visions. It's something that happened, I'm looking for it."

The padre shook his head.

Lloyd kept on. "This ain't the one, I know that. Rains too much here. I reckon it was somewhere in the desert. That sound right?"

"I do not know of such things. It is late. You will stay here?"

"You got something to eat?"

The shake of the padre's head came sharper this time. "There is no food."

"I seen them indians threshing wheat outside. I figured there'd be something to show for it."

The padre gave no answer.

Lloyd scanned the room again but there was no food, nothing to arrest his interest. "It don't matter to me where I stay."

"You will stay until morning. Now drink the wine, it is good for you."

The Karankawa slept in their blankets in the courtyard. One remained awake. He sat just outside the barracks with a rattle made from deer hooves. When the padre led Lloyd out from his quarters and under the arches to the adjoining room, the native stopped his shaking and stood and disappeared beneath the eaves.

"The barracks are full," said the padre. "They come in, more every day." He carried a chamberstick with two candles burning. In the entryway he stopped and looked about as though he'd never entered before. The floor was native soil, unboarded, unpaved, not an even surface visible. A rawhide cot took up the center. It rocked when the padre touched it. "The comfort we must provide ourselves," his lips gleamed in the candlelight. "We are men in the darkness." He raised a hand and brought his fingers to Lloyd's cheek.

Lloyd flinched and jolted back.

They stood for a moment with the chamberstick throwing light between them. The flames twitched, shadows shifted on the cratered floor.

"You gonna leave now?"

The padre waited the space of several breaths. His eyes did not blink. The habit was too large for him, the bottom rested in the dirt. He stretched his neck from the collar like a turtle from its shell, his lips parted. Then he blinked, bowed his head and left.

On the cot Lloyd closed his eyes, but sleep did not come. His head was heavy from wine. From the padre's quarters came the sound of slapping, and Lloyd opened his eyes and waited. The sound came again, the smack of a hand across flesh. A whimper followed. Other noises, faint through the adobe mud.

He left the cot and stuck his feet in his boots and pushed open the door.

In the courtyard a child walked naked in the dirt. He held the hoof rattle in his hand and when he saw Lloyd under the arches he dropped it and ran with his unwashed hair swaying in a tangled mat behind him.

Lloyd held still, watching. When the boy was gone Lloyd moved. His footsteps soundless. Along the arched corridor were several double doors with chains wrapped through the handles. At each one he would stop and put his nose to the crack where the doors met to sniff and fumble at the locks, until the fourth, where the smell of bread through the gap caused him to drive his shoulder into the wood, the chains clanking, wood popping at the hinges, the Karankawa stirring from their blankets and rising finally to the commotion of the broken doors, of Lloyd squeezing through the gap and emerging like a frantic animal with the bread loaves clutched against his chest, the padre staggering from his quarters, drunk and naked and hairless in the moonlight with his red lips glistening, shouting in Spanish while Lloyd shot through the courtyard and under the belltower and into the empty night where no one followed.

He stopped running a quarter mile out and shoved the bread into his mouth. His breath had not returned; he panted through his nose while he chewed. When he finished he continued on, pausing on high ground to look behind. When certain he was not followed, he laid himself out on the ground and slept.

Two days later Lloyd walked within view of the second mission under the presidio's command. It was smaller than the first, the corral empty. Landless indians wandered across the grounds. They filled the chapel and the housing. Flies, attracted by the excrement accumulating in piles beyond the cemetery, filled the mission grounds. Lloyd swatted them away with a hand while he wandered in search of the padre in charge. He found him bent before an altar. He spoke no English.

"No hay comida," said the padre when Lloyd pointed to his mouth and stomach. He watched more of Lloyd's gestures, watched Lloyd pull at invisible reins, and shook his head. *"Caballos tampoco. Ve al presidio."*

When Lloyd reached the presidio four days later the binding around his boot had worn through and the sole flopped and dragged through the grass, forcing him to raise one leg higher than the other. The contorted highstep resulted in an odd, uneven gait that caused a pain to flare in his hip and spread up his back.

It had rained, his shirt was wet. The thread was worn at the shoulders and his clavicles protruded against the fabric. He came stepping unevenly out of a stand of sycamores with the wet rags clinging to him and his eyes deep-set with hunger, a figure no less pitiful than the Karankawa kneeling at the presidio gates and wailing songs of misery.

A Mexican soldier met him outside and questioned him in Spanish. Lloyd mimed a few gestures but the soldier only muttered and dismissed him with a wave of his hand.

Lloyd returned to the sycamores. The sun flared. It steamed the puddled water and lent a thickness to the air that was unpleasant to breathe. He sat in the shade and watched the soldiers smoke cigarillos along the eastern wall. Indians milled about the presidio grounds, ragged, nearly naked. Their cries went unheeded. Newborns, strapped to their mothers' backs, stared at the uniformed men without comprehension of their fates, nor that of their mothers, who begged with hands outstretched at the riders stomping past.

Wagons arrived; Mexican peasants come to peddle their crops. A wagon pulled by a team of four oxen and carrying white men trundled through the gates and disappeared beyond the walls.

Lloyd rested his back against a trunk and waited for evening to settle. The traffic had reduced the grass to dirt, and when the soldiers paraded in formation that evening they raised a cloud of dust that hovered over the presidio like a copper ball imbued by the rays of the sun. The walls turned orange, the indians' faces the color of polished leather, and when the dust finally settled and the soldiers retired, only the wailing remained in the night.

Here Lloyd rose and left the sycamores. He circled the fortress with his odd gait and worked his way to the back, where all day he had seen soldiers lead horses and return without them. The corral, when he came upon it, was long and narrow and in it were the horses of two hundred soldiers, their coats an array of colors twitching over slabs of muscle in the moonlight. He squatted in the grass and counted the soldiers on patrol. They came and went. He counted again, lost count. He crawled forward until he could smell the dung on the air, the horses' hides perfumed in sweat. Their tails sashayed, breath curled from their nostrils. Two soldiers patrolled from opposite directions. When they met they leaned against the corral and lit cigarillos and spoke in Spanish, and when they were done they laughed in the way men do when they boast of conquests. Embers fell from their smokes and glowed red and died in the dust. When they resumed their vigil they adjusted their weapons. The metallic clanking carried far in the stillness.

Tucked in the grass, Lloyd sat while the constellations spun and set like a thousand distant suns over the edge of the world. More soldiers came, more laughter. Further on, past the barracks, carts and wagons sat with their tongues in the grass. He searched for some animal outside the corral, horse or mule or donkey, something unsecured, it did not matter, but all the beasts in the employment of man were trapped within the enclosure.

His belly ached. Night dwindled on, lice bit at his neck. At another meeting of the guards in which they declined to smoke and instead exchanged only a brief word before continuing on, Lloyd rose from his haunches and slunk forward. He kept his back bent low. At the corral fence the horses showed the whites of their eyes and pranced back from him. He shuffled the length of the fence with one hand tracing the wooden beams, and when he reached the gate he stopped and slid the crossbar from the racking. The gate swung open in a miserable squeal of wood over stiff hinges. A child cried out. Someone shouted. Men took up their carbines and called out in the darkness. They came running, boots on the ground, and Lloyd bolted from the corral gate and fled, bent to the ground, stumbling into the grass on his broken footwear. A firearm cracked behind him and he fell from the shock of it, then bounded up again and hurried like a crippled, flightless bird, jerking epilepticly at each gunblast until he was out of rifle range and running directionless along the horizon.

The following morning he met Gil Pucker. He'd spent an hour wandering a streambank before climbing a rise to consider his options. From the high point he searched out the most westward mission, but the cedar breaks obstructed his view. To the east lay the Sabine, the hut, and employment with Bodeman should he want it. He turned his head one way to the other and, with a hand over his brow to shade the sun, he saw him.

He was no taller than Lloyd. A few years younger, sixteen perhaps, and just as famished by the way the clothing draped his frame. It was not likely his own. The shirt went untucked. It hung past his wrists and waved like a skirt above his knees. The pant legs dragged in the dirt and the boy would stop every so often to roll the shirtsleeves up and yank his britches back above his waist. He followed Lloyd's trail. He'd lose it, plain as it was, stop, look around, pick it up again.

From behind a shrub Lloyd watched the boy advance. He waited until he was no more than ten feet out, and spoke. "You got some cause for following me?"

The boy recoiled. His sleeves fell over his fingers and he waved his arms which gave him the appearance of a scarecrow thrashing in the wind. "I ain't following you," he said, and tugged up his pants.

"I left a path clear as day through the grass," said Lloyd. "There weren't no hiding it. I know what it is to look for sign, I seen you doing it."

"Thought I was following a trail, that's all."

"Well I ain't got no money and I ain't got no horse. No food or water neither. So there ain't no use following me."

"Why ain't you got a horse?"

"Sold it."

"You said you don't got no money."

"Done spent it."

The boy scratched his chin where a few wisps of hair had sprouted. He looked out at the expanse of trees and grass and turned back to Lloyd. "Which way you going?"

"Same way I been going."

"Maybe I'll go with."

"I don't need no company."

"That's indian country out there."

"Yeah."

"Ain't it dangerous?"

"Yeah."

"You ain't got no gun, do you?"

Lloyd stayed silent. He sat where he was and waited.

"Didn't think you did," the boy smiled and lifted his shirtfront. From his neck hung a saddlebag with a strap so long it rested against his sunken belly. A curved wooden handle protruded from the top. "See this here," he said, and pulled out a flintlock pistol nearly a foot and a half long. The boy used both hands to lift it, such was its weight. The barrel alone measured over ten inches.

"I see it," said Lloyd.

"This here's a Springfield Model 1817."

"You gonna shoot indians with it?"

"You funnin?"

"I'm asking you."

The boy turned the weapon on the empty plain and sighted down the barrel with one eye closed and his face scrunched tight. He swung it in an arc, this way and that, then tucked it back from where he'd drawn it, his arms tired. "Damn right I am."

Lloyd stood. He looked once to the east where the Sabine flowed some sixty miles distant, then turned his back on it. "I got to get going," he said.

"Hey wait," the boy scampered after him. "What's your name?"

"Lloyd."

"I'm Gil."

"Alright."

"Gil Pucker."

"I heard you."

"It alright if I walk with you?"

"You do whatever you're of a mind."

They came off the rise and walked the afternoon through a valley of cross timbers, Lloyd high-stepping and Gil holding his pants up. Cockleburs stuck to their trouser legs. They accumulated in such profusion that the two wayfarers appeared swaddled in living carpets; two drifters plagued by the weight of nature.

Lloyd walked in front. He kept his eyes forward, he could hear the boy behind him. At an overrun riverbank they stopped and chased down bullfrogs until they'd caught a meal's worth. The sun was getting on and the heat had begun to relent.

"You got a knife?" Lloyd said. He'd loaded his arms with fallen branches and dumped them in a pile. The boy stood staring at him with the bullfrogs laid out on the ground and their necks all twisted off.

"Course I do. You ain't got one?" he said.

"No. Ain't got flint neither."

"I got flint." Gil drew a knife from the bag beneath his shirt. In the bag was a length of flint. "Why ain't you got a knife?"

"Sold it."

"What, you done sold everything you had?" When Lloyd didn't answer, Gil laughed. "Bet you wish you had one now."

Lloyd squatted. He broke the branches across his knee and set the smaller twigs aside for kindling. He took the flint and knife from Gil and from his pocket drew a wad of brown material.

"What are you doing?"

"Making fire."

"I know that. What you got there?"

"Fungus," said Lloyd. "Birch." He formed it into a ball and set it in a trough of bark peelings and struck sparks. It took. He held it eye-level and puffed at it, then returned it to the ground and fed it twigs, Gil watching all the while. When the fire became stable Lloyd handed the boy back his knife and flint. "Here. Dress them frogs out."

"Where you from, anyway?" said Gil.

"Up yonder," Lloyd pointed vaguely into nothing.

"How far?"

"Far."

"I'm from Mississippi," said Gil. He slit the frog bellies and scraped the viscera out with two fingers and when he was done he raised the carcasses with their slime and blood drooling over his dirty fingers and held them out to Lloyd.

"I ain't ready for them yet," said Lloyd. "Here. Sharpen this stick so's we can cook them."

"Is there American forts up that way?"

"What way?"

"Whatever way you're from."

"There ain't nothing where I'm from. What do you want with forts?"

"I figure I'll join up. Soldiering."

"You could've done that in Mississippi."

"They won't take me there."

"Why not?"

"On account of this."

Lloyd looked up from the fire. The boy drew the Springfield from the saddlebag. He held it by the curled handle with a hand on each side of the wood as though he were in prayer. He twisted his wrists and the barrel traced circles in the air. He smiled at Lloyd. His teeth were small and set apart from one another.

"What about it?" said Lloyd.

"I killed a man."

"What for?"

"For a disagreement."

"Them his clothes you're wearing?"

Gil dropped his chin and took in his attire and looked again at Lloyd. He shrugged. "Anyway, they won't take me on account of that. Besides, a soldier's life ain't no better than a nigger's in Mississippi. They'll put you to doing the same work."

"What work you figure on doing?"

"Hunting indians."

"What indians?"

"Any of 'em. All of 'em. You soldier after indians, that's how you make rank, and when you make rank you make pay. Now there's a way forward for a man."

"That's how you figure it?"

"That's how it is."

Lloyd lifted the stick of impaled frogs from the fire. The legs swayed and came to rest. "There's a man by the Sabine hiring on. Name of Bodeman."

"That ain't no deal right there. You seen them indians they's hunting? Ain't much left of 'em. And I heard Bodeman don't pay. Army is who pays. Once you make rank."

Night had come. They sucked the meat from the bones and

tossed the bones in the river. Lloyd set what wood was left onto the embers and laid himself out with his back to the fire. Before sleep took him, the boy spoke.

"What are you doing out here anyway?"

Lloyd opened his eyes. The last whips and whistles popped from the fire. Its final throes produced no warmth. The burs had worked their way through his clothing and the spines poked his skin from neck to ankle, the flesh a festering puckered red, swollen and itching and strangely cold. Without turning over he said, "Looking for a horse."

"Army'll give you a horse."

"I ain't joining the army."

"New boots, too."

"If I don't find me a horse soon I'll be dead before I run into army folk. You too."

"Was that why you was at the Spanish fort yesterday?" said Gil. "I seen you."

Lloyd rolled over. "You seen me?"

"At the fort. I know that was you trying to steal them horses."

The coals went silent. One last speck of crimson flared and faded, and through the smell of ash Lloyd grunted a muffled concession.

"So what then?" said Gil. "You give up on it?"

"No."

"The fort ain't getting no closer."

"I'm going to sleep," said Lloyd. "Let me be."

At noon the day following they came upon the most westward mission of the presidio's command. From three miles out they saw the horses. Three geldings corralled together, all unsaddled. The grass within the fencing had been trampled to dust. From one end to the other the beasts paced a worn and hardened path. They craned their long-veined necks through the boards and ripped tufts of bluegrass from the earth and not a soul stood watch over them.

Lloyd stopped walking. Gil continued forward and Lloyd called him back.

"What are we waiting on?" said the boy.

"We're just waiting."

Gil stood with his shoulders slumped. "You think they got food there?"

"They ain't gonna give us no food."

"They give them indians food?" When he said it his eyes swung to the bent figures draped in rags sitting motionless against the mission walls.

"I reckon not."

"Then why they there?"

"Cause Bodeman would kill them if they were anywhere else. Now sit down. Sit and watch."

They spent the day in a thicket of shinnery oak and stared slack-eyed at the going-ons of the mission which were few. A uniformed Mexican emerged once with a bucket of water for the horses and did not show himself again.

In the branches not far from where they sat, a pair of swallows had built their nest. The hatchlings chirped and squealed all that afternoon. They quieted a moment when Gil threw a rock but started up soon enough again. As Lloyd watched, a red-shouldered hawk dove through the canopy like cannonball fire and seized a shrieking chick from the nest. The adult swallows screeched and flew berserk through the branches and they'd not yet calmed when the hawk returned to tear the second from where it lay. When the hawk departed the parents fluttered back and stared at the empty nest. They hopped about a while, their chirps simply empty echoes, and in the silence that followed Lloyd slept.

At nightfall he woke. He turned to Gil and roused him. Half an hour it took to cross the distance to the corral gates. In that time, as the horses came better into view, he chose which would be his own. There was no saddlery, no harnesses or bits or even a blanket, and no time to look for such things. He flipped the gate latch and followed Gil through, and when they rode out they did so bareback, hunched over the horses' crests with their arms wrapped about the veiny necks and no one but a few beleaguered Karankawa to watch them go.

Three

Out on the plains Gil screeched into the night. He whooped and hollered and when they finally stilled the horses his celebration had not ended.

"Goddamn I said goddamn," he panted. "They didn't do nothing, Lloyd!" He whooped again and the horse under him laid its ears back and side-stepped. "You see that?"

"See what?"

"You see what we did? We took them! These is our horses now." His breath came ragged. He looked back from where they'd come and gestured obscenely into the air.

The animals had worked themselves into a lather and their coats shone white in the moonlight. They flared their nostrils and bent their heads and shook them while their ribs heaved against their riders' legs. Lloyd scratched his neck and waited. When his horse's breathing calmed some he nudged it onward. Gil followed.

The once sporadic sections of grasslands disappeared. Thickets of trees replaced them, post oak and pine, dense and impenetrable. They skirted stands of bur oak that grew thirty feet into the air and crookened their path such that four hours riding took them only a few miles west. At a low spot where water pooled they stopped and let the horses drink.

"We gotta keep moving," said Lloyd.

"Why?"

"Get us some distance."

"You think they'll try following us?"

"I reckon they will."

At this Gil stopped his grinning. "They will?"

"More'n likely."

Gil twisted around on the horse's spine. His mouth hung open. He blinked his eyes and leaned over the animal's haunches but there was nothing to see but shadows in the darkness. "What'll we do?"

"They ain't got but one horse left, and it weren't much," Lloyd answered.

"They gonna catch us?"

"Not if we keep riding."

In eleven days they came out of the forests and onto open land sitting bareback atop their horses like bone-whittled marionettes. Their eyes were sunken and the scraping of cartilage could be heard quite plainly beneath their skin. Nothing more than water and a few wild onions had passed their lips.

They struck a line due west and rode in silence, their talk long since having waned. Herds of grazing buffalo raised their heads far out on the plain to watch them pass. Gil drew the Springfield and sighted down the barrel and made noises like a child at play with a stick.

One evening they picketed the horses with cordage Lloyd had

woven from strands of stinging nettle. Head bent before the fire, he spun the extra fibers into twine and began the construction of yet another snare.

"Them ain't working," Gil picked his teeth for some forgotten morsel. He waited for a response and got none. "Why you keep making 'em?"

"That's trapping."

"Well it ain't caught nothing."

"If it does, you gonna ask to eat?"

"Yeah."

He placed the finished trap along an old varmint run. The others he propped with sticks along the forest floor, then returned to the fire and laid his body out beside it. In the morning he checked the traps and rode out no less hungry than when he'd bedded down.

Some days later, where the cross timbers yielded to grasslands, they sighted a band of indians that in no way resembled the Karankawa. What sorrows afflicted the aboriginals begging at the mission walls had no presence here. Their skin was left bare to the sun. It glistened bright as malleable copper. Strong backs, strides a meter long, heads founded on necks of thickened muscle. They walked in procession northward, their wares portaged on the backs of dogs.

From the cover of trees Lloyd and Gil waited. When they'd passed, Lloyd turned to remark on them, but the boy had hidden himself behind the last few scattered trees.

Two days later they rode into the outpost of La Chureca. A sign once bore the name. It had been nailed through a section of clapboard and driven into the ground, and sometime thereafter had been set fire to. It sat crookedly on the plain like a blackened shriveled finger, pointing to a collection of canvas tents and half-completed structures that numbered fewer than a dozen. The most principle of these was a trading post. Two unfinished blockhouses framed the entrance. The proprietor owned, in addition to the post, a face that resembled a skull wrapped in uncured leather. His nostrils huffed when Lloyd entered.

"What you got to eat?" said Lloyd. He stepped through the doorway and stood sniffing the air in a fruitless appraisal of the interior.

The man held a bag of beads in one hand. Beside him on a deer hide were piles of them. He set the bag down. His nostrils huffed again at Gil's entrance. "Either of you carrying money?" he asked.

"No," said Lloyd.

"Something to trade?"

"No."

"Then get out."

The floor was unboarded. One lone shelf of goods stretched along the wall. Under it were sacks of cornmeal and flour. Lloyd took a step in the dirt and eyed them. "I'm only asking."

"Only asking."

"What I said."

"You ain't come to buy-- you got no money. Ain't come to trade, neither."

Lloyd considered this. His head was heavy and his knuckles hurt. He looked again at the bags of flour laid out in the dirt and scratched at the lice in his crotch.

"You've come to beg," said the proprietor. "And I don't serve beggars."

"I got something," said Gil.

As the man thought to form a response, Gil lifted his shirt. Beneath it hung the saddlebag. The Springfield appeared in the boy's hands and the man's leather face cracked. Beads rolled off the deer hide and scattered onto the floor. Gil smiled. He showed the white nubs protruding from his bleeding gums like tombstones spaced equidistant along a crusted lava ridge. "This here ain't for trade, you ugly son of a bitch. Now you got lard to go with that flour?"

The proprietor nodded at the pistol.

"Where?"

"The barrel," his voice wavered.

"Lloyd, grab up them bags. This bastard does something, you tell me. I'll shoot him." Gil twisted the top from the lard barrel and let it drop. From the shelving he snatched a blanket and scooped mounds of white lard into it with his free hand. A smaller barrel sat next to the first. Gil wrenched its top open and looked inside, then upended it and dumped out several strips of jerked meat over the wad of lard.

Lloyd stood at the shelving. A sack of flour he held pressed against his tattered clothing. He waited while Gil tied the blanket ends off, then the two turned for the door when through it suddenly appeared an indian in white man's clothing. His black uncut hair hung long past his shoulders.

Gil tripped and fell back and came up again with his eyes wild like a spooked doe. He shook the gun at the indian. For a piece of time no man spoke. Lloyd moved first with the sacks still clutched against his ribs. He edged up the wall to the doorway and the indian stepped aside and let him pass. When he'd gone through, Gil followed. The gun sagged in the boy's hand, such was its weight. In the street the horses wandered untethered with the nettle cordage dragging at their hooves. The two wrangled themselves onto their backs, the stolen goods clutched to their persons, and galloped past the slack-jawed inhabitants of La Chureca and out into the empty grasslands.

By their own accord the animals slowed to a walk several miles out. Gil returned the pistol to its bag. He wore the same grin; the same small teeth sitting alone along a blackened ridge.

All the day following they searched for a suitable rock. Flat and wide. They'd have stopped where they found it had the woodlands not petered out, but they had, and what stretched before them were hills stacked one after another under multitudes of grass waving endless under a vacant skyline. Lloyd dismounted and pried the rock from its resting place and rode with it over his thighs like sacred plunder. It dug into his skin all that evening and again the next day, until they found both wood and water together, the flat rock to complete the trinity.

The jerky was gone, eaten. Lloyd built a fire. Gil watched stupidly from behind with his arms idle. The sparks took to the kindling. It burst in a crimson rage, crackling, snapping, stretching upward to lap at the drywood. Lloyd tipped the rock into the flames with his foot and waited.

When he kicked it free some time later its color was grey-white like pine smoke in winter. The biscuits fried on its surface contained no leavening. No salt for flavor. They were flat, queerly shaped. They stuck to their teeth, to the roofs of their mouths, and they washed them down with water and ate more and burned themselves rather than let them cool. When they'd eaten them they mixed handfuls of flour and lard in their palms and wetted the batter in the stream and cooked more.

While they sat masticating there appeared a rider. A black nub in the otherwise featureless distance. Tendrils of dust rose behind the horse, each hoof emerging from a miniature cloud, the pace cautious. Over the saddle pommel he carried a coat stitched together from animal hides, fox and beaver and mink and skunk, a patchwork of colors and textures all cut to puzzling shapes and sewn one to the other like some barbaric interpretation of Joseph's coat of many colors. He stopped a ways out from the fire and waited to speak until the dust plumes settled.

"Mind if I partake of your fire?" his voice rattled like stones in gravel. "I'm a bit hard up, myself."

His mane was long, his eyebrows heavy. Wire-like hairs curled from his nostrils and disappeared into an uncut beard. He spread the coat of pelts over the grass and sat upon it and inhaled through his nose while he engulfed a biscuit. He told them his name was Jim.

"You ain't et in a while," said Gil.

"No," said Jim.

"Us neither."

Not until he'd eaten did he surveil their meager encampment. With his brows heavy and brooding he took in his surroundings: the unsaddled horses, the sack of flour. The snare traps rested alongside the stolen blanket. He allowed them his attention, then combed through his beard for crumbs and licked his fingers when he found them. His horse wandered about with the others.

Lloyd and Gil sat watching him.

"That's a funny coat you got there," said Gil. "Where'd you get all them pelts?"

"Trapping."

"Why you stitch them all together like that?"

"Them's pieces that won't sell. Look here," he lifted an edge. "They got cuts and such in 'em. Stains, mange. But they'll keep a man warm, and I ain't one to make waste."

"Ain't hard to stay warm here."

"It's hard in the mountains. Hard in the desert at night. You ain't got to go much further and you'll see."

"You was trapping in the mountains?"

Jim nodded.

"Where's the hides that'll sell?"

The man put Gil under a stare. He held it until Gil's eyes broke and wavered, then he twisted around on the coat and pointed from where he'd come. "Gone," he said.

"Gone where?"

"Goddamn savages."

"Karankawa?"

'No. Karankawa don't got no fight left. They're mostly dead. These was Comanche. Caught me coming out of a draw and killed the mules straightaway. All my furs was on 'em. Lost that. About lost my own hide; they was close enough they stripped my rifle, my packs, everything but the coat. Stuck me with a lance but I done took one by the hair and pulled him from his horse and tore his eye out and that seemed to take the fight out of 'em."

Lloyd and Gil sat in the grass and waited for more but Jim had finished his account.

"They stuck you with a lance?" said Gil.

Jim patted the back of his shoulder then turned and showed the bloodstain. Gil leaned forward with his mouth hanging open. Blood had soaked through the cotton and stiffened a section of fabric. The boy frowned. His eyes glazed over and he breathed through his mouth.

Lloyd, chewing the last of his biscuit, watched these reactions. When his mouth was empty he took a swallow of water and said to Gil: "You still itching to join up?"

"I ain't scared."

"I would be."

"Well that's you."

"Yeah, that's me."

They looked across the grass at each other. The shadow of a carrion bird flitted between them and they lifted their eyes skyward.

"Who's joining up with who?" said Jim.

Lloyd pulled his eyes from the heavens. "He reckons he'll latch onto the army. Says he'll fight indians and get rich."

"You make rank, you make pay," said Gil.

"That true?" Lloyd asked.

"I never met no rich soldiers," said Jim.

"Regular soldiers don't make nothing," said Gil. "I'm talking about them that's fighting indians. I met a man who done it. Said there's money to be had."

Jim shrugged. "Trapping's easier."

Lloyd regarded the unwashed trapper, aging in his years, weaponless and penniless, his voice rattling like charred wood, his body perched on a coat of mange-ruined pelts with crumbs of stolen flour dotting his beard.

"You seen 'em?" Gil asked.

"Seen who?" said Jim.

"American soldiers. West of here."

"There's not but a handful. You ain't in American territory no more; this here's Texas. Belongs to Mexico."

"There's American settlements though."

"A few. Mexes ain't happy about it."

"So ain't there no forts?"

"Fort Tackett is a week's ride north of here. That ain't nobody's territory. There's soldiers garrisoned up thataway. Every time word of a raid or a killing or a raping or some such mess reaches them, they mount up and go hunting reparations," Jim ran a hand down his beard. He put his eyes on Gil. "I seen 'em. And I'll say this, them men ain't no better than the savages they's fighting."

"Why do you say that?"

"Because it's true."

Gil glanced at Lloyd then bowed his head. In his fingers he spun a blade of grass.

"You joining up too?" said Jim.

"No," Lloyd answered.

"You a trapper?"

"I done some."

"You make them snares?"

"I did."

"Them ain't the first you've made. There's craftsmanship there. Folks think braiding a snare is easy, but it ain't. Especially out of nettle like you done. Somebody had to teach you that."

Lloyd's response was only to suck the lard drippings from his fingers.

"You got a knack for it," said Jim. "Keep at it-- I reckon you'll do alright."

"A man ain't got no future trapping."

Jim considered this. "It's not what it once was," he said finally.

The buzzard kept its interest up, gliding on sightless currents. Its shadow withdrew beyond the men along the angle of the sun. Bellies were full, supper finished. Conversation withered.

Jim stood and gathered his coat. "There's a couple hours of daylight left," he said. "I thank you for the biscuits." He walked to where his horse had wandered and draped the coat of pelts over the pommel and climbed into the saddle with his two hosts watching on.

"Hey," Lloyd came forward. "You seen any missions out there?"

Jim glanced down from his height astride the horse. A stream of wind picked up tendrils of his hair and whipped them over his face. "What do you want with missions?"

"I'm just asking."

"There's nobody in 'em."

"But they're out there? In the desert?"

"Aye, there's a few. But like I say, there's no one in 'em. Those times have passed." His voice rattled away in the wind. He turned the horse's nose and nudged the animal forward. It took a plodding step. A quiver rippled over its hindquarters and the trapper bobbed in the saddle, his hair matted in strings and elevated in the breeze. Not once did he look back.

For a long while Lloyd and Gil stood watching him go. When the forms of animal and man had amalgamated into one unfocused speck no larger than a sand gnat, Gil threw a fist into the air. "That son of a bitch can burn in hell."

"You done missed the chance to tell him."

"He thinks he's better than me."

"Why you say that?"

"You weren't listening?" Gil jerked his head sideways in asymmetry to his body. "Saying army folk ain't no better than a damn savage." He turned and paced, then looked out over the grasslands to where the trapper had vanished. "Goddamn his eyes.

And his stinking hides. He ain't no better than me."

The wood they'd collected had burned away. No more lay in sight. The moon swelled out of the east while the sun tarried in handing over the night, and the two pushed down swaths of grass and laid themselves on this bedding before the day had truly ended.

"Hey," said Gil. He turned under a sky still laced in orange tendrils. "What was you asking about missions for?"

"Nothing," said Lloyd.

"Then why was you asking?"

"I was just asking."

Gil rolled back over. "Well he's a son of a bitch."

In the night Lloyd woke. He heard Gil rustling. He heard him rise, heard his boots stamp down stalks of bluestem. Lloyd remained on his side with his limbs curled into his belly. The night was cold. When Gil called for his horse and rode it eastward at a trot, Lloyd shifted some and was asleep again before the batter of hoofbeats faded.

By morning Gil had not returned. His horse had trampled a path through the vegetation that lined up in near mirror image to Jim's trail. Lloyd shielded his eyes against the sun and studied it. He rubbed his shoulders; the morning was slow to warm. After a while he walked to the stream and drank, then bundled together the lard and the meal and the snare traps, and threw it all over his horse and climbed up after.

He'd not ridden ten paces before Gil's shouting reached him from the far ridge. Shrill like a mad woman. He came charging over the plains leading Jim's horse by the reins, his oversized shirt whipping in the wind. He jerked the frenzied animals to a stop before Lloyd. So fraught were the beasts they spun in circles and reared up on their hind legs, Gil clutching a mane, his own eyes wide, his mouth stretched open in victory.

Lloyd directed himself away from the commotion. He waited until Gil had brought the animals to a halt, and the two stared at each other over the horses' ears.

"Well?" said Lloyd finally.

"Well look!" Gil's smile contorted his face. Underdeveloped teeth stood arrayed in exhibition. The emotion at his eyes sought to match his grin. He held the reins of the stolen horse overhead in a champion's pose.

"I'm looking."

"This is a damn fine horse right here. Worth fifty, sixty dollars, easy." He was breathing heavy, grinning.

"You pay Jim that much?"

"Course I didn't."

"Then how'd you get it?"

Gil lowered the reins. His smile cut lower. "I stole him. Just like you showed me."

"I didn't show you nothing."

"Course you did. I took him just like we took these ones here. He'd done built a fire, led me straight to him. He didn't know nothing till I was clean gone."

"Where is he now?"

Gil squinted. He shook his head. "Where I left him."

"We gotta take that horse back."

"What the hell you mean?"

"Take it back."

"This here's worth money."

"It'll get us shot."

Gil's lips curled right down. His sleeve cuffs hung over his knuckles. "What do you mean? He don't got no way to foller us."

"He's but a couple day's walk from the trading post."

"So?"

"So what do you think he'll do when he gets there?"

"He won't do nothing. He ain't got no money. No gun, no horse. He ain't got nothing, Lloyd, he was robbed. Twice," he laughed at this last point.

"That leather-faced feller is there," said Lloyd. "He got guns, horses too I reckon."

Gil sat astride his horse and stretched his neck from side to side. He looked back over the grass down the length of the plain.

"You can't just go stealing without nothing happening," said Lloyd. "Specially from a man like that."

"What, Leatherface?"

"Him too. Both of them."

"Them Mexicans didn't do nothing."

"That was army. Weren't their horses."

"Still, we stole 'em. I don't see no difference."

"We needed them horses."

"We need this one."

"No we don't."

"It's worth fifty dollars."

"I ain't getting shot for it. Come on," Lloyd started in the opposite direction.

"Lloyd…"

"Come on."

They rode with the sun stinging their eyes. Two hours due east and not a word between them. They kept distance between one another. The way forward was carved through grass from Gil's previous trip. When the bluestem gave way to buffalograss only a few inches in height, the way was still clear, for smoldering like a black wart on the flat sheet of earth lay the remnants of Jim's fire.

A ring of singed grass lay around it. The stale smell of old burn. They pulled up and stopped and stared, and after a while Gil said, "This is where he was."

"I can see that," said Lloyd.

"You figure he's headed for the trading post?"

"I reckon he is." Lloyd rode his horse in a half-circle around the fire and rode it back.

"He ain't got but a few hour's start on us."

Lloyd made no comment.

"What are you looking at?"

"Sign," said Lloyd.

"I don't see nothing."

Lloyd swung off the horse and squatted on his haunches away from the fire. His eyes swept the ground. He put a hand to his brow to shield the sun and looked to the horizon.

"Trading post is thataway," Gil pointed.

Lloyd stood and took the horse's reins in his hand and pulled it north, eyes on the ground. He stopped and bent again, straightened and walked forward.

"Where are you going?" said Gil. "Why don't we just keep riding? He ain't got far."

"He didn't go that way," said Lloyd.

"You said he'd go to the trading post."

"He will."

"Trading post is thataway," Gil repeated.

"Come here," said Lloyd. He stood a good thirty yards from the fire. He took a knee and signaled with his finger. "See that?"

Gil's makeshift belt had come undone and his pants were falling. He jerked them up and cinched the belt and ambled over to

Lloyd. "No," he said.

"Come around to this side. You need the sun on the other side of the track. Shadows come out that way."

Gil contemplated the grass. He frowned.

"That's his boot heel," Lloyd traced an arc in the dirt.

"That ain't much."

"It's what it is."

"Where's the rest of it?"

"You ain't gonna find no more than that," Lloyd said. "'Less he's walking in sand."

They mounted up again and rode northeast in the virgin morning. A turpentine sky bereft of clouds. The black vulture outlined in it's sweep. Aside from the bird there appeared no living thing under that empyrean save for the two young men, the horses they rode, and the lice they carried with them.

Shortly Gil pulled the stolen horse to a stop along with his own, and set to complaining. "Why we going so slow?"

Lloyd looked back. "Sun's rising. Makes it harder."

"What are you even seeing? I don't see nothing."

"Sign."

"What sign?"

Lloyd only pushed his horse on. Gil trotted up to him.

"Why don't we just ride to the post? Where old Leatherface is."

"You gonna deal with that man?"

"I ain't afraid."

"But you gonna deal with him?"

"You think I'm scared?"

Lloyd stopped. "Best thing is to find Jim while he's alone. Give the horse back."

"We sure doing a lot of wandering. I say we just ride direct."

"He didn't go direct."

"Why not?"

"Cause he ain't no fool."

Gil scratched his neck. New hairs had begun to sprout. He tickled at them. "How do you know he went this way? You say you see tracks. I don't see nothing."

"Get off your horse," said Lloyd.

Gil dismounted and followed Lloyd a few yards from the horses until Lloyd stopped. The boy itched himself and stood swayback, hands on his hips. Lloyd's finger hovered over blades of grass, short and squat.

Gil shook his head. He flipped his hands over. "I don't see nothing," he said.

"This here," Lloyd touched a flattened area no larger that the ball of his thumb.

"What about it."

"That's him."

"That ain't nothing."

"Only thing that'll flatten a spot like that is a man or a hoofed animal. Here," he took four steps and turned around and bent over. "Look," he pointed to where he'd stepped and pointed back to the original spot. "Same thing."

Gil knelt in the sod and put his face against the tracks as though cataract-afflicted, his palms in the weeds like a man struck dumb and crawling ape-like in the wild. After a while he turned his head with his cheek to the ground and narrowed his eyes at Lloyd. Then he rose and slapped his palms against his trousers. "Where'd you learn all that?" he said.

"All what?"

"Reading sign like that. Bootheels and such, where to put the sun. This here."

"That's how I growed up."

Gil scratched his throat where a few lone curls of hair grew. "What else you see in that sign?"

"He keeps turning around. Looking back. He ain't but an hour out. If you'd quit your bellyaching we'll catch him by noon."

They remounted with the spines of the horses biting their groins, the beginnings of thirst in their throats. Overhead the buzzard lost interest. It drifted off on unseen currents.

By noon they came upon spotted stands of blackjack oak. Clumps of cedar elm. The ground stuttered and bare between them. In one such open area marched Jim, robed in his gallimaufry like some misplaced viking crusading through the Texan plains. He turned frequently, and when he spied them he stopped and stood waiting.

Gil dropped the reins of Jim's horse. He put his own to a trot and passed Lloyd with his shirt billowing off his back.

Jim waited in the heat with his hair hanging flat against his ears. The man was a mass of hair. Pelts and hides, bearded, browed. His hands hung empty at his sides. Gil reached him, slowed his horse.

Lloyd, from a distance, saw Jim step back. He did not see Gil reach into the saddlebag hanging at his belly; the fluttering shirt hid the boy's movements. He saw only the arm emerge with the Springfield extended. He saw Jim bend his knees, caught with nowhere to flee. He saw Gil steady the pistol, saw him pull the trigger. The flint sprang forward, struck the frizzen. The pan flared. Jim spasmed, the crack clapped over the plains. It reached Lloyd a moment later, and Jim was already staggering backward. Gracelessly. The trapper's hands grabbed at his neck and he fell on his knees and dropped forward and remained still under the pelts, his arms and legs folded strangely beneath him. Smoke wafted from Gil's pistol. Notes of charcoal in the air.

Lloyd jinnied his horse. It took a minute to cross the distance. Gil stood over the dead man with his pistol drawn and made intimations of gunfire while his other hand squeezed his crotch, all the while spewing from his mouth a diatribe of filth wrapped in a vernacular not wholly familiar to Lloyd.

The boy spun when he heard the horse approach. Like he'd forgotten who all was there. "You see that?" he hollered, his voice pitched high. He swung back around and pointed the pistol at Jim. "You think you're better than me? That's my horse!" He spat. The ball of sputum landed in the dead trapper's hair.

Lloyd dismounted. He knelt before the man, rolled him over. Blood covered his shirtfront. The tip of his beard was soaked red.

"You see that?" Gil said again. He was only a few feet from Lloyd, nearly shouting.

"Why'd you do that?" Lloyd let Jim's shoulder go. The man's face rolled back into the grass with his eyes open and the blades poking into the wet orifices.

"He ain't gonna say nothing to no one," said Gil.

"He's dead."

"Goddamn right," Gil flashed his nubby teeth. "I killed him." He lifted his shirt and stowed the weapon. "Horse ain't his no more." He bent to where Jim lay dead, and shouted: "You hear me you son of a bitch? It ain't yours no more!" When he stood straight again he was laughing.

Lloyd took a step back.

The two horses twitched their tails and snorted. Jim's horse came walking in from where Gil had released it.

"We'll sell it," said Gil. He hitched up his trousers that had begun to fall again. "Split it, fifty-fifty."

"That ain't mine," said Lloyd.

"It's as much yours as mine. I wouldn't never have found him without you. I ain't never seen a man read sign like that. I bet don't even no indian read sign like that. Fifty-fifty, Lloyd. That's what partners do."

"We ain't partners."

"Sure we are."

"We ain't nothing. You only been riding along with me, following me. I don't want no part of this."

Gil rocked his head a might. His eyes seemed to cross. A frown settled between them. "We're horse thieves," he said.

"We ain't nothing. I'm leaving. You go your own way now. Go join the army, do whatever you're of a mind, but I ain't no part of it."

Lloyd grabbed up the braided reins and threw a leg over the horse's back and turned the animal around. The snares had fallen away, only the sack of flour and the blanketful of lard remained. He put his heels to the horse. At fifty yards he heard Gil call out. He stopped the horse and looked back. The boy stood with his arms slack and his head cocked oddly, his face small and bewildered. A pool of blood had formed beneath Jim's dead body, and the edge had nearly reached Gil's feet.

Four

The cold settled in that night. It came on a northern wind, down off the high mesas, gushing through the valleys and over spindly creosote where it whistled past the leaves in a siren song whose end Lloyd waited for but never came. Huddled into the lee side of a gravel esker, without flint and without fire, it found him. It whipped down his neck beneath his collar. It found the damaged boot sole and robbed the warmth from his toes. He shivered and slapped his arms, cupped his fingers over his mouth and exhaled his lungs into them. His temples throbbed. He lied awake with his eyes pinched shut against the cold and curled his knees into his ribs.

While the night was still young he picked himself up from the gravel and unstaked his horse and rode back the way he'd come with the sack of flour resting in his groin.

It took him until morning to retrace his path, a bit longer. The sun had broken.

Jim hadn't moved; he was still dead. The buzzards had found him. They'd pecked his eyes from his skull and stood with their claws tangled in his uncut hair, jabbing their beaks into the hollowed sockets and ripping strands of sinew from them. Lloyd threw a stone and they scuttled off in squawks and ruffled feathers and paced some distance off like wild angered chickens. He squatted in the puddled blood and unlaced the man's arms from the sleeves and gathered up the coat and slung it over the horse's withers, then walked back to where the body lay and flipped it face-up. It smelled of fresh meat. The shirt was stained in blood, the trousers also; the puddle had grown down the length of the corpse. Lloyd felt along the shirtfront. The blood was not yet dried. It stuck to Lloyd's hands like unset mortar. Finding nothing in the shirtfront he stuck his hands into the trouser pockets and fished around and came up empty.

"I know you got the makings," he said aloud. The buzzards stretched their wings and waddled closer.

He found it tied around Jim's hips; a sack bound by string hanging just below the waistband. In it was a set of flint and steel. A pouch of untanned leather was nestled into the first. In this was a mass of sourdough starter. Lloyd sniffed it and closed it up and tucked the findings into his own pocket. The remaining clothing from neck to ankle held nothing. At Jim's feet he pried the boots off. He swapped them out with his own and stood and took a few steps and nearly tripped for the size of them. He shoved his feet back into his own and left the others tipped in the dead man's blood.

By evening he'd outridden the stands of cedars, and in a week's time the grass began to wither and turn spotty. It clutched the soil in brittle, stubborn clumps, and each mile westward it bent still more until it caved to an ocean of parched earth that seemed to take delight in its destruction of all things verdant. From it rose crags of bleached rock. Cretaceous strata overlain by conglomerations of sandstone and granite. Presiding over the palisades stood high-walled mesas that cast their shadows long and dark across the piled scree laying jumbled at their bases. Atop these plateaued escarpments grew sagebrush, yucca and pinyon pine, dwarfed and lonely on the peaks.

Lloyd wove his horse through the bottoms, his lips chapped and peeling. The days saddled him in heat, the whisper of the wind was there to steal it back at night. He would wake cold and shivering beneath the furs with his eyes red-rimmed and crusted, his mind wrapped in hallucinations bounding rampant in the cage of his dry and thirsty skull. No man or beast did he see. Only lizards darting among the rocks. He would drop from the horse and chase them through the sand and eat them raw without fire, more to quench his thirst with their salted blood than for any satiety rendered.

In small increments he ate the lard. A scoop at sunrise, another when he bedded down. The starter he fed with pinches of flour. He wicked the morning dew from agave leaves and trickled it into the pouch and kept the fermenting masa close against his skin, waiting all the while to find the water with which to make his bread. What might burn he ripped from the ground and carried with him. At night he'd light it and stare into the flames and never was there enough to last till morning.

On the day the lard ran out he followed a dry arroyo littered with sheaths of broken limestone strewn amiss like slag heaps left untended and unwanted by some ancient cult of desert masons. Cholla and ocotillo sprouted through them. The horse sniffed at the stalks with a hopelessness borne out in each miserable stride as Lloyd urged it down the embankment through gravel dunes and over shelves of precambrian sediment that overran its hooves and came to rest in plumes of dust.

The watershed where they emerged was empty and arid and striated by primeval channels, its tattooed crust left naked to the air. He turned the horse up its length and listened to the hooves scrape stone-like across the floor. They echoed out along the talus ghats and settled over the basin. Lloyd attempted a swallow of his own spit but his tongue was dry and swollen and he only hacked up a cough at the attempt. His mind drifted, thoughts did not fill it.

Near sundown he found water. The horse smelled it first. It balked and stumbled and attempted a run, and nearly fell in its disorientation. Lloyd snapped forward. Out of a dreamstate. Alert suddenly on the animal's scraggled back he put a hand to the flour, grabbed the coat. He jerked his head around. His eyes sought movement, he found none apart from the horse's head tossing in exaggerated jounces and craning its neck out over its hooves as though by stretching its head forward it might bypass the constraints of its physical wreckage and drink prematurely the liquid beckoning yonder.

They topped a ridge, horse and rider and, descending the other side, came within earshot of water chortling on rocks. Lloyd let the horse choose its path. It took but a minute to find, the sun low and blinding in their eyes. The stream was narrow, the water shallow. Grass decorated its banks. Desert willow, juniper, limbs hanging over shaded havens. Soapberry roots caught the passing current. From distant horizons, under snow-capped mountains, the stream bore itself. It scored its route through far-off forests and into desert country, and where it flowed there opposite the watershed ridge Lloyd fell to his knees and drank.

When he lifted his head he saw the mission. There beyond the willows where the grass gave back the desert. Only when his body stopped shaking did he realize what it was. He forded the shallows and climbed the streambank and walked some hundred yards on droughted legs until he stood before the adobe walls painted red in the setting sun. Shards of old pottery filled the dry bottom of a fountain. The door had fallen away. The facade was cracked, his fingers grazed it as he entered. Light flared through the hollow windows. It shot tangerine beams beneath the rafters and turned the floating dust to pixies.

He beheld the half-ton vigas laid lengthwise atop the walls with an awe befitting such sacred ground, and stepped forward. Eyes aloft on the boarded ceiling. His foot landed in a hole and he pitched forward and fell amongst mounds of upturned earth. The flooring had been hacked up and stripped and peeled away. Chopped and splintered planks lay against the walls. He pushed himself upright. He walked along the wall edge where the ground was flat and he looked again at the ceiling boards, then ducked through the doorway, past the fountain, and scrambled down the streambank where he pushed against a wrist-thick willow limb until it cracked free. He dragged it back up the bank and into the ransacked mission. Standing on a mound of dirt he jabbed the branch into a ceiling board. Dust sifted down. He jabbed again and took another look. He did this for a long while, working up a sweat while the sun set, dust falling, coating him, and when the beam finally gave he started on the next. He worked until he couldn't see, then set the stick against the wall and walked into the night.

Beside the stream the horse cropped grass. Lloyd spread the coat beneath the soapberry branches. The cold had come in already. It brushed over his sweat-drenched body and gave him a shiver. He snuck his arms through the coat sleeves and plumped the flour sack under his head and shut his eyes.

In the morning he knocked three more boards loose from the vigas and stood there staring up at the hole. He stretched his arms up and guessed the distance. For a while he shoved more dirt onto the pile but, consisting of mostly sand, it only avalanched off.

Outside he found the horse where he'd left it. He pulled it across the stream and up the bank and past the fountain. It fought some at the doorway. Lloyd tugged, clucked his tongue. The horse bowed its head.

Inside, the paneless lancet windows clove the sunbeams in two. Pale sky beyond. Smell of must, stale dirt. The horse centered at the altar space and all silent in the chapel like some bare and hollowed stable made incandescent in the morning light. Beside the beast stood Lloyd with his hands over its withers. He lifted himself to its back and bent a knee and steadied a boot across its spine. He raised his broken boot and set it beside the other and held himself in a crouch while whispering reassurances to himself or to his horse, he knew not which.

With a leap he caught the ceiling boards and pulled himself through.

The roof pitched down at a hard angle. Heat collected in the crawlspace. It stung Lloyd's nose and he opened his mouth and sucked in hot gulps of air while he crawled about in the blackness with his hands groping before him like some blinded beggar clawing at the air. He crawled up one side and down the other and repeated the loop again. The space was empty save for the heat. He stuck his head down through the hole and panted in the chapel air and set about on another fruitless search.

When he reached the hole again he stuck his head through and saw that the horse had left. He lowered himself down, feet first, and hung vertical for a moment before he dropped.

Outside by the stream he made bread. He kneaded flour and starter with water and covered it with his shirt and set it in the sun. He watched it for a while then stripped off his rags and bathed himself in the passing water. While the day wasted, he wandered the mission grounds and fished pottery from the fountain. Remnants of some forgone tribe. The larger pieces he scrubbed clean. In the evening he built a fire and set the dough in the shattered earthenware and listened to the crackling of the juniper wood while the smell of baking bread encircled him.

Four days he spent there. On the morning of the fifth he filled the empty flour sack with grass and rode out. Upstream, northward. The horse indifferent.

He'd travelled not but a mile, keeping to the shade of the waterbank, when he came upon the ruins of a burned-out cathedral whose dome had once been constructed of tule thatch and had thereupon caught lightning. The scars of the fire ripped down its walls and blackened the stone in great long sweeping scorch marks. Topped over the soot were the piled droppings of sparrows. Their excrement streaked the walls in long thin cutlines; white brushstrokes through burnt canvas. They roosted in the empty campanario and camped out under the alcoves. In great black twisting clouds they flew, morphing and stretching and coiling in upon themselves, and when they descended they did so by the hundreds in single-minded fashion to alight upon the ledges where the tule thatch once connected. Left open to the sun, the interior withered. The pews cracked, sand filled the aisles. Nests replaced votive candles. Down the length of the tabernacle the earth had been shoveled out and piled in heaps, the pews ripped from their moorings and tossed in an unlit pyre.

Through it all walked Lloyd. He leaned into the baptistry and climbed up the altar steps, and after standing a moment with the flock of sparrows strangely quieted by his presence, he left.

Days of hunger followed. Nights of desert sound, of far off coyotes and the clicks of bats. He kept the horse watered. They drank together before bedding down, man and beast, and together listened to the water ripple southward in the dark.

He searched for sign and found mostly the scratchings of sparrows or the vague disturbances of lizard tails in sand. Once he rode through sixty yards of pronghorn tracks where a herd had grazed both sides of the stream and filed out across the desert to where he could not imagine. Days he never counted turned and died and were born again.

When he found human tracks they were not indian moccasins, but bootheels stamped in sand. He reined up and ran his eyes over the horizon. The horse twitched an ear. He clucked at it and nudged it on.

For a time the bootheels followed the river, their owner kneeling here and there-- a hunter's repose-- then turned west and walked the length of a ravine. Lloyd followed. The tracks took him past a stand of acacia and wound up a slope layered in petrified terracettes clear up to the ridgetop. He crested it, and there past the horse's ears the signs of man lay scattered upon the plain. Buildings sat skewered in every direction. In the center was a sawmill. It stood like a fulcrum from which the town had been flung. The stream he had followed all these days coiled around the far side of the ravine and cut its path along the northern edge of the settlement. Grass grew beyond it all the way up the valley to where limestone cliffs tore up through the ground.

Lloyd dropped from the horse and pulled it off the skyline and sat in the gravel and watched. He sat for a long while. Long enough for the sun to flip the shadows and lengthen them. In all that time he saw no movement. He counted the buildings, thirty-one total. Mostly adobe huts, something that resembled a trading post, a wood-faced storefront, a corral with a livery attached. Across the stream was a clapboard cabin. Something barn-like beside it.

In all that isolated valley Lloyd saw not one soul, man or animal. He stood and began to clamber his way down the shaleslide. Halfway to the plain he stopped and crouched. A drove of goats was being driven up the far-side of the valley by a rider on horseback. They went running and bleating before the horse and crossed the stream and trotted into the barn beside the cabin.

He sank back to his haunches and waited. His horse set to snorting and carrying on and he turned and hushed it, though it paid him no mind. He turned back and faced the valley. The rider was two miles off but he could see plain as day it was a woman. She'd followed the goats inside and was several minutes coming out again. Lloyd rubbed his jaw and puzzled at it and finally gathered up the horse's reins again and led it down the slope and into the mouth of the village.

At the first few cabins he stopped and stuck his head through the windows. Dark and stale and cold. Dust over everything. He led the horse up what might be the center lane of town, up where the larger buildings were clustered around the sawmill, and tied the horse to a hitch post. The footprints crisscrossing the dirt he did not miss. He saw them as clearly as a hawk sees a vole, and when he came off the horse he stood and read them. Old tracks, faint and faded.

The building closest bore a sign made illegible by blowsand. Different feet at different times had crossed its threshold; he saw these tracks as well. He pushed through the batwing doors and stood staring at an empty barroom with the hinges creaking behind him.

The first thing he noticed was the floor. It was made of plankboard and held no dust. He saw it by the light angling through a section of unfinished roof, pouring through the hole down over the trusses and making small shadows in the broom marks streaking the boards. The tables were clean. The bar that stretched the length of the room showed signs of a recent polish. Behind it sat bottles on shelving. He walked the length and came around behind the bar and picked up a bottle and held it to his eye and shook it. He replaced this and took up another. The next several were empty and he continued on, bent like an alchemist with the empty bottles in his hands when the bald man appeared next to him.

Lloyd felt his shoulders jerk. He snapped back with a bottle raised in each hand, caught between the shelving and the bar, the man grinning toothless before him.

"Find anything in 'em, it's yourn," said the man.

Lloyd lowered his arms. By the light through the open rooftop he saw the man was not truly bald, but had been scalped. The skin had grown back and sat in a thin wrinkled layer over the bone. What hair remained hung like wet string over his ears and down his collar.

"Ain't nothing in 'em," said Lloyd.

The man cackled and shook his head so the hair floated and settled back. "I know it," he said. "Fancy a drink?"

"Drink of what?"

The old man turned and waved for Lloyd to follow. He walked in a hunch. At the end of the bar he bent and pulled up a jar wrapped in cheesecloth and set it over the bartop. He squinted an eye at Lloyd as though the two were complicit in some unspoken secret, and unwound the cloth and dropped it on the bartop.

"What's that?" said Lloyd.

"Drink."

"I ain't got for what to pay you."

"Money?"

"I ain't got it."

The man adjusted his shirt collar. "It don't matter. I wouldn't know where to spend it." He turned his back on the rows of empty glasses and put the jar to his lips. His eyes veered to their corners and he stared at Lloyd while his throat pistoned up and down. Some of the brew slipped past his lips. Lloyd watched it run down his jaw. The smile seemed to remain all the while, and when the man finally peeled the jar away and held it out, Lloyd saw this was so.

"Go on," the scalped man said. "Take it."

"What is it?"

"I done told ye. It's drink."

Lloyd peered down the jarmouth. He gave it a swirl. The liquid sloshed against the glass and ran down in thick legs like wet cornmeal. Despite the smell, Lloyd's belly twitched. Saliva collected under his tongue. He drank, chewed some at the mealy bits, and set the jar back over the bartop.

"Go on then," urged the man. "Have at it."

Lloyd scraped his tongue across his teeth. He chewed the granules and breathed through his nose.

"I'd drink the whole thing were I as skinny as ye."

Lloyd took the jar up again and let the gruel ooze down his throat. He chewed and swallowed and sucked it back. When he set it down it was half-empty and the old man was grinning his toothless grin.

"Welcome to Milltown," he said.

"That what you call this place?" said Lloyd.

"That's right."

"Where's everybody at?"

"Well now," the man wiggled his lips over his bare gums and considered. "Bruder and the Sampson boys taken off hunting. I don't know where Clyde's at, he might be dead. He got the consumption-- I ain't seen him in a while. Black Paw took out with some hides to trade and he should've been back a week ago. Don't know what's keeping him."

"What about everyone else?"

"Who else?"

"All these houses here. And them buildings--everything's empty."

"I don't know where they gone to."

"Who built 'em?"

"Don't know that neither. I reckon it's got something to do with the mill there, and the quarry up yonder. Black Paw maybe knows, but he don't say much." The man took the jar between his hands and lapped down a couple mouthfuls. "Thinking to stay on?"

"What for?"

"Look what we got. We got water, we got the mill. They's game in the high country. Folks headed to Californy will stay put once they see this here. Get ye'self a free house done been built. I got me a whole dang bar here, didn't cost me a dime."

Lloyd looked into the shadows. The sky had turned dark with evening.

"Get in early, might get ye'self on the town council. Bruder, he's sheriff. They done made me mayor," the man cackled a toothless laugh and pushed the jar across the bartop. "Go on now, share a drink."

They passed the jar between themselves and became drunk. When they'd emptied it the old man shuffled off to a corner and brought forth another. In the darkness his skull gleamed bluish-white. He spoke of enterprising things, every last one riddled in incoherence. When he wandered out back to relieve himself Lloyd snuck through the front. He slid the coat from the horse and left the animal tied at the hitching post while he weaved drunkenly up past the sawmill with the pelts swinging from his shoulders.

A fair distance from the woman's cabin he stopped and sat in the dirt and closed his eyes. Acid gurgled in his pipes. He breathed through his nose, kept his throat tight. After a while whatever curdled in his belly came to rest and he opened his eyes.

It was a glassless cabin window he stared at. Candle flames fluttered through it when the breeze ruffled the curtains just right. He sat watching until she extinguished them, then he watched the house in darkness.

He nearly fell asleep right there but for the squealing of a wagon axle.

The driver came from the east outlined in blue moonlight. The draft horses leaned into their traces on legs long exhausted, through the stream and up the bank. The wagon tipped. A wheel spun loose in the air a moment and thudded back to the ground. The load rose over the sideboards, careened against the ropes, and the whole outfit-- animals and wagon and driver-- with their huffing and creaking and squalering, seemed to Lloyd in his drunkenness some primitive beast lumbering berserkly between the adobe walls.

It all came to rest in a cloudy mist. Heat wafted from the animals' backs and hung shimmering in a silver aura about them. The driver jumped off the bench. In the moonlight he was nothing but a blotch of shadow, no face or features, just a tall thin shape moving lithely in the dark. He slipped under the shafts and gathered up the hame and collar and reins like he'd done it a thousand times before and led the horses away to the corral. Several minutes later he returned. Over a dozen trips it took him to unload the wagon. He piled his wares against his chest and hoisted them over the sideboards and into an adobe hut that looked no different than the rest. Back and forth. Lloyd watching.

When the driver finished he left the wagon before the hut and walked north. Through the edge of a ghost town. He turned before the stream and walked past the barn and stopped at the cabin door.

Lloyd stood up. He tottered from the change in position, crossed his arms for warmth, narrowed his eyes across the distance.

The rapping on the cabin door carried in the night. The door opened. The man stepped forward. Two figures merged there in the frame, muddled by darkness and by Lloyd's inebriation. They disappeared behind the door and all that was left awake in the night was Lloyd Raymond Reed, wrapped in his patchwork of hides.

The feeling of pins piercing his head woke him. He turned on the floor and opened his eyes. Red walls. Adobe brick. Abandoned and stale and all of it scented in the smell of hardpacked earth. He rose and walked outside. After a minute standing in the sun he reentered the hut and shimmied out of the coat and walked back out again.

Eyes half shut against the daylight he made his way to the saloon. His footsteps landed shallow in the dust. The boot sole scraped and flapped and molested him.

In a portal beam of sunlight sat the scalped man, the table

before him covered in corn. To his right a massive piece of earthenware rivuletted by the etchings of some ancient hand. At the creak of the batwings he squinted and looked up. His cheeks were full of kernels. He motioned Lloyd in with a wave, then bent and spit into the pottery and wiped the spittle from his lips.

"I knew ye'd stay," he said.

"Yeah?" said Lloyd. "How you figure?"

"Left your horse in front."

"Where's it gone to?"

"Black Paw took it. He's a man good with animals. Took it to the corral, said he'd brush it down and let it graze."

Lloyd stood just out of the sunlight. He scratched his belly.

"Hungry?"

"My head hurts."

"Is ye hungry though?"

"I'm hungry."

"Good. Hunger wets the mouth. Now take a seat and help me and I'll give ye a drink to thank ye."

Lloyd sat. "What are you doing?"

"Making brew. Come round to this side. Here. Don't swaller it. Spit in here," the old man tapped a knuckle against the pottery.

Lloyd rolled corn over the tabletop with the flat of his hand. "What's all this?"

"That's what makes the chicha."

"That's what we drunk last night?"

The old man smiled. Yellow meal coated his gums-- he had hardly any teeth. "Now you gonna chew or ain't ye? I reckon ye'll go twice as fast seeing as all ye teeth is settin' pretty."

"You want for me to spit in there?"

The old man nodded.

Lloyd rolled his hand about and watched the man stuff his mouth and gum the kernels. After a while he joined in. They chewed and spat together beneath the unroofed trusses. After an hour of this the old man put a hand to his face. "My jaw gets weary," he tipped the pot and lowered his head to the rim. "That's enough-- it'll start a batch. Let's share us a drink now." He scooted off to the bar and came back with a jar same as the night before, covered in cloth.

Lloyd leaned back from it. "That your spit?" he asked.

"Some of Clyde's too."

Lloyd sat still.

"Chew this here corn with me and ye can drink ye own spit in a couple weeks," the man put a hand to his scalped head and laughed. He watched Lloyd tip the jar back and nodded in approval. "Black Paw come in last night, said he near lost the wagon load over the stream. Horses was about beat. Would've been a sorry thing to lose the corn like that."

While the old man rambled, Lloyd swallowed more chicha. It filled his belly, and by and by the vice loosened about his head and he drank more freely until the fermented corn piled up thick to his ribs and he sat back breathless.

"Bruder and the Sampson boys'll be back soon," the old man was saying. "They been out a few days now. They'll have fresh meat-- they's good with rifles."

"I ain't hungry no more," said Lloyd. He put a hand to his stomach as if to pacify an angry beast within, and as he did so he swayed on the stool.

The old man laughed and spewed bits of gruel over the table.

"Who's that woman?" Lloyd blurted into the man's cackling.

The old man took hold of himself and narrowed his eyes. His

smile twisted some. "Molly? I forgot to mention her. She ain't bad to look at, is she?"

"She the one up by the stream?"

"Ain't no other one."

"What's she doing here?"

"Waiting for a man," the chicha-maker grabbed his bald skull with both hands and bent and shook with laughter, and from his nose bubbled yellow snot eerily similar to the corn gruel.

"I ain't seen her up close," said Lloyd.

"She ain't yourn, nohow. The captain's been courtin' her. Working at her like a dog works a bone. I 'spect were he to find another man's paw marks on her he'd be liable to run him through."

"I ain't done nothing."

"Like ye said, ye ain't seen her close. She ain't young no more but she ain't old neither." The man reached for the jar. He slapped the side of it and shook it over his mouth until the last clumps sludged over the rim into his mouth.

Lloyd stood. "I need to get my horse." He turned and smacked into a table and fell. The old man screeched and clutched his head, and Lloyd drew himself up and forged an unsteady route past the bar and out the batwings while the old man's hoots warbled out behind him.

By the edge of town, slunk in the shade of an abandoned hut, Lloyd watched the cabin. At a quarter-mile distance his eyes struggled to ascertain the features of her face, but the body beneath the dress was enough. He watched her draw water, noticed how she bent and rose. How her hips stretched the fabric. She disappeared inside the cabin long enough for Lloyd to fall asleep and when he woke it was with a start, for rising in a half-shell over the plain was the dust of three riders. Like phantoms they materialized from the bowels of the limestone cliffs. Two spare horses accompanied them. Lashed across each was a fresh kill, the blood dripping along the horses' shanks, the horsemen erect in their saddles with the air of victory all about them.

As they came abreast of the cabin the woman stepped out to watch them pass. From where Lloyd sat he saw their shapes flicker between the adobe walls, down the main street and past the sawmill where they drew up in a commotion of noise and clatterings and the hollering of voices. The chicha-maker stumbled out to greet them, the sunlight brilliant on his skull. He lifted his arms to share in their victory, and before these men he appeared small and ragged.

Lloyd turned from the scene. He crept back through the scattering of huts to where he'd spent the night. To where the coat awaited him. He curled into the mottled hides and tucked the flour sack beneath his head. As he dreamt his body lurched. Visions of snow on tree-lined crags. When he woke, the remnants of his dreams dispersed like smoke through leaves. Only a feeling remained, something parasitic that he shook off along with the chill of night. He clutched the coat about his shoulders and stood and ambled out in careful steps, for his bootsole had dislodged itself yet further, and to walk without stumbling he was forced to swing the foot far forward and pull it back as each stride landed.

In such lopsided fashion he reached the saloon. Again through the batwings, starlight in the trusses. The smell of corn fermenting in the pottery. He bent over it, then pulled his nose away and hobbled among the tables.

From behind the bar he drew a jar and threw aside the cheesecloth. The taste now familiar, the smell less acrid than what frothed within the pot.

He chewed and swallowed and licked his lips. When he'd

reduced the chicha to a quarter-jar he dropped it on the bartop and sprawled himself across a table where he wallowed in the pleasure of satiety. His toes were cold, his torso warm beneath the coat. He lolled his head from side to side and parodied a laugh. When his belly settled he forced down the last quarter-jar and returned cross-eyed to the hut. He tripped twice on the way. The bootsole doubled up and the sound of his body toppling to the ground was the only sound the night produced.

Well into morning he was woken by Black Paw's voice in the window. It worked his way into his dreams. He sat up with his head in a sunbeam and as he turned toward the light he thought he might be sleeping still. Then he saw the gun barrel.

It protruded from a silhouette of hair, the barrel long and black, the hair long and black, the barrel motionless in space, the hair hanging over the indian's torso clear to the window ledge.

"What's that for?" said Lloyd.

"To kill you, should I need to."

Shadows moved outside the doorway. Lloyd swung his head to them, then back at the indian.

"That's Bruder and the Sampsons. They'll shoot you too. Now you carrying a weapon?"

"No," Lloyd reeled some with his eyes squinted against the sunlight. His mind half wandered yet in snow-laden dreamfields.

"What's in that bag?"

"This?" Lloyd touched the flour sack.

"What's in it?"

"Grass."

Black Paw considered this. "Stand up," he said.

Lloyd looked down the rifle barrel. He rolled over and drew his knees up under him. His head was heavy. It hung unwieldy from his neck. He stood up and accommodated the coat around him.

"I'll ask you again if you got a weapon."

"I said I ain't got one."

"If it turns out you do and you draw it on us, I'll surely kill you. I'd rather not, but I will."

Lloyd swallowed, blinked again. "I seen you somewhere?"

"You surely did."

"What do you want?"

"Step outside where we can talk to you."

Lloyd did as he was told. The indian called to the shadows outside the doorway. When Lloyd crossed the empty portal into the sunlight, the three men outside had guns waiting for him and Black Paw was coming around the side of the hut with the stock of his own still lodged against his shoulder and the barrel no less black than before.

"This him?" said the bigger man among them. He held a rifle trained on Lloyd's shirtfront.

"That's him."

"You sure?"

"I haven't forgotten him. He's still got the flour sack," said Black Paw. "He ate the flour and stuffed it with grass. Been using it as a pillow."

"Alright," the big man ran his eyes over Lloyd's face and down the coat. "What's your name?"

"Lloyd."

"You get that flour over in La Chureca?"

"I don't know what it was called."

"You pay for it?"

"What's it matter?"

"Black Paw says you stole it."

Lloyd looked at the indian. If he was told the man was forty-five or seventy-five he'd have believed either one. "I took it on credit," he said.

"On credit," said the big man.

Lloyd sniffed.

"That why you and your partner ran out of Henry's waving guns around?"

"Who's Henry?"

"The man you two robbed."

"I didn't rob him."

"You want to blame it on your partner?"

"He ain't my partner."

"Black Paw says you stole it. Says he was at Henry's when you did it. Saw you clear as day."

One of the Sampson boys nudged Lloyd with his rifle barrel and jabbed his head toward the big man. "Tell Bruder where you got the coat."

Lloyd drew it tight over his shoulders.

"Where'd you get the coat?" said Bruder.

"East of here a ways."

"You steal that too?" said Bruder.

"No."

"You kill for it?"

"No."

"You didn't kill Jim Crudger?"

"I ain't killed nobody."

"Why's Jim laying dead outside La Chureca with a bullet hole in him?"

"I said I didn't do it."

"You're wearing his coat."

"It wasn't me."

"You gonna say you took that coat on credit too?"

"No."

"Where's your partner?"

"I told you he ain't my partner."

"You just ride with him."

"He was just following me. I don't hardly know him."

"I expect you're gonna tell us it was him shot Jim Crudger."

"It was him."

"See there?"

"It was."

"And you ended up with the coat."

Lloyd closed his mouth. He breathed through his nose and looked down the four barrels and blinked. The Sampson boys fidgeted. They might have been twins, no older than Lloyd.

"What are you doing here anyway?" said Bruder.

"Just passing through is all."

"Old Crazy says you've been here two days and not sober for even one."

"Who's Old Crazy?"

"The man whose spit you been drinking," said Bruder. He kept the gun pointed at Lloyd's chest. "Why don't you come with us."

"Where?"

"Down by the sawmill."

Lloyd's legs stayed put beneath the coat.

"Go on now."

The men's breathing the only thing audible under the sky.

Black Paw made no perceptible movement, but all four men's heads turned to him, Lloyd's included. "Walk in front of us to the land office," said Black Paw. "You do anything else, I'll shoot you."

Lloyd walked. The men followed, barrels loping like hounds at his backside. They circled down the adobe lanes and came out abreast of the sawmill. Old Crazy with his scalped head pushed open the saloon doors and squinted with his mouth all skewed up and his shoulders hunched and watched the four men direct Lloyd into the land office across the lane.

The ceiling was raised up high and there were tables covered in dust. Bruder's voice guided Lloyd past them and around a support post to where they stopped at an open stairwell. The steps were carved from the earth and led into darkness.

"Billy," said Bruder, "Go fetch us a candle."

The Sampson boy had been gone but a minute when Black Paw said, "We'll need more than a candle."

"Go ask Molly for a couple lamps," Bruder said to the other Sampson bother. "And make sure they got oil in 'em."

When the two young men returned, Bruder touched the lit candle to the lamps and prodded Lloyd down the stairwell with the firelight flitting off the cellar walls and making shadows out of nothing.

The room below was not six feet high and one half of it was sectioned off by iron bars. Hinges ran down a section and from these opened a gate through which Lloyd was ushered. He entered and turned and watched through the bars while they hunted the key in the shadows. When they found it they locked the cell gate, and Bruder sent the boys out to tend to the skinning of the antelopes.

Inside the cell there was nothing. A table furnished the other half of the room. Bruder set the lamps on it.

"What'll you do with him now?" said Black Paw.

"What'll I do with him?"

"You're sheriff."

"That was a lark," said Bruder.

"It's no lark now."

"And Old Crazy is mayor."

"You took the title."

"Title," said Bruder.

Lloyd watched this exchange with his face in the bars. The cellar had a chill to it. He crossed his arms in the coat.

"I guess we'll wait for Stroud to show up."

"You expecting him?"

"As long as Molly's here I expect he'll come around."

The indian's face remained square in the lamplight. Unmoving.

"Speaking of which," said Bruder, "she was asking about you. 'Shouldn't he be back, shouldn't he be back.' I don't know what the hell for, you done fixed all there was needed fixing. Lord knows she's got nothing to pay you with, less she plans on giving you a goat." Bruder cocked his head but Black Paw provided nothing in response. "What were you watching her for anyway?" said Bruder.

Lloyd looked at the indian.

"I'm talking to you, boy," said Bruder.

"What?" said Lloyd.

"Black Paw says you was settin' up by the huts spying on Molly."

"I wasn't spying."

"You was watching her."

"I was just looking."

"Just looking. Like hell. You figure on stealing a goat?"

"No."

"You figure on something worse?"

"No"

"You steal that horse? Decent enough looking horse with no

saddle on him. You don't even got a proper bridle on him. You steal him?"

Lloyd dropped his head.

"The hell with it," said Bruder. He stood off the table. "Let Stroud deal with him."

They extinguished the lamps and ascended the stairwell by candlelight. When they closed the hatch all was dark. Lloyd sat with his legs crossed in the dirt and soon he was stretched out asleep in the silence of the cellar.

Later that day Bruder returned. He carried with him a waterskin made of cow bladder, a rag and a chamberpot. He passed the waterskin through the bars. Next he handed Lloyd the rag in which was wrapped a strip of antelope meat, and finally the chamberpot. Lloyd gave no thanks and Bruder waited for none. The big man turned his back and climbed the stairs and shut the hatch behind him, taking with him light and sound and any sense of dimension in all that sightless void.

Blackness returned. Dark enough that time, no matter its duration, inured Lloyd's eyes not one degree to it's profundity. By feel alone he made his prison's acquaintance. He ran his hands along the wall and up into the corners. He held the bars and shook them, stamped his feet against the floor. The meat he chewed and swallowed. Later, his colon cramping in response, he took a squat and shat into the chamberpot and used the rag to wipe himself.

Between sleep and fits of wakefulness he swam in weightless empty. His throat clenched up but he kept away from the waterskin. Darkness robbed him of his bearings. Lacking proprioception, he stumbled into the chamberpot and overturned its contents, and like a man plagued by queer misfortune he turned disoriented into the wall and smashed his face against it and toppled back into his feces.

He crawled his way to the bars. Hands tight around them he hollered out. The voice he heard reflecting off the cellar walls rang weak and foreign in his ears, and he laid himself against them while the vice cranked tighter around his skull.

The hatch opened.

Firelight jumpy on the walls.

Shapes of blurred edges, of legs meeting steps. Bruder's legs, Bruder with an oil lamp in his hand. He held it out and followed its light and stopped beside the bars where Lloyd's face was pressed between them.

"You letting me out?" Lloyd's words rasped from an unused throat.

Bruder lowered the lamp. He swung it wide and brought it center, but whichever way the light cast its shadows it mitigated naught Lloyd's anguish.

"I come to fill that waterskin."

"You ain't gonna let me out?"

"Not now I ain't."

"How long I been down here?"

"Couple days."

"You can't keep me in here, there ain't no light."

Bruder looked into the cell. "You done kicked over your pisspot," he swung the lantern around in search of the waterskin. "Hand me that bladder."

"There ain't no light, I can't...," Lloyd's voice rose and fell and lifted and dried up.

"It's right there, hand it over." Bruder took it. He hefted it twice in his hand and shook his head. "You drink any of this? You need to drink water. Here's why you say *No* when Old Crazy unwraps his corn spit. This right here. You look like Clyde 'fore he died. Drink some water." He shoved the waterskin back through the bars. When he turned, the light turned with him.

Lloyd called out, "Leave that lamp here."

"How am I to see my way out?" said Bruder.

"You can see."

Bruder looked at the lamp and looked at Lloyd. "You gonna pay for the oil?"

Lloyd's adam's apple bolted up and down again. His head jerked with the attempt at a swallow.

"I'll leave it," said Bruder. "I got to get. Later I'm coming back-- I got some questions for you."

When he'd gone Lloyd watched the lamp flame burn eternal. There was no glass; the fire stood straight in the open air. After a while Lloyd puckered his lips and blew softly and waited, and the air carried, and Lloyd gripped the bars in a panic at the flame's lurching and twisting and the fluttering of its death, and when it righted itself and grew bold again he laughed a soundless laugh and sat relieved against the bars.

Bruder returned while Lloyd slept. The hatch banged closed and Lloyd sat up in the pelts. The man had brought another lamp. He set it on the table with the other and sat himself on the flat space beside them. He looked at Lloyd.

"You drink that water?" he said.

"I drank it," said Lloyd.

"Them hallucinations leave you?"

"I ain't had no hallucinations."

"Like hell," Bruder gripped the table edge. "I want to ask you about that horse. You steal it?"

Lloyd laid back down.

Bruder came off the table. "I can take that lamp back with me."

"What do you want with my horse?"

"I assume its owner wants it back."

"Why do you think I stole it?"

"Man who shoots another man dead for a coat don't think nothing of stealing a horse."

"I didn't shoot that man."

"Black Paw reckons you did."

"He's a liar."

"Black Paw ain't no liar. Hell, he saw you steal the flour, he was right there."

Lloyd rested his chin on his chest.

"Why don't you just say what you did."

"What are you gonna do?"

"I'm only asking."

"Ain't you a sheriff?"

"No."

"I thought you was."

"I'm not."

"What's all this here then? Why you got a jail if you ain't no sheriff?"

"This was here before I ever shown up. Never thought I'd use it. Now tell me; you steal that horse?"

"What if I did?"

"Then I'll try to get a man his horse back."

"What'll you do to me?"

"Nothing."

"Nothing?"

"That's what I said."

Lloyd turned his face to the light. "Alright. I stole it."

"Alright," Bruder said. He nodded and pursed his mouth.

"Where from?"

"From some soldiers over by the Sabine."

"Americans or Mexicans?"

"Mexicans."

Bruder sucked air through his nose. It didn't quite whistle.

They stood each of them in the glow of the lamplight and the iron bars between them and the ceiling low against Bruder's head. No sound in the cellar.

After a while Bruder said, "Well I ain't gonna ride clear across Texas to give some Mexican soldier his horse back."

"You'll let me go then?" said Lloyd.

"No," said Bruder.

"You ain't got cause to hold me. All I done is took some Mexican's horse."

"There's Jim," said Bruder.

"I didn't kill him."

"I ain't the one to say you did or didn't."

"Then what are you doing holding me?"

"Waiting for Thaddeus Stroud. Captain Stroud."

"What'll he do?"

"He'll do whatever it is he does." Bruder took the second lamp from the table. At the steps he said to Lloyd, "I'll bring you some grub later."

"Bring me that indian," said Lloyd. "He's lying. He's lying!"

Later, when Bruder descended the stairwell with a plate of food in hand, Lloyd rose like a waif in his cell and asked to see the indian. Bruder set the plate in the dirt by the bars and poured a dram of oil into the lamp body and turned and climbed back up the stairs while Lloyd's demands ricocheted off the stunted ceiling. They continued as though they'd never stopped, thrown against the dirt walls and withstood like ocean waves by Bruder when he returned that following day to empty the chamberpot. The big man lowered his head and pushed it like a plow into Lloyd's complaints. That day and the next, and the day following. By and by Lloyd grew hoarse. He drank the water and ate what was served and mumbled words to Bruder of which Bruder recognized few.

At a point in time, day or night he knew not which, Lloyd told Bruder in a clear voice he would kill Black Paw.

Bruder set down the chamberpot he'd come to empty and squinted at where Lloyd sat wrapped in his pelts in the shadows. "Now why you go and say that," he said.

"Cause I will."

"You gonna kill Black Paw."

"He's the one done this to me."

"He didn't kill Jim Crudger."

"Neither did I. And he's saying I did."

"Sure looks like you did."

"Only cause I got his coat. What about my tracks?"

"What about them?"

"If Black Paw found Jim, he'd have seen my tracks there too."

"I'm sure he did."

"Well?" said Lloyd. "Can't he read no sign?"

"What is there to read? Jim's dead, and your tracks are all about. And then there's the coat."

"I come back later for the coat. The kid that was riding with me is the one who shot him."

"Black Paw said it was you."

"He's wrong."

Bruder looked through the bars but said nothing.

"They'll shoot me or they'll hang me for that," said Lloyd.

"I reckon they will."

"I'll kill him," Lloyd said again.

"Is that what you'll do?"

"I will."

Bruder clucked his tongue against his palate. "You won't do no such thing. You know it and I know it."

"What do you know?"

"I know what I see," said Bruder. "I see a young man ain't done nothing in his life but rob and steal and make destruction on the earth and all the while sour and ornery and set against goodness."

Lloyd leaned forward. The pelts leaned forward with him. Out of the shadows and into the lamplight.

"You think you're a big man," said Bruder. "Tell me, what have you done in your life? You gone and got drunk. Made you feel big. Maybe you paid some whore to let you mount her, made you feel like you done something."

Lloyd's face drew tight. He listened and breathed through his mouth as though he'd been running.

Bruder snorted. "And you settin' there saying you gonna kill Black Paw. Like hell. I'm starting to come around to the idea that maybe you never did kill Jim Crudger. You got a lot of gripe in you, but there ain't much below it. You even know what you're capable of? What it is you might do should it really come down to it?"

Lloyd waited.

"You don't know. I can hear it when you speak. You spit fire and fury and it's all empty. I'll tell you something, Black Paw ain't like us. That's a man, when he speaks, he means it. Recollect now us standing there outside the huts. I tell you to get to walkin', and you just stand there. Then Black Paw says get walkin' and what do you do?" Bruder paced down the length of the cellar and came

107

back. Shadows whipped in angled response to the lamp. "I'll tell you something since you're just setting there and you got all the time in the world. I'll tell you something a man once told me, I ain't never forgot it."

"Yeah?" said Lloyd.

Bruder sat himself on the table with his crown inches from the ceiling. He set the lamp back down and curled his fingers over the table edge and looked at Lloyd. "Within each man there lies a monster."

Lloyd breathed. Bruder breathed. Bruder went on.

"Folks may not believe that, but it's true. They don't believe it cause most ain't seen what lies way down inside 'em. But it's truly in us, black and ugly. It's in you and it's in me. Only we ain't seen it. Don't wanna see it. But once a man does, he knows what he's truly capable of. He knows what foulness he's made of, and when he says he'll do something he says it not as a threat but as an admission of what wretchedness sits inside him. Man like that, you can hear it when he talks. That's why when Black Paw tells you he'll kill you, you know it. Why when he tells you to stand up you stand up, he says walk, you walk. He ain't asking you; he's pleading with you. 'Help me keep it away,' he's saying. Cause Black Paw seen his monster."

Lloyd crawled closer to the bars. "What's he seen?"

Lamplight outlined Bruder's frame in a dancing aura. His chest rose in his shirt. "Was a time this country looked mighty different. Long time ago. Then the Spanish came, brought horses with 'em. Most people living here took 'em up, those that didn't fell behind. Black Paw's people fell behind. Got their hunting grounds stole, their women stole, war brought on them. But it weren't the other tribes did 'em in in the end, it was the damn Spanish. Trawling the earth like a pack of dogs after a bitch, ever last one crazed up by gold like they could smell it. You think about that-- what nonsense that was. Thinking they was gonna find a city built of gold, when every man they saw from Mexico City to here weren't dressed in nothing but a breechcloth and hunting rock squirrels with a goddamn spear. Carrying their wares on the backs of dogs. Think about that foolishness," he looked away as if he saw the scene playing out in the shadows of the cellar. "That's how Black Paw's people left the earth."

Lloyd crawled forward the last few feet and stuck his nose between the bars. "How?"

"In chains or dead. He weren't no more than a boy. Saw them murdered before him and led away like cattle. Him hiding in the bushes. I can't imagine it myself. What I'd do like that, alone like that. What Black Paw done; he followed. Trailed right behind the Spanish soldiers, watched them beat his kinsmen, rape the women. Watched them unshackle the ones couldn't keep up and drop them dead along the wayside. Trailed them halfway through Mexico, something ugly brewing in him all the while."

Bruder sat with his hands clutched around the table edge and his breath coming heavy through his nose. His eyes wandered.

"What'd he do?" said Lloyd.

Bruder's head came up out of a distant place.

"When them soldiers got back to Mexico they didn't have no gold, but they had a few indian slaves. Those that hadn't died anyway. They come back like heroes, full of stories. The city of gold was just beyond the bend, they said. They'd reach it on the next trip, they said. So there they was all piled up in the garrison, celebrating their victories. Soldiers, townsfolk, viceroys. A banquet of vittles, the whole town populace dressed up for dancing, and

Black Paw outside watching. One double door on the garrison. A monster inside him. He found himself a crossbar and barricaded the door and set fire to the garrison and burned every last one alive. Killed all them soldiers. Killed the townsfolk. Women was in there, children too I reckon. And him sitting there watching," Bruder bent his head. "I can't imagine the smell."

"They all die?"

"The whole damn village. Over two-hundred souls. He hung around for some time after, doing what in the ashes I don't know. Group of missionaries traveling through picked him up. Lucky, maybe. Maybe not. They brought him East, put him in school, learned him English. They didn't know what the hell had happened. Black Paw never said. Anyway, he come back out West at some point. You can't stick no indian in civilization and expect he'll stay. He's been here ever since, no people, no nothing, just the memory of what he done. I reckon that's why he lives like he does."

"Like how?"

"Fixing Molly's gate. Patching her roof, tending her goats. He hauls corn back from East Texas so Old Crazy can make his damn chicha. Used to hunt for Clyde. He takes my furs in, doesn't ask a thing, just does favors for folks like it was his life's work. Maybe it is. What I do know is that Black Paw's a man who knows what he's capable of, and when he talks you can hear it. Black Paw don't make no empty threats. He seen his monster."

Bruder uncapped the bottle and poured a shot into the lamp base still full of oil. His hand seemed to shake, or maybe it was the wiggle of the flame, Lloyd couldn't tell. He watched from the cell and scratched his neck and waited until Bruder had capped the bottle again.

"There ain't no gold then?" said Lloyd.

"What?"

"You said them Spanish soldiers was hunting gold."

"Aye."

"They didn't find it?"

"Down Mexico way there was plenty. Not up here. Only gold ever found up this way was stolen from Mexico. Hell, Black Paw seen it. All that time he was trailing them soldiers and they were out marauding and killing, he told me one time he seen it."

"Where?"

"Seen a man run out and bury it somewheres."

"That don't sound likely."

"Black Paw don't lie."

"Yeah, well," said Lloyd. "Seems like everyone's got a story about gold hid somewheres."

"This one's real."

"I heard a better one."

Bruder blew through his lips. They fluttered in contempt.

"If he seen it get buried," said Lloyd, "why don't he go back for it?"

"That's Black Paw. He said to me once he ain't got no reason for it. I don't know. I reckon it's guilt that keeps him from it. Likely figures he ain't worthy. He said to me he'd go dig it up if he had a reason. I said, 'What would that be?' You know what he told me? He said if he had him a woman and child he'd go dig it up," Bruder laughed suddenly. The sound warbled deep and rippling in the confines of the cellar, and when it died out the big man shook his head. "Black Paw ain't never gonna have no woman and child. Just look at where we are."

For a moment Lloyd considered this. He sat hunched in the furs with his neck craned back and tilted somewhat, and after that moment of consideration passed he let his head down some. "I'll kill him all the same," he said.

Bruder's arm flashed in a blur. The oil tin came flying across the space to smash and clatter against the bars. Lloyd splayed backwards in a spasm that knocked his head against the wall. Bruder lunged from the table in a great raft of blasphemy fired through hardly decipherable syllables all broken and jagged in his rage, Lloyd holding his skull, the ceiling crushingly low, the cellar like the belly of some dusty beast churning in slow digestion in the must, and all back to blackness where Lloyd sat alone and scornful in the hollow of his foul cell.

Five

The hatch door opened. It slapped against the floor when it dropped. Lloyd sat up. A ricochet of voices pattered off the stairwell walls. Lamplight pushed against the darkness. It hugged the ceiling and shimmered forward to surveil the cellar, and where it fell against the steps it fell too on a pair of boots polished black and smooth.

They came down into the confines of the cellar and the men held their lamps out before them and regarded Lloyd as one would some foreign creature wheeled into town by a traveling circus. The man with the polished boots boasted a uniform with buttons running in a line down his chest and a red sash long faded tied around his waist and hanging off to one side. He was clean-shaven. As he stood there studying Lloyd through the cage bars he smiled. His teeth were straight and flat. The light gleamed against their whiteness.

"How long have you been holding him?"

"A few weeks," answered Bruder.

"It smells longer than that."

"He don't always hit the chamberpot direct."

The captain shifted. His smile remained. "You could have taken him out and shot him if you're so sure of his crimes."

"That ain't for me to do, Captain."

"That's for me, is it?"

"Well."

"I've got sixteen guns in the street. We can have him buried by noon if that's what you want."

"You don't need to take it like that, Captain. You're the closest thing to law we've got. I'm only trying to do the right thing."

"And what's the right thing?"

"I thought you'd take him up to La Chureca. See if Henry recognizes him."

"What good will that do?"

"If Henry says it's him, well then, that about settles it. It's him."

"You said you already know it's him."

"I don't know for sure. But he's wearing the coat, and the man who found Jim Crudger dead said he found this young man's tracks all about."

"Are you positive the coat belongs to the trapper?"

"There ain't no mistaking it."

"That's enough for me. We can hang him or shoot him, your choice. La Chureca is out of my way."

"Hell, Stroud, I'm trying to do the right thing."

The captain stroked the smooth of his face.

"Just take him up to see Henry," said Bruder. "It ain't so far out of your way. It's the right thing to do. That's what Molly figures anyway."

The captain turned on Bruder. Lloyd saw the lips close, the teeth disappear. Only the two men's breath, the sounds of small movements. Lamp flames burned between them. They wavered some when the captain lifted a hand. Bruder snaked the key from a pocket in response, and the two men pulled Lloyd like an old woman from the cell; thin and frail beneath the coat.

They carried him up the stairwell and into the street and when they came into the light of day Lloyd wrapped an arm against his eyes and croaked at its harshness. He fell to his knees where they dropped him. Under the coat he was hot. He heard an order given and heard the shuffling of feet in response. A hand grabbed him and pulled him across the lane and he was set down with his back against a post. The squeaking of the saloon doors whined out beside him.

A long while he sat there with his face buried in the crook of his coat sleeve. When he finally let loose the tension of his arm against his eyes and allowed daylight to sneak through, it poured in on orange beams that flickered at the edge of his vision. He pulled his arm away and breathed in the sunshine while soldiers paced in and out of the saloon with glasses in their hands and their drunken conjectures cut with laughter. Lloyd counted a dozen and lost track. He looked for Bruder or the Sampson brothers or Molly, but saw only cavalry milling about the abandoned town. Mostly his eyes searched for Black Paw, but he too was gone.

"Best guzzle that down," one soldier said to another. The two sat in the shade of the saloon wall not far from Lloyd.

"Burgess said we'd be here a while."

"Five minutes."

"Five minutes what?"

"That's how long it'll take the captain to wet his pecker."

Laughter.

"Maybe he'll dip it in twice and we'll get ten."

More laughter.

Boots clapped the plankboards. Hinges creaked. The waistline of the man emerging measured as wide as his shoulders. "You fancy a lashing, McKenny?"

Lloyd watched the soldiers flinch before they answered.

"No, sir," said McKenny.

"Captain Stroud allows you a drink and you repay him with insult?"

"No, sir."

"You, Price?"

"We was just funning, Lieutenant."

"Keep it up and the captain will stand you up alongside this louse trap and shoot you all the same."

The two soldiers appraised Lloyd sitting in his coat of mottled pelts. A cursory inspection brought no comfort to their faces. Unshaved faces rimmed in dirt, grime in their nails. They ran him up and down with unhurried glances, then turned back to the lieutenant.

"We really riding to La Chureca?" asked Price.

"Those are the orders."

Their faces turned again to Lloyd. Glasses touched their lips and they swallowed through coiled beards and turned away again. When the batwings whined again, Old Crazy came through. He held a glass of chicha against his chest. He stepped around in front of Lloyd and squatted with his bald head shining white in the sun and looked up like a grasshopper at the soldiers gathered round.

"You'll not begrudge a man a last drink, will ye?"

The lieutenant only snorted.

"Go on now," Old Crazy stretched the chicha forward. He watched Lloyd take it and eye it and rest the edge on his lips, and when the slop came over the rim the old man smiled his toothless smile and beat his arms against his ribs. "I never cottoned to Jim anyhow," he said.

Captain Stroud returned on Lloyd's second glass. He marched a path down the center lane, past the mill, his spine straight, his face to match. He said nothing, only fetched his horse. The lieutenant called the men to attention and they rose and staggered out of the bar and assembled their horses and pack mules, and in a commotion of dust Lloyd's stolen horse appeared. They threw the coat over its back in place of a saddle and heaved Lloyd up like a doll, too frail or too drunk to mount it himself, or perhaps already taken for dead.

With Captain Stroud riding lead they filed down the empty street to the edge of town where Lieutenant Burgess barked at the men to ride sharp, and before Molly's cabin they paraded themselves, all sixteen soldiers throwing furtive glances to see if she watched from behind the curtains or if their display of gallantry went unnoticed and unendowed of recognition. By twos they crossed the stream; each man and his spare. The pack mules followed, the tents and poles, the luggage careening on their backs, supply wagons jerking, and Lloyd behind it all watching drunk from his pelt-robed steed. A soldier tasked with guard duty stuck beside him. They paid one another little mind. Lloyd's hands were left unbound, his feet hung free; nothing to keep him in the company's command but the vast unfolding desert glowing red beneath the sun.

At the quarry road they turned and looped back eastward. Molly's cabin was left behind along with any residue of military formation. They rode as they were dressed; each to his own. Not a single uniform matched. Aside from the captain and his lieutenant, nary a soldier could lay claim to a complete outfit that might pass as military regalia. Some wore buckskin leggings. There were jackets fashioned out of myriad animal hides. Soldier hats and continentals and bicorn navy caps and any headpiece that might import some sense of stature were festooned upon their heads. In the vanguard rode a Paiute scout on a white horse. He wore breechcloths made of woven sagebrush and across his shoulders was a cloak of rabbit fur, and this costume appeared no less formal than any other in that motley ensemble.

They held their trajectory until nightfall, at which they stopped in the shelter of a shale outcropping. The pack mules were unloaded, poles were planted in the ground, canvas tents raised. Drunk as the men were, the ride had sobered them. They carried out their tasks without need of the lieutenant's reproach. Ashes of old cook fires lay like craters rimmed in moonlight. Two of these were relit. Lloyd's hands and feet were tied with rope and he was left to find comfort in the sand, unattended and unnoticed until morning, at which the restraints were unwound and he was shoved once again upon his horse.

Like wolves they rode through scraggled stands of prickly pear. Spots of purple cenizo adorned that jagged hell as though placed there by a woman's hand to deliver it from misery by the sole bequest of beauty. The Paiute brushed a hand against them and their petals fell and lay like garlands on the trail. In a water hole tucked in a ridge they filled their canteens and watered the animals and rode on. Out through the cenizo, onto the sun-baked basin.

Lloyd, seated on the coat, squirmed and twisted. The horse's spine splayed his legs. His eyes wandered. He was given enough water to keep his throat from suffocation, the food not more than scraps.

Not until the third day did he realize it was Gil Pucker staring back at him. The boy sat a different horse than either of the two he'd stolen, and in place of the ship's sail wrapped about his torso he'd been given a fitted shirt and a faded army jacket. The same oversized trousers swam about his legs. He rode just behind the lieutenant and the Paiute, and every quarter mile he'd twist in the saddle to squint back at Lloyd.

That night the company built their fires over ancient rings. As they'd shot no game, the captain allowed them a run on the whiskey. They tied Lloyd's hands behind his back and left him sitting cross-legged on the ground. He stared at the fires, watched the soldiers tip the bottles back. He watched Gil scuttle closer, the boy crouching and nervous as he crossed the campgrounds, holding his trousers up as though in doubt of the belt's steadfastness. When the boy reached him Lloyd's leaned back, but a few inches were all the distance the ropes would allow. The Springfield tucked in Gil's belt appeared oversized and toy-like against such slight a frame. He hunched over Lloyd as though bent from crippled vertebrae.

"How'd they get you?" he hissed.

Lloyd shrugged.

"They're taking you to La Chureca," Gil waited for a response and none came. The hairs on his face had been shaven or clipped and the skin was smooth and soft. "They gonna see if that old man Leatherface recognizes you."

"Yeah," said Lloyd.

"You know he will."

"I reckon."

"If he does, they'll shoot you. What with you having Jim's coat and all."

Lloyd nodded.

"What'll you do?"

"I don't want to be shot."

"You gonna say something about me?"

"You're the one that killed him."

Gil turned. The sound of soldiers laughing met him, and when he faced Lloyd again his mouth was drawn in a grimace. The small round teeth sat same as before. "You can't prove that," he said.

"It's true."

"You ain't got to say it though."

"I ain't getting shot for something I never done."

"They gonna shoot you anyways."

Lloyd eyed the Springfield. The handle rested in the curve of Gil's belly.

"They gonna shoot you anyways, Lloyd. Ain't no reason to involve me."

Lloyd looked away. Gil huffed some and twitched and turned finally and found himself a tin cup of whiskey amongst the men. He drank it and stared at Lloyd from the fire until he lay drunk and unconscious in the sand.

In the morning they broke camp and lashed the tents to the mules and marched into the sun with their faces red and swollen. Lloyd rode in back and ate the dust of sixty animals. Through it he saw Gil turn. The boy's face scrunched. The Springfield in his belt.

In two days they descended a limestone ridge into a valley covered in bluestem and grama, leaving the desert behind like a bygone dream. The horses and mules dropped their necks and wrenched the grass from the shallow soil in disobedience to the men's commands. The heels jabbing their ribs and the lashes over their hindquarters were a bargain offered and taken. The men dismounted and whipped the animals harder, but still they wouldn't move. They only brayed and kicked and tore half-starved at the grass.

Seeing the futility, Stroud gave the order to halt. The soldiers wandered under the sky without direction or purpose. When they raised their heads and looked upon the escarpment of limestone rising out of the west in dry and barren crags they turned from it like sinners turns from a woman's wrath, and stared out instead upon the friendlier eastern pastures.

Not a thing there was to bind them together on that empty plain save for the pretense of uniforms and the recalcitrance of the animals, until four arrows rained down from the limestone cliffs. They whistled softly as they flew, and when two of them implanted themselves in the grass some ten feet apart it was with dull whumps that turned every head except the mules, who only twitched their ears and grazed on.

A cry came out of the ensuing silence and all heads turned to John McKenny. A cry of indignation. He gripped his forearm in one hand. Pierced clean through was an arrow shaft.

To his left the Paiute's white horse pranced forward. The Paiute swayed dead in the saddle. His body tilted and he spilled to the ground, the rabbit furs red with blood.

Captain Stroud shouted a command which Lieutenant Burgess repeated and the soldiers quickly obeyed. They pulled the animals in line with the supply wagons, steadied their rifles over the sideboards and nestled them in the creases of saddles, the bayonets extending out like the noses of basset hounds sniffing up at the ridge. The sudden flurry of commotion, the creaking of the wheels, it ended abruptly in a settling of dust and a long stillness and the eventual call of high-soaring birds overhead.

From behind his horse Lloyd studied the cliffs. He waited in expectation of something more, and when nothing followed, the captain called for the surgeon to be brought forward. In the supply wagon was a medicine chest. The wounded arm was bandaged, its owner insistent on keeping it. The surgeon rinsed the hole with aguardiente and gave the man the bottle.

Upon council with the lieutenant, Captain Stroud selected a dozen men to take to the backs of their horses, the name Osmond Culkin first among them. They took out in a tight grouping, horses at a gallop, and Lloyd stood with the four remaining soldiers and watched this ensemble of avengers cap the ridge and run along the rim a ways and turn and disappear within its bowels.

Wagers ensued forthwith.

Francis Price ventured that John McKenny would lose his arm, and McKenny, unstabled by the liquor, turned his carbine onto Price and held it steady with his good arm and swore to kill the man who would cut his bone or take the bet.

"Francis won't take your arm, John," said the surgeon. "Now hear me. I'll give any man two to one that Osmond comes up short."

Price snorted.

"It's a fair bet," said the surgeon.

"Fair as a whore's fanny."

"You doubt him?"

"The damn Paiute would have had a hard time of it. And Osmond ain't much of a tracker."

"He's decent enough," said the surgeon. "You, Linus?"

"I ain't a part of this," said the wrinkled soldier.

"Give me three to one," said McKenny. "And promise you won't take me arm."

They laid their coins on the wagon bed, Mexican and American and strange foreign tender, knowing not their value save for what they'd buy in drink and vice.

"Why you reckon Stroud took the boy?" said Price.

"Gil?" The surgeon clinked the remaining coins in his pocket.

"Aye."

"The captain's taken a shining to him."

"Maybe."

"See's himself in him."

Price waited.

"Not in any physical way," the surgeon clarified.

"In what way then?"

The surgeon fondled his pocket. He drew forth the coins and fingered them. "I'll lay three of my big ones against three of yours that if they do catch up with them, and that's only if they do, mind you, that that boy will kill himself one."

Price looked hard at the surgeon. He pursed his lips. His eyes moved around their orbs and he looked up at the ridge like he might see the new recruit and somehow judge his nature, and in so doing he nodded slowly and agreed to take the bet. The two drew out a separate square on the wagon into which each man placed his coinage.

Price thumbed his silver onto the space and counted out his remaining monies. "Linus?" he said.

"I ain't a part of this," repeated the old man in the floppy hat.

"You're a part of this as much as any man."

"Leave him," said the surgeon.

"I'll leave him. You, John?"

"That boy Gil don't look like much."

"Exactly," said Price. "Looks like a damn scapegrace."

"You two see what he did on the Clearwater?" said the

surgeon.

"I weren't watching," said McKenny.

"I was," said the surgeon.

John McKenny sucked on the bottle. He wiped his lips and looked at his arm. "I don't know. He ain't been with us but a few weeks."

"That mean you ain't betting?"

"Don't matter anyways. Like Price says, Osmond ain't no Paiute."

As Lloyd listened on, Francis Price raised the flat of his hand to him. "How about you?" he said. "You fancy a wager?"

They turned all four upon him, even Linus, who claimed he had no part in these proceedings, and assessed Lloyd's meagre outfit. The horse sniffed the ground. The coat of mange decorated its back. Lloyd silent like a piece at auction, his clothing soiled into one flat color.

"He ain't got nary a thing to wager," said McKenny.

"He'd do well to risk them boots," said Price. "It'd be a favor to him should he lose."

McKenny laughed and kissed the bottle.

"You want to wager them boots, fella?"

"Why don't ya'll let him be?"

"I thought you weren't a part of this, old man."

"You needn't torment him."

"I'm just funnin'."

"He ain't laughing."

"John's laughing."

"Francis," the surgeon raised a hand.

"I'm just having some fun is all. Goddamn. Should have gone up the ridge yonder, I'd have had more fun chasing down savages than setting here with a bunch of Marys."

"Hey Francis," the wagon sagged under McKenny's weight. He rocked against it and held out the empty bottle. "I'll lay you a wager."

"Go on."

"I'll take that they put him against a wall. You take hanging."

Price dismissed him with a hand. "I'm not the one that's drunk."

"Ain't nothing wrong with that wager, Francis."

"The captain likes the sound of rifles. I know it as well as you."

The four men looked upon the condemned again and the jest left their faces.

"Is it ya'll who'll be doing the shooting?" said Lloyd.

"Aye," said the surgeon.

No more words were spoken there on the plain. Linus Tate took to his horse and made a loop around the pack animals and sang to them in his old raspy voice. Francis Price and the surgeon raised the tents and asked nothing of John McKenny, who stared at the cliffs with the empty bottle to pacify his lips.

When the company rode down from the highgrounds that evening the surgeon had unloaded wood from the supply wagons and let water from the barrels and put it on to boil. The soldiers rode in silent and dust-covered and each of those who had stayed behind knew the surgeon had won his bet. Osmond Culkin striped the gear from his horse and found a quiet place in the shadows, far from the captain's fire. Scant food there was; hard tack and goat butter bartered from Mexican soldiers. They ate in silence and no one ventured to probe the captain's mind.

In the dark Gil came scuttling. Bent like an insect. He crouched beside Lloyd where Lloyd could smell him.

"You thought any more about it?"

"There ain't nothing more to think."

"They'll kill you anyway. You know that, don't you? It don't matter what you say about me."

Lloyd watched the cookfires crackle.

"You don't need to say nothing about me."

They popped and spat.

"Ain't no reason for it."

Red columns twisting.

"There's another way."

"What way?" said Lloyd.

"You just don't say nothin' about me. I'll get you out of this." He stood and was gone.

Lloyd looked away from the flames and into the night and he was blind and cared not. He tipped back and felt the beginnings of dew seep through his shirt. Cold on the thin grass. Wet.

Lieutenant Burgess shook him. "Captain Stroud will see you."

Lloyd sat up. "My feet are tied."

The lieutenant looked down. "There's slack enough. Get up."

They walked past dying fires smoldering in the earth, the lieutenant's gait firm, Lloyd shambling behind in severed paces, the rope slackening and snapping and the boot sole scraping violently beneath. They halted at the captain's tent. A lamp lit the canvas like the orange translucent belly of a bug. Lieutenant Burgess lifted the flap. Inside the tent the flame glowed and wobbled. Captain Thaddeus Stroud sat cross-legged on the floor. To his right Gil mirrored the position. The lieutenant put a hand to Lloyd's shoulder and Lloyd sat. The four faced each other in a square, the lamp flame breathing.

The captain smiled. His teeth were beautiful. His boots were polished and the polish coated Gil's fingers.

"What is your full name?" he said.

"Lloyd Raymond Reed."

"Speak up."

"Lloyd Raymond Reed."

"Have you ever met a Paiute before?"

"Some."

"Not like this one. He was a barbarian and a sinner but he could sniff out a trail like a coonhound."

The lamp burned calm. Lieutenant Burgess arched his back and exhaled. Gil sat hunched over in a posture of subservient cripple.

"I'm going to ask you some questions and you'll give me clear responses. Gil Pucker says he knows you. Says you can read sign. Can you read sign?"

"Yes."

"Speak up."

"Yes."

"Can you read it like a Paiute?"

"I reckon."

"Where'd you learn it?"

"I don't recollect. I just always knowed it."

"Someone must have taught you."

"My pa."

"Where is he?"

"Dead, I reckon."

"You reckon?"

Lloyd turned his chin. "He's dead."

The captain waited, then continued. "He was a trapper?"

"Yes."

"And you trapped with him?"

"Yes."

"You know the land west of the Missouri?"

"I know it."

"You trapped the Rocky Mountains?"

"Yes."

"How far?"

"All over."

"You know the tribes there? One from another?"

"I know which is which."

"You know the tribes here in Texas? The Mexican lands to the Colorado River?"

"Some."

"You speak their tongues?"

"Which ones?"

"Any of them."

Lloyd sniffed. His eyes fell on his untethered sole. Eyes directed at the boot, he said, "I speak Shoshone and Cheyenne. I can get by in Crow. A few trading words in Modoc, same with Nez Perce."

"How about Apache? Or Comanche, or Kiowa."

"No."

"Not a word?"

"I never done no trading with them."

The captain leaned in. His supple lips turned hard. "What is your opinion of them?"

"Which ones?"

"The whole lot of them."

Lloyd hesitated. "I can't say I got one."

The captain's eyes held the fire's reflection. Unblinking. "That

Paiute was a good scout. A savage, but a good scout. John McKenny is going to lose an arm, and that won't stand." He looked at Gil sitting a head lower and at the lieutenant, then back to Lloyd. "I'm to take you in to La Chureca so Henry can tell us what we already know. After he confirms it was you that robbed him and murdered that trapper and left him dead on the plain, I'll have Lieutenant Burgess assemble the men and I'll stand you against a wall and I'll wrap a cloth about your eyes and when I tell the men to aim and fire they'll aim and fire and you'll be executed without so much as a six-word eulogy."

Lloyd's chest rose and fell. Gil hinged forward at the hips. The boy's eyes blinked wide as a mule deer's.

"I didn't kill him," said Lloyd. "I ain't never killed nobody in my life. This here's a misunderstanding. Some lying indian--"

"I don't give a damn if you did or didn't. Folks want to see a man pay. You're wearing the coat-- you pay." The captain paused and watched the effect of his words. He looked at Burgess and back at Lloyd. "That's what I am supposed to do. But there are greater things, Mr. Reed, to which a man might aspire than to carry out a sentence of retribution. More noble causes. There's a land that stretches westward, this very ground," he drilled a finger into the canvas floor, "its soil rich, its pastures a thousand miles long. I've seen forests that cover a hundred thousand acres only to unravel a hundred thousand more. Herds of buffalo number the same. There is a bounty of wealth immeasurable, and not a hand to work it nor a plow to turn it clear to the Pacific Ocean. It sits unused and wasted, and it is an insult not only to common sense but to the sanctity of the American Destiny. In place of progress there exist only barbarous tribes that run dimwitted and half naked and leave nothing for posterity save for their own heathen offspring which breed like feral dogs and are no better than such and dare I say worse. We make trade with them, introduce culture, enlightenment, salvation, and they turn from it and pay us back with war. John McKenny lost an arm today, and I lost my scout. These acts will be atoned for."

A shot of wind flogged the canvas. The men's shadows convulsed and the men themselves sat like quarried stone struck dumb by the captain's oration. When the wind departed and the shadows stilled, Stroud offered Lloyd his terms.

"There are four of them and they are on foot. Lead me to them and there will be no stop at La Chureca. We'll ride straight to Fort Tackett. I'll enlist you, feed you, pay you," he looked at Lloyd's feet, "provide you a new pair of boots. A bath and a bed; a soldier's life. An opportunity for good. It's that or the cloth over your eyes and my command."

Lloyd's head sank and rose and by such slight motion an affirmation was assumed.

"Lieutenant," said Stroud. "I want to be on that ridge at first light. I'll reward those mongrels yet, and young Mr. Reed here will earn his stay of execution. May there be no doubt," he showed his perfect teeth to the light, "in the darkest hours we are shown our providence."

The moon gleamed at three quarters its cycle and the flat barren ground atop the limestone mesa shone like beachsand beneath it. The soldiers sat hunched and lost in their saddles and breathed clouds of steam into the predawn while far down on the valley floor the captain and his lieutenant could see the speck that was the surgeon tend to the makings of a fire. A carpet of grass poked through the earth where the supply wagons sat. It bent in silver strings, and through it waded the surgeon to the wagons and back.

Some fifty yards from the captain and lieutenant, Lloyd walked the mesa top. Their words drifted in the thin air.

"He should have taken that arm last night," said Burgess.

"It's McKenny's arm," said Stroud. "If he wants to keep it another day, so be it."

"He's wasting wood."

"There's more ahead."

"What if these four we're chasing only mean to lead us away? You don't think maybe there's more hiding out? Got their eyes set on the supply train?"

"No," the captain said without looking at his lieutenant. His eyes were watching Lloyd. "These here are what got away in the Clearwater."

"I didn't think any got away."

"Well here they are."

"You think they followed us?" said Burgess. He considered his own question. "Well there ain't much left of them."

Lloyd turned again and walked to the two men with his head bent.

The lieutenant watched the crooked gait and the boot sole scraping. His lip curled up like he'd come upon something foul.

"Tell me what you see," said Stroud.

"Ain't nothing to see," said Lloyd. "Everything's trampled out. Up in them rocks is where they sat with their bows. Them tracks is all that's left."

"And then?"

"Where'd the sign lead before ya'll rode over it?"

"Two miles north is where Osmond lost it."

"You ride over that too?"

"Watch your mouth," the lieutenant interrupted.

"I'm just asking," said Lloyd.

"You ask with respect."

The captain raised a hand to quell Burgess. He frowned at Lloyd, standing in the moonlight. "Would you rather we begin there?"

"I reckon we ought to."

They crossed the plateau in the tracks of the previous day's excursion. As the sun crested, it birthed the shadows of thirteen men and thirteen horses all panting steam into its rays. They gathered where the trail ended and watched Lloyd ride his horse out away from them and stare across the mesa top. He swung a leg over the horse's croup and dropped to the ground and walked a hundred yards west then turned and looked back. He cared not of the ground beneath him. With his head raised, he seemed to be staring at the company like some insolent country dotard, the coat enormous on him, his dirty head poking through the top. After some minutes of this the soldiers began to comment. Stroud watched with his jaw unmoving. Only his knuckles, white on his reins, lent indication to his temperament. He looked at Gil and Gil looked away and back at Lloyd who was now hobbling slowly in a northern arc, stopping sporadically with his hands lazy on his hips.

The captain urged his horse forward. He walked it out over the empty ground to where Lloyd stood and leaned low in the saddle. "Tell me what you're doing."

Lloyd gave the captain a tired look and turned away. He cocked his head and only his eyes moved. "You ain't gonna see nothing looking straight down," he said finally.

"And staring ahead?"

"Pick up their shine."

The captain made no comment. He set a hand on the butt of his pistol and when Lloyd looked up he saw the captain's face set hard and the weapon unsheathed a half an inch from his belt.

"That's it right there," Lloyd raised an arm. His finger drifted out.

"That's what?"

"What we's looking for. You ain't gonna see it standing on top of it."

The captain followed Lloyd's finger. His hand remained on the pistol. "I see nothing."

"Well," said Lloyd. "That's shine. And that's where they gone to." He turned at the waist and his outstretched arm came around with him. He stopped with the finger laid against the western skyline. "Ain't hard to pick up, seeing as there was four of them. We ought to ride now while the sun's low; easier to catch the shadows in their tracks." He walked away from the captain and the captain's pistol and the captain's stone-cut jaw and climbed up the horse's back and trotted off in the direction he'd pointed.

The company followed. They hung a good distance back for the first several barren miles until they reached a gravel slope. Lloyd took to his feet again and wheeled about, the coat heavy on his back. He pulled the horse along a ways and paid no mind to the company of men judging his aptitude through unlearned and simple comparisons to how the Paiute had plied his trade. When he mounted up again and turned southwest the lieutenant made to voice his concern but Stroud waved him off and they rode on.

By noon the soldiers had placed their bets and were it not for

Gil there'd be no takers, for none but he owned confidence in Lloyd's meanderings. Their quarry was lost to them; this was clear. That evening they slept like animals on the ground, without fire and without food. The captain's hand returned several times to stroke the pistol, and the lieutenant offered up no reason not to use it. The following morning they again followed Lloyd like an armed rabble in the pilgrimage of their unproven prophet.

Once that day Stroud stopped him to interrogate his logic, and Lloyd pointed to stones dislodged from their beds and other small pebbles he claimed were pushed into the dirt. The captain examined this evidence. Nothing but dirt and rocks lay about. He rode back to where Lieutenant Burgess waited and related what was said, and the lieutenant passed this on to the men and they turned to Gil and questioned if he had the means to pay, for each man knew now that the nit-infested vagrant leading them was an impostor.

When the sun was again low they had taken a pace that made the horses sweat, and when it finally sank they did not stop but rode under moonlight. When Lloyd drew to a walk the soldiers did likewise. The commotion of their movement ebbed. A measure of quiet arrived. Enough for the men to gather round Gil and demand payment. He dithered. He had not the money. The men began to rumble and the lieutenant barked an order to quiet, and suddenly on the wind they caught the smell of burning sagebrush.

The young braves had built their fire between a wall of upthrust boulders and a stand of barrel cacti. Lloyd, out ahead, saw it first. Not the fire, but its light; climbing the wall in orange pantomime. Stroud spurred his horse and the company rode down into that cove, a pack of jackals charging, the four boys caught with their bows unreadied, four orphaned teens, their screams sliding up the wall, jittered and choked with blood, Gil off his horse, stabbing with his bayonet, the captain like a madman in the firelight, his teeth so straight and his face so handsome and his satisfaction so thorough it lasted all the following day, all the way over the mesa tops and down the cliff faces and into the valley where the wagons waited and the mules grazed and where the surgeon met him with whispered words.

In that late hour Stroud gave the order. The surgeon propped the saw blade over a fire and when it turned an ashen white the men seized John McKenny in his sickbed and pinned him where he lay, two men on each limb and another on his head. They cinched a tourniquet about his arm and deafened their ears to his cries, for he'd been given the bottle entire and was a fool to have drunk it in one go. Beneath his elbow they slid a flat stone. The blade touched the skin. The surgeon rehearsed his mark, and in one swipe he reached bone. Two more saw lengths; one for the ulna, another for the radius, and the blade sunk through the meat below and scraped against the stone and the severed arm dropped and laid in the dirt with the white empty palm facing up and everyman's eyes upon it as though it held something they might see if only they could eye it fiercely enough.

From the wagons Francis Price drew a shovel and took the severed limb with him out away from the packmules. He touched the fingers once by accident and a shiver ran over him.

In the morning the company broke camp. When the horses and the wagons and the soldiers and the packmules had vacated the ground, Lloyd twisted for a backwards look from his horse. An empty valley against the cliffs. Two arrows stood from the grass as markers of their passing.

The Paiute also. He rose not from death, and where he had fallen he remained.

Six

Fort Tackett's upper spires rose several yards above the dull green canopies of post oak clustered along the north Texas border. Its walls were constructed of that same lumber, its gates as well, and the company trailing Captain Thaddeus Stroud through them appeared more a lost desert tribe or renegade band of buccaneers than any company belonging to such a place. They were unbathed and foul-smelling. Dried across their clothing was the blood of war. The soldiers stationed there stood back from their labor and watched them file in, and when the last had entered they drew shut the gates and resumed their tasks with the flurry of rumor to bless their day.

In the courtyard by the flagstaff Lloyd swung off his horse. His legs and thighs were brittle, he'd abandoned the coat at the captain's orders, and what cushion it had provided went with it. Further orders compelled him to follow Stroud into the belly of the fort, down musty unlit hallways to a bench outside Major Hangel's office. He sat where he was told and flinched when the captain shut the door behind him

Through the gap underneath Lloyd heard the major cough.

He'd heard this species of cough before and it was the kind that preceded death. He scooted down the bench and bent sideways and faced his ear to the floor.

"You're back."

More might have followed were it not for a fit of coughing. When it subsided Lloyd heard Stroud respond, "Two men shy of what I left with."

"What happened?"

"One took a ball of shot through his belly. Another took ill of what I don't know and there was nothing the surgeon could do."

"This happen on the Clearwater?"

"Yes."

"How did that turn into a fighting matter?"

"They're all fighting matters."

"All to you," the major hacked something from his lungs.

"If I had the men I've been asking for they'd be less inclined to resist. I should have a company of one hundred men. I would settle for sixty, yet here I am sent out with not even one quarter that many."

"You'd only spill more blood with sixty men."

"Not our blood."

"Goddamnit, Stroud. We are not at war. You have a clear duty and that is to offer support to American settlers in Mexican territory. Mexican territory, Captain Stroud, and those indians you hunt down are Mexican citizens."

"Hunt down?"

"Do you not? Would you have me pronounce it more delicately? I am not blind nor am I deaf as to what goes on."

"My duty is to the United States and its people."

"And the natives are to be cut down like dogs to serve this

duty?"

"They are an impediment to our progress."

A laborious grating resonated under the doorway that to Lloyd sounded as equally a seizing of the major's throat as an ejaculation of disgust.

"Men who roam the earth like vermin will be culled by those who govern."

"Enough. Go away from me, I've heard it all before."

"And what of my men?"

"What of your men?"

"I lost two in the Clearwater. The Paiute as well."

"What of that boy that came wandering in? I gave him to you, didn't I?"

"That's one. And a fine soldier I'll make of him. I picked up another in the desert; an army of stragglers I'm making. Allow me another forty and I'll make a company of men worthy of Washington himself."

"A company of men who'll take any vice the devil extends."

"I'll be the judge of them."

"We're all judged, Captain. All of us."

Silence followed. Lloyd scooted back up the bench. The door opened, Stroud came through. He shut it behind him and motioned for Lloyd to follow.

He was led across the parade grounds to the store houses where Lieutenant Burgess waited with a pair of boots and an army issue jacket, all of which had previously adorned some poor fool now dead. A musket ball had torn through the jacket breast. Lloyd poked his finger into the hole rimmed with the dead soldier's blood and pinched the stained cloth between finger and thumb.

In the barracks the lieutenant pointed to a cot and ordered

Lloyd to polish his boots and present himself in the morning dressed and ready. Lloyd obeyed. He rubbed them clean with the sleeve of his new jacket and set them beside the cot. When the soldiers of his company came in that night he lay with his eyes closed and the jacket clutched about him. They looked him over and retired to their cots and his eyes did not open when they spoke.

The following day he was enlisted under his full name, issued a Harpers Ferry Hall rifle, model 1819, and introduced to the routine that was to be his routine every day. At bugle call he would rise and dress and stand in formation with his company. Roll call followed. Report to the stables at stable call to feed and groom the mounts. Water call. Mess call. Bread and mush and molasses. Fatigue call; cutting firewood, hauling water, shovel work that blistered his fingers past the point of bleeding. A warning was given to him by Linus Tate not to report ill to sick call-- Lieutenant Burgess considered every last man a malingerer. Drill call, in which the men practiced battle formations and marched up and down the parade grounds, turning and marching, standing and stopping, up and down and back again, no man's movement sovereign unto himself until the bugle sounded for mess call and they would break from their lines and march into the mess rooms to spoon thin gruel down their throats and rinse it back with water. Rations were tight, they were told. They grew tighter. Afternoon stable call. Another water call-- the horses cared for like deities. They would parade again and assemble again, and when the flag was lowered and the last trumpet faded they would return to the barracks, not built-up but chiseled-down, left with that thin fraction of night before they slept to recover whatever sense of self-determination fermented yet within them. At times they would fall broken into their cots and at others they would tend it by lying awake and cajoling one another like a pack of jackals jostling for hierarchy and establishing bonds through insult and mockery.

On one such occasion John McKenny revealed a bottle of rum stolen from the trade store. He'd been assigned there on fatigue duty-- the reward for his sacrifice-- and during a moment at which Mexican soldiers and a band of Osage bearing sacks of pemmican came to barter, he'd slid the bottle down his britches.

That night in their barracks they lit candles and slid a cot around. A man named Clemons drew out a deck of cards and dealt the cards upon it. A fair number were missing, they all knew it. As for the game they played it mattered not, for in the end each man was a loser and so was poured a dram from the bottle. They called Lloyd from his cot and he too was dealt a card. They turned the deck and his number was lower, and their eyes sparkled in the candlelight as they watched him down the rum.

"Give him another!" someone shouted from the darkness.

"You'll not get drunk and murder us in the night, will you Lloyd?"

"There's none of us owns a coat worth stealing," answered Price.

They laughed, and Gil laughed with them, though had the sound his laughter made been heard above the others it would have turned their heads.

When the bottle ran dry their vice turned to gambling. They played until the cards had thoroughly separated the lucky from the luckless, then abandoned them and set their wagers instead on the ambiguities of the future. Foremost among these was how soon Captain Stroud would lead them back out the gates, away from one misery and on to another.

"He don't like it more than anyone else," said Clemons. He

shuffled the partial deck in his fingers.

"He don't like what?" said Gil.

"The rules. All the marching and the calls. You seen how we done it when no one's looking and it's only the captain to give the orders."

Francis Price leaned over the cot. "If he don't get an order he'll make one up. He'll want to see his lady."

Clemons bridged the deck. "How many days will he drive us off course so's we can stop in Milltown? Now that's a wager."

"Better one is who'll be first to vomit up that corn spit. My money's on Linus."

"I ain't a part of this."

"You is if you drink it, old man."

"There's a better wager to be had," said the surgeon from his cot, "and I'll lay my money on it."

They turned and stared into the shadows where the surgeon lay. Clemons bridged his cards again.

"About the woman?" said Price.

"Aye. About the woman."

"A dunce's bet, Surgeon. You'll lose your money. She's his if she's anyone's."

"He's not made a wife of her."

"Not every man pines for a wife."

"It's true. Some men only seek their comforts."

"That's how I figure it."

"Only," said the surgeon, "he's not yet enjoyed that woman's comforts."

They sat and considered this. The cards stopped fluttering. John McKenny tottered on his cot, drunker than any other. He'd had the largest share of rum; to the thief went the spoils. He held the empty bottle to his face with his lips pressed against it and narrowed his brow at the surgeon. "If I had me arm back I'd bet it against you."

"You'd only lose it twice."

Price scoffed. "It's a silly bet. There's no way of knowing such a thing."

"What the hell do you think he's doing in there with her?" said McKenny. "He ain't drinking tea, he's putting it to her. You're a fool to think otherwise."

"It's in his face," said the surgeon. "He leaves that cabin with a serious face and doesn't look a man in the eye until he's been two hours in the saddle. Think back now. A man fresh out of a woman's arms walks with an easy step. He walks lazy, he smiles. Captain Stroud is always smiling-- a handsome devil he is. But fresh out of that woman's cabin he stares at the ground and his jaw is clenched up tight."

Price raised the candle from the cot and let its light search out the surgeon. "Is that an honest wager you're proposing?"

"It is."

"With no way of knowing."

"If it's as you say she'll end up with child."

"There's no certainty in that."

"No, Francis, there is not. There is no certainty…"

"You're drunk," said McKenny. "All of you. Blow out them candles. I've marching to do come morning."

Sleep came quickly, aided by alcohol and exhaustion, but not to Lloyd. The rum mixed poorly with the mess hall gruel. He bolted outside and fell to his hands and knees and sent the contents of his stomach splattering into the grass.

The surgeon only glanced at him on his way to the privy. When he returned, Lloyd was still on hands and knees spitting strings of bile from his lips.

"You going to retch, you retch quiet-like," the surgeon rebuked him. "They catch you drunk and we'll all take a lashing."

Lloyd's body swayed over the pile of vomit. He took the rag the surgeon offered and wiped it across his mouth. "I ain't even supposed to be here."

"Well you are."

"It's that damn indian's fault."

"What indian?"

"Black Paw."

The surgeon stepped back while Lloyd heaved another stream of vomit into the yard. "Who's that?"

Lloyd wiped his face again. "He's the one that got me into this. He found the trapper dead, said I done it. But it ain't true."

"No?"

"That was Gil," Lloyd spat again. "Gil killed him."

The surgeon rubbed his jaw. He watched Lloyd shiver and wobble. "And now you're here."

"I ain't supposed to be."

"Doesn't matter. You're in this now, there's no getting away from it."

"I'll leave."

"No one leaves. If it were that simple we'd all be gone."

Lloyd came up to his knees. He looked at the surgeon standing over him. "I'll kill him."

"I wouldn't advise it. The captain's taken a shining to him. That boy was shaped from the same filth as he was."

"Not Gil. Black Paw."

The surgeon tilted his head. "The indian?"

"He's the one done this to me."

"You said Gil killed the trapper."

"He did. But Black Paw's the one accused me of it."

"Your ire's misplaced, boy."

"Ain't nothing misplaced."

"If you've got a bone to pick with anyone it's Gil."

"Gil didn't do nothing to me. He didn't put me here. What he did was to Jim and Jim ain't here no more to argue about it. I'm only here cause that lying indian."

"You were wearing the coat, weren't you?"

"So?"

"So he sees the dead trapper, your tracks everywhere, and you with the coat. What else was he to make of it?"

"That's right," Lloyd pointed a finger at the surgeon. "The tracks was everywhere. Mine and Gil's and Jim's. The story was all right there, all he had to do was read it."

"Not everyone can read sign like you."

"If he can't read sign he should have said so."

The surgeon shook his head. "I'm telling you, your ire is misplaced."

Lloyd ran the rag across his mouth. "Black Paw can tell me that before he dies."

A week later, nine Mexican soldiers appeared at the gates of Fort Tackett. They drove a wagon in whose bed was laid out a French trapper, wounded and bandaged and moaning at every bump of the wheels. One of the Mexicans claimed to speak French. A man in Stroud's company by the name of Joel Viker held a tenuous grasp on Spanish. By this chain of tongues the Frenchman's story was born.

He'd spent the spring trapping the Weminuche country off the Rio Grande, high up in the Rocky Mountains. His luck was good; before the autumn leaves fell his canoe was full. After a week of paddling he came upon an outpost some ways upriver from Santa Fe that he'd not seen the year before. A group of American missionaries had built cabins from rough cut lumber and were bringing salvation to the Comanches there. The Frenchman planned to stay a night-- he stayed three weeks. There was a girl, he was lonely. He'd have stayed longer had the girl survived the attack. It came with a knock on the cabin door; six Comanche men, their sons and daughters dead from measles. They carried with them hatchets and jawbone clubs. Cabin by cabin they clubbed down the whites, nineteen total, the Frenchman fighting his way to the river and escaping in his canoe, beaten but alive. The soldiers at the Santa Fe presidio found him and sent him east, and those who received him, being no fools themselves and seeing this as an American problem, brought him to the gates of Fort Tackett and left the situation of the dead missionaries as one the Americans could address.

When the account was finished, Stroud walked across the parade grounds and through the officer's quarters to Major Hangel's door. The conference lasted no more than a few minutes. He came back across the grounds, past the flagstaff, and standing straight with his knees together and his boots polished as if he'd prophesied the moment would come, instructed Lieutenant Burgess to ready the men, for they'd be leaving at sunrise.

They readied the horses; two to each man. Forty pack mules and four supply wagons into which were packed and stowed, among other things, eight kegs of salt pork, ten half barrels of flour, two barrels of fat, two boxes of candles and a bag of wicks, three kegs of whiskey and any other bottles the soldiers raided from the trade store, two-hundred pounds of ammunition in varying size and shot, and a shovel for each man.

Stacking the shovels, Lloyd asked Linus Tate their reason.

"Pray he finds his treasure in the ground," replied the old soldier. "For if he don't, he'll find it in the blood of the savage."

In the morning the company gathered before the gates. Their horses and wagons and mules covered the parade grounds clear to the store houses. Captain Stroud called up Gil, and there before the men repeated a ceremony of words and pinned a chevron on the boy's breast. When the captain announced him Corporal Pucker, Gil pulled his lips back from his small round teeth and trained his smile on Lloyd.

Seven

Outside the gates of Fort Tackett, the regimented order of garrison life marked by bugle calls and scripted drills disintegrated. Not into chaos, but a chaotic new order. The men stopped shaving. All but Stroud and the newly appointed Corporal Pucker, who mirrored the captain like a smitten imbecile, drawing the blade each morning across the few stray hairs that sprouted through his pimpled skin, shining his boots, smiling when the captain smiled, frowning when not.

As for the rest, they reverted to a primitive state of man just as domesticated hogs will do when escaped to the wild. Stubble covered their faces. Dust covered their clothing. Shirts went untucked. Could they have grown tusks they would have. They cared more for their horses than themselves. The watering and feeding and general care bestowed upon the stock was all that remained of garrison life, and there was no bugle call that drove them to it.

In two week's time their metamorphosis became complete. They looked no more improved than when they'd ridden out of Milltown and across the desert, onto the plains, into the cross-timbers, and through the gates of Fort Tackett. In reverse order they retrod their path, and only Lloyd Reed might have considered himself any more improved than when he'd first traveled it. He sat a saddle. Harpers rifle over the pommel. Bridle and reins. New boots. He rode not toward his execution but to something else, though the manner in which he rode bore no difference to the ignorance of cattle steered through the slaughterhouse gates. He understood only that he was in the company of soldiers. Any notion that he was part and parcel to them, that this moment was not one of many acts but the play entire, did not land upon his consciousness until Linus Tate snuck a bottle of whiskey from the wagons and spoke his mind out loud.

They'd come out of the post oak to the edge of the blackland prairies where all that separated them from desert was a plateau of rolling plains and the autumn winds blowing them flat. Kiowa tracks littered the ground. They'd ridden over them all that day, and in the evening Lieutenant Burgess assigned Lloyd and the grey-haired soldier to guard watch. The two circled the remuda on foot while the company slept. On the fourth loop Linus stopped. He took Lloyd's elbows in his fingers. "We could saddle up our horses," he said. "Take spares and some grub."

"Where you reckon on going?"

"It don't matter where we go, just that we go."

Lloyd looked across the rising vapor of forty mules and forty horses and into the old man's wrinkled eyes. The fingers still had his elbow. Whiskey drifted on the old soldier's breath.

"Ain't nobody would find us," said Linus. "You're the tracker. Osmond can't read no sign."

"I'll be leaving. Not before we get to Milltown though. There's a man there I got to settle something with. Besides, I got a month's pay coming."

"You got no idea what's coming. You ain't seen hell yet but you'll see it and you'll see far worse if you keep on. Stroud will take you with him. You'll be part of it; there won't be no turning back. You'll have done what you done once you done it. You understand? Them boys you tracked down weren't nothin. They weren't nothin." He wheezed a cloud of liquored breath into the night and it rose and swirled into the steam of eighty herded beasts huffing under starlight. His eyes wrinkled. Lloyd pulled his arm from the man's fingers and walked on.

At midnight they swapped with the Virginians. Lloyd walked back to the rows of tents that held within them the eighteen soldiers that composed Stroud's company and shut his eyes beneath his blanket. He didn't sleep. He saw the boys' screams sliding up the wall and the fire screaming and Gil stabbing and the captain's teeth gleaming there in the cove on the mesa top, and when the sun rose Lloyd rose and rolled his blanket and rode out in single file with McKenny's empty sleeve swaying in front of him and the surgeon behind him and his eyes open and looking as though he'd woken from a bare and joyless sleep.

Across the plains they pushed the animals. Over plateaus that sat at the edge of the atmosphere and down into broken canyons in whose crevices ran tributaries winding their way down from the high country. Along one of these nameless waterways stood a collection of shacks. The peasants who lived there raised their brown faces at the sound of hoofbeats rising off the canyon walls. When they saw what rode out of the draw they filtered into their homes and shut their doors behind them.

At the edge of town the company parked the wagons. The mules set to cropping grass, and Stroud ordered the horses brushed down and watered before setting foot in the cantina. When this was done the company drew straws. Osmond Culkin and the Virginians drew short. The rest walked on foot into the alleyways of shacks to the low door of the cantina where they ducked their heads and entered one by one.

The floor was hard-packed dirt. Candlelight fought the darkness. In it sat a few old Mexicans who pulled at their cigarillos and watched the Americans crowd around the tables. The counter was no more than an overturned wagon bed perched across two pillars of bricks. The man behind it spoke no English. He looked at the ancianos and looked at the American soldiers and he set his hands over the makeshift bartop and spread his fingers wide.

Before him stood Stroud. He raised a hand and wagged a finger at the soldiers crowded behind him and instructed the barkeep to pour each man a drink.

The barkeep overturned his hands. *"No hay,"* he shook his head and looked again at the old men seated in a cloud of smoke.

Stroud glanced at them and back to the barkeep. "Whiskey," he said.

"No hay nada pa' tomar. Mire," the man opened his arms in a show for Stroud to inspect the empty shelves behind the wagon top. When the captain didn't move, the barkeep reached to the end of the planks and slid over a box. He raised the lid. Inside were neatly stacked rows of hand-rolled cigarillos. He held the box up to Stroud and gave it a wiggle, and his eyes again drifted pleadingly to the ancianos sitting silent at their table.

Stroud took it. He drew out a smoke and passed the box to Burgess. Then he turned to where a candle burned on a table and plucked it from its melted wax. He lifted it to the paper protruding from his lips. The soldiers and the barkeep and the old men watched the candleflame bend, saw it lick the cigarillo and the cigarillo crackle and glow red. The captain exhaled and the barkeep nodded and attempted a smile.

"*Mujeres?*" said Stroud.

The barkeep's smile waned. He shook his head. "*Tampoco.*"

"Town like this always has women in it."

"*No hay.*"

"You best not hide them from us. It's not your people protecting you from the savages-- it's us. We do it. Least you could do is show appreciation. Men go too long without womenfolk, they sour. Makes the work harder."

The barkeep looked to the faces of the old men and at the soldiers standing round and found in them no clarification of the captain's English.

"*Mujeres,*" Stroud repeated.

"*Se lo juro que no hay, señor.*"

"He swears there ain't no women," said Viker.

"There's nothing but old men and cigarettes," said Burgess.

"Let's have one," said Viker.

Burgess still held the box. He opened the lid and Viker plucked up a cigarillo and lit it.

"It any good, Joel?" someone asked.

Viker blew the smoke out over the soldiers' heads. He smiled. "It's good."

Stroud turned. "Bring a keg of whiskey from the wagons. Price, go with him."

They rolled it down the slope and through the doorway and heaved it over the wagon boards. Burgess hammered a spike into the bung and ripped it out and twisted the spout flush into the hole. From behind the bar they fetched dusty mugs and filled them with whiskey, and when each man sat content with a drink and a smoke, they poured servings for the old men and the barkeep.

Lloyd was last to sit. He found himself at Stroud's table. Gil sat beside the captain. He laughed at the captain's jokes.

One of the ancianos became inebriated before the others and he came and sat in the empty space across from Stroud. He was small and wrinkled and his eyes were half closed with whiskey. He smiled and raised his glass and when he spoke the soldiers bent forward to make out his garbled tongue.

"Is very good," he proclaimed.

The soldiers raised their glass to his.

"Here no have whiskey. Only cigarillo."

"No women either?" said Clemons.

"Yeah," said Gil. "Where you got the women hid? The *mujeres*," he gleamed at his Spanish and turned to see if the captain approved.

"*No hay mujeres.*"

"Just cigarettes," said Clemons.

"*Les gustan?* You like?"

Clemons took a drag. He blew the smoke at the anciano. "I guess I do."

"I make trade in Aguas Claras. Los indios very poor. Trade for nothing."

Stroud's mug clapped the table. He put down his cigarillo. "Where'd you say? *Dónde?*"

"*En Aguas Claras.*"

"The Clearwater?"

"*Las Aguas Claras,*" the anciano repeated.

Stroud half-rose and shouted through the smoke. Joel Viker came running. He stooped beside the captain's table and Stroud pointed to the Mexican. "Tell me what he's saying."

The table leaned in to hear the anciano pronounce what he'd pronounced three times already. He said it a fourth, and Stroud gripped Viker's collar. "Is he saying the Clearwater?"

"I believe he is."

"When was this?"

"Cuándo?" said Viker.

"Hace dos semanas."

"He says two weeks ago."

"Ask him again."

Joel Viker repeated the question and the anciano muttered the same answer, and this time there showed a mix of fear and confusion in his wrinkled eyes. He sought to explain himself with a slurred diatribe which none there would comprehend, and at length Stroud raised a hand and quieted the old man.

"They're all *muertos,*" said Stroud. "All the indios. *Todos.*"

The anciano's head quivered. *"No todos,"* he said. "Many dead, some alive. *Se escondieron en la Misión de Las Tres Marías. Allí están todavía."*

"Did he say mission?"

"I believe he did, Captain."

"There's a mission we missed?"

"I can ask him."

"Ask him."

By this time the soldiers had gathered around and stood sipping their whiskey while Viker interrogated the Mexican. The barkeep and the townsmen fell silent at their table. Someone coughed in the smoke. When the exchange was over Joel Viker confirmed that an abandoned mission by the name of Las Tres Marias lay somewhere off the Clearwater. A few wickiups housed some fifty Apaches within view of the old Spanish ruins.

The men watched their captain's face. He sat considering this news in the privacy of his mind. His eyes darted about as if watching some silent events unfold within it. The cigarillo in his fingers burned out. He flicked it to the floor and his eyes ran over his men until he found Lloyd sitting at the end of the table.

"You know the Weminuche country?"

"I know it," said Lloyd.

"How long do we have until it snows in the passes?"

"It's different every year."

"Do we have six weeks?"

Lloyd blinked under the scrutiny of his fellow soldiers. "I reckon."

Stroud nodded. What he considered next in that private conference he held within himself was settled shortly. The men knew the verdict before he spoke it. He stood from the table and ordered them out of the cantina and back up the slope, the keg sloshing half empty as it rolled along the ground. Though the day was on its way to evening they hitched the wagons and saddled their horses and drove their coterie southward and back to the desert, the men riding inebriated in the low-hanging sun.

They slept that night without discussion. The following evening when their drunkenness had left them and the captain and his lieutenant were out of earshot, they sat around the fires and ventured to share with each other their minds.

"I'd not have wagered that any of 'em got away," said Price.

"If you believe a drunk old Mexican," said McKenny.

"What cause would he have to lie?"

"Keep us from the women."

"What women?"

"There was women in that town," McKenny said. "I smelt

'em."

"There weren't any women."

"I said I smelt 'em."

"You should've pulled them out from hiding then."

"Well we ain't there no more."

Francis Price stuck a leg out toward the flames and twisted his boot against the heat. "I still don't see how any got away in the Clearwater," he said. "Maybe the old Mexican was out of his mind. Maybe Joel misunderstood him."

"I know what he said," Joel Viker shot from the end of the fire.

"How would we have missed fifty of them?"

"It's what he said."

"Keeping us from the women," McKenny belched. He raised both arms and the sleeve of one drooped and swayed in the light. "He no more than said it and the captain up and runs to finish the job."

The surgeon sat not far from Lloyd, cleaning his musket on the ground before him. He pushed the ramrod through the barrel and when he pulled it out again the knot of flax tow emerged soiled in black powder. He held it deftly in the air, and when he spoke the men listened. "It wasn't the indians we missed that turned us south. It was mention of the mission."

The men nodded at this. Again the surgeon with his wisdom.

"What's he care about a mission?" said Gil.

"It's a notion he has."

"It's a fool's errand," said McKenny.

"The captain's convinced of it."

"Are you?"

The surgeon fit the tow over the ramrod and once more twisted it through the barrel. He looked at McKenny and he looked at Gil. "Stroud believes there's gold buried in a mission somewhere. At every one we come across he sets us to digging."

Gil's eyes found Lloyd across the fire. Lloyd bowed his head.

"It's a story goes around," the surgeon went on.

"A tale," said McKenny. "It's a tale that goes around."

"Either way, it goes around."

"What's it say?" said Gil.

"The way I've heard it," the surgeon paused to re-accommodate the tow, "there was a group of American soldiers sometime back not much different than us. Thirty, forty years ago. Maybe more, no one knows."

"No one knows," said McKenny.

"Let him tell it, John," said Price.

"That was back when this was Spanish land. Spanish soldiers, Spanish priests, everyone combing the country for gold. The Americans had found it. Coming up from Mexico they ran into the Spaniards, made a fight of it. Way the story goes, they buried their treasures in an abandoned mission before the Spaniards wiped them out. Every last one." The surgeon spoke these last words and lowered his head to the cleaning of his weapon. The story was told.

Gil sat with his mouth agape. His brows furrowed together. He put a hand to the Springfield sticking up from his belt and rubbed the polished wood. The men picked at their teeth and watched him.

"Why didn't them Spanish soldiers dig it up?"

"They knew nothing of it," answered the surgeon.

Gil stroked the Springfield. "How did the story get out if everybody died?"

"Ha!" McKenny erupted. He stood and flapped his empty sleeve. "You see that, surgeon? Even our Corporal Pucker can see the foolishness of it."

The surgeon shrugged. He finished reassembling the weapon. When the final piece was laid he said, "I'm not the one who makes you dig."

They kicked the coals across the ground and drifted to their tents. Lloyd's stride landed evenly, one leg matching the other, the soles of his boots bound tight. Before he reached the tent he'd share with the Virginians, Gil caught him.

"Hey, wait," the boy stepped in front of Lloyd. "What do you know about all that?"

"Nothing."

"You was asking that son of a bitch trapper about them Spanish missions."

"I was just asking."

"What for?"

Lloyd pushed past him.

"I know you know something, Lloyd. I'll tell Captain Stroud on you."

Nine days of riding brought them to the Clearwater. On the tenth they found the mission. It was tucked behind a knoll, out of sight form the river. Not half a mile away the ground was littered with broken bottles and the remains of army campfires. They left the mules and wagons on the same site they'd staged them two months prior, and Stroud led his men up the hill. He rode in the lead with his rifle balanced on the pommel. Before he topped the rise, a bare-chested boy of perhaps fifteen years came running up the other side. He rounded a stand of rocks and he was close enough that Lloyd could make out the freckles traced along his nose. In his hands were a bow and arrow. He wore moccasins made of deerskin. He stopped. Stroud stopped. The company halted their horses and the jangle of tack and saddlery faded and all eyes were on the boy standing before them with his bowstring notched and the arrow pulled half-taut. The jackrabbit he'd been hunting sprang from a stand of ocotillo, and Stroud swung the rifle off the pommel and shot the boy square in the chest. The boy's arms flung back and the arrow sprang loose. It skittered over the sand. His body fell and his head bounced hollow on a rock and Stroud walked his horse up to where he lay and looked down. He turned to the line of men strung out behind him and shouted, "Any younger than this we keep." Then he drove his heels into the horse's ribs and charged over the lip of the knoll, and the commotion of bits and hooves and metal jangling saddlery followed him over.

Lloyd rode in back. He came over the rise just as Stroud trampled his horse over an indian woman. She fell beneath the hooves and her limbs flailed violently and lay still and broken and the horse trammeled on, the company fanning out behind the captain. They fired their rifles into the dozen wickiups scattered there beneath the knoll and the women came running from them with infants at their breasts and their men caught weaponless in the open. Lloyd saw Gil pull his Springfield and discharge it into the back of a woman's head. She fell forward and the baby she carried fell with her and cried in the sun and a horse rode over it and its cries were over. A man carrying a tomahawk appeared between the wickiups. He swung at the riders sweeping past. The blade caught McKenny's empty sleeve, it sliced through. Price's horse struck him and the tomahawk clattered to the rocks. One of the Virginians fired on him then dropped to the ground and drove his bayonet through the body. Linus turned in circles. Children ran naked into the desert. A man with burn scars over his face went running after them and Lieutenant Burgess fired into his back and dropped him. Yapping dogs ran forth to snip at the soldiers' heels and these too were shot and killed.

The smell of gunpowder hung everywhere. Dirt and blood. The soldiers dropped from their horses and walked through it. They stepped over the fallen Apaches and ripped open the wickiup flaps and fired upon those hiding within. Lloyd saw Clemons yank a young squaw out by the hair. The soldier looked up the battleground through the gunsmoke and dragged the woman up into the rocks beneath the knoll and he threw her to the ground and the two were lost from sight.

Some of the children that had fled into the desert had stopped running and were looking back. They turned and ran again when they saw the horses charge their way.

Lloyd's own horse danced beneath him. He held the Harpers rifle at his shoulder. His finger slid inside the trigger guard and slid back out. The confusion of screams and gunfire clapped in his ears. Other sounds filtered in, he struggled to hear them, they were far and distant and he had no sensation of his body beneath him.

Children were being gathered. They sat across the soldiers' legs. Some cried and some only sat staring with their eyes wide open at the remnants of their massacred tribe strewn about like dolls dropped in untenable positions. Even as they rode there burst a man from a wickiup and he was cut down by John McKenny's rifle blast, him balancing the weapon in his one hand, the indian spinning and crumpling, and even then some of those children did not cry but only gawked in silence from the soldiers' laps.

Lloyd had not moved from the base of the knoll. He held the rifle out, the stock still flush against his shoulder. Captain Stroud rode up through the patches of red yucca and stopped beside him. He reached out and gripped Lloyd's rifle barrel and held it a moment. His eyes met Lloyd's. He measured a head taller and his shoulders that much wider. His mouth tight. When he let the barrel go it was with a fling of his hand.

The screaming inside the wickiups was fading. Soldiers took to their horses and rode out from the village. The last of the children running naked in the desert were snatched up and brought to the base of the knoll with the rest. A single gunshot smacked and echoed against the rocks, and Clemons stood and rejoined the company.

Stroud walked his horse out away from Lloyd and made a count of the soldiers and all were accounted for. Next the children. Lloyd could see the captain's head dropping and lifting as it moved from one to the next. When he'd counted out fourteen he nodded in approval and ordered Lieutenant Burgess to take a party of men back over the knoll and return with a wagonful of shovels.

In the interim the children set to grieving. For their parents laying twisted up in death or for the greater misfortune imagined but unknowable yoked about their necks, Lloyd knew not. Neither did the soldiers. They turned their backs to the children and paced about and kicked stones. Some wandered into the mission to assess what toil awaited them. Not one man addressed another in all that endless crescendo of sorrow until Burgess whipped the mules over the ridge and the party was blessed with an intermission from anguish as all heads lifted to watch the mules skittering in their traces, the lieutenant riding heavy on the brake. He hollered them down the slope and when they reached the base in a plume of disorder he turned them and brought the team to a stop at the mission doors.

Shovels slid off the wagon boards in twangs of metal brushing metal as each man took up his instrument. The children's sobbing revived. It followed the men inside. Francis Price entered. After a minute he came back out and shouted over the racket to where Stroud sat on the wagon bed. "There's half of them big enough to handle a shovel, Captain. It'll stop their yammering if it'll do anything else."

The captain agreed. They hauled the older children up by their arms and herded them into the mission and set them to digging, one strike of the lash across a child's back to serve as both instruction and incentive for the rest. Just as Price had reckoned, their sobs found replacement in the grunt of labor.

Lloyd dug with them. The callouses raised in Fort Tackett had not yet softened on his hands. He turned the shovel with practiced ease and when he paused to rest the sounds of the children at work were loud and haunting in that narrow space. Their whimpers painted the cathedral hall. He arched his back and stared upward. The ceiling was nothing more than bundles of reeds laid over crossbeams. He looked back down at the children and at Osmond Culkin tossing soil. The Virginians hit solid material and became excited. They dropped their shovels and dug by hand, and when they revealed a buried rock they cursed and flung the thing against the wall.

Linus Tate held a shovel. He stared across the cathedral floor. His eyes met Lloyd's over the heads of the children and Lloyd turned away and bit his shovel into the earth. He dug until a voice close to his ear startled him.

It was Burgess at his elbow. "Stroud will see you."

The captain sat on the wagon bed with his boots off. On the ground crouched Gil in a smudge of polish. He was sent away by a flurry of the captain's arm, and as he went scuttling off he took a backwards look at Lloyd.

Stroud pulled his boots on. Beside him lay the Harpers rifle. He cinched the laces and picked up the weapon. "This rifle hasn't seen a shot fired since we left Fort Tackett."

Lloyd tucked his thumbs in his belt and his eyes slid away.

"It's a fine weapon," Stroud ran a hand along the breech. He traced the barrel with his fingertip and followed the bayonet out to its point. "Not every man has a rifle such as this. The surgeon is stuck with his musket, the Virginians kept the Fergusons they wandered in with. See here?" the captain pointed. "The breech raising up as it does-- not having to ram a ball and wad down the barrel-- a man can load and fire nine shots a minute if he's quick. Nine shots. And yet you didn't fire a single one." He waited for Lloyd to respond and when nothing followed he called for an explanation.

"I didn't know why we was shooting them," Lloyd said finally.

An expression Lloyd hadn't seen before crossed the captain's face. It flashed and was gone. "Because I gave the order," he said. "Did you hear the order?"

"Yes sir."

"You're a soldier; you follow orders."

"Yes sir."

"The next time I call on you to fire your weapon you'll fire it."

"Yes sir."

"I tell you to do anything, it doesn't matter what it is, you don't stand and wonder why, you carry out the order. I won't give it to you twice. You understand that, Private Reed?"

"I understand."

"Anything."

"Yes."

"I say walk, you walk. I say dig, dig. I say kill that savage, you kill him."

Lloyd breathed. Head bowed, eyes on the captain's sash, eyes on the buttons. Stroud bending, his face bronzed by sun, level with Lloyd's.

"You understand that?"

"Yes sir."

"Get your shovel and dig up that floor."

After sunset they piled the shovels in the wagon and followed it up the ridge and back down to the Clearwater. The children slogged behind, bound wrist to wrist, ankle to ankle. Their cries stopped. They walked out of sync. The youngest among them stumbled and brought down those directly forward and back, and Burgess barked an order that each child interpreted in his or her own way.

What fires were kindled that night burned without conversation to ring them. They served their purpose and when the food was cooked and eaten they were extinguished from the earth with no more fanfare than had been given those souls lying dead beyond the knoll. The children of the slaughtered slept on the sand. Burgess and Linus Tate stood watch over them.

On his way to his tent Lloyd passed them. He slowed his walk. The children's eyes followed him and he hurried on. Outside the tent he crossed paths with the surgeon. The man's step came faltering; a bottle hung half empty at his thigh. Lloyd stopped him. "What are we doing with them kids?"

The surgeon wove on his feet. He worked a knuckle over his eyelids and blinked at Lloyd. "We left them alive," he said.

"What's he gonna do with them?"

The surgeon pulled away. "Sell them," he drawled. He sucked at the bottle and stumbled on, and Lloyd watched him careen up through the tent stakes and out onto the flats beside the Clearwater.

In the tent the Virginians slept. Lloyd wormed through the flap and it was not for the foulness inside that he remained awake staring at the canvas and pricking his ears to the night sounds. He thought he heard the children whimper, but he did not; they were far down the beach. He thought he heard them moan, but when he slid back out the flap and froze quietly in a crouch in the darkness he heard nothing. He waited anyway, hunched like a thief among the tents.

When he rose he was quick with motion. Through the stakes, around the smoldering coals. Before he slid the shovel from the wagon he looked both ways and down the beach. Linus and the lieutenant smoked beside the sleeping children. The red nubs of their cigarettes unfurled like tiny pumping suns. He plucked up his shovel and scampered through the rocks, taking the long way around camp and climbing the knoll until he reached its summit. The encampment below sat along a black string of river, the tents and wagons small black dots, yet still he could hear the mewling of the children. It followed him clear to the mission, through its rotted gates, and when he swung the shovel at the reeds above, the children's bawl grew louder, louder until they were screaming sharp and grievous and their throats were choked and hiccuping and uncontrolled and he swung at the reeds and the reeds fell and he swung and he stumbled and he gripped the shovel and he swung and he tumbled and he sat there in the fallen reeds and cried until the weeping of the children was overtaken by his own anguished rueful bleating.

———————

They filled the barrels at the river and untied the children and set them on the backs of mules. Stroud rode his horse down the line. His boots reflected the world in the morning light. He eyed the captives and took in his soldiers without a word of reprimand to their disheveled state. He turned and trotted his horse past the wagons and alongside the mules where they stood laden down with the canvases wrapped around the tent poles and lashed to their backs. When he rejoined Burgess at the head of the train he raised an arm and pointed it forward and the whole ensemble kicked off in one sudden motion all down the line. They cut up from the riverbank and stamped flat the ground another mile into the desert whereupon they reached the village that three months prior had housed over two-hundred souls and retained now nothing but their burned-out wickiups, row upon row, the ashes blown out over mounds of graves that stretched along the flatlands like some geometric artwork in a bowl of barren earth.

Some minutes it took to pass them. When they were through, Lloyd turned his head for another look. The sun made shadows off each one. Not a single other rider save the children lifted an eye in reverence to that scene.

Their route was southward, away from the Clearwater. It cut through gravel and past rock ledges in whose shadows they rode. Dust covered them. It coated their teeth and mixed with the sweat in their ears. At the watering holes they found only dust, cracks of mud. The horses attempted to lick at the muck and the soldiers drove them on. The last known spot of water resulted no differently. By then one of the boys had taken ill. He'd fallen off the mule and Joel Viker had swept him up and thrown him back on. He was not trampled underfoot, but died the next day, and when he fell that second time they could see he was dead and they marched on and left him with his face in the sand and his black hair limp and shining bright like an aureole of raven wings to mark his little head.

Several days later they tacked east and joined a road well-trammeled which they shared with Mexican peasants hauling carts of tubers. Unshod vagabonds portaged bales of hay on their backs. Ancianos journeyed beside them on copper colored feet, all walking as though some dire purpose called them remote along the road.

Late in that day's breast they reached a vast presidio towering before a Mexican city hemmed in high-walled gates. They bore the hunger of hard driven men and not one addressed another except in snaps and jagged gestures. At the gates they grouped tight and waited. The children stared around at the dark-skinned soldiers and the commotion of animals and campesinos and carts and weaponry and elements of rustic modernity they'd never seen and couldn't fathom. The city behind the fort sat in a plume of dust and noise.

In all that waiting no man swallowed. Some held pebbles in their mouths and they sucked on these and stared at the rooftops with their lids half shut and dust clinging in their nostrils.

A soldier came to inform them in Spanish that Colonel Martinez would see them shortly. Stroud grunted a response. The soldier stamped his feet and swiveled and faced the presidio. He remained at attention while Stroud's horse snorted behind him. The sentry's posture seemed a misplaced formality with the Americans bunched behind him in a shambled filthy mass, and when Martinez arrived he waved the soldier away. He smiled at Captain Stroud and extended a flask of water. Lloyd could see even from where he sat that his smile was not quite as handsome and his teeth not quite as straight as the captain's. Stroud took a sip and passed it to Burgess who drank and passed it down the line.

Colonel Martinez's eyes ran over the dusty uniforms and over the children perched atop the mules' backs. He stretched his fingers along his belt. His elbows swung outward. "You have been very busy, Captain Stroud. Much trade you bring me."

"Good trade," said Stroud. "You'll get rich off me."

"No so good," Martinez's mustache turned up in another smile. He signaled to the children. "These Lipan Apache. Lazy Apache."

"They're all the same."

"No same. No work hard."

"They'll work as hard as you drive them," said Stroud.

The Mexican colonel shook his head. "No work. Very lazy. Many people give me complain last time."

"I brought you strong young bodies. These ones here are just as good."

"I cannot make you same price *señor.*"

"Name it," said Stroud.

They began the haggling in English numbers, which Martinez knew complete, and all the while the colonel continued to smile and shake his head and look amused until Stroud, his own politeness long vanished, threatened to shoot the children there before the presidio walls and leave them for Martinez to deal with. At this there came a break of silence. The two officers regarded each other while the children fussed on the mules. When the haggling resumed, Lloyd saw clearly the captain had gained the edge. When they shook hands on the final terms they came included with the stabling of the mules and horses, the barrels filled with water, and an undetermined quantity of aguardiente from the Mexican storehouses. Martinez drew a purse from his waistcoat and counted out a pile of coins and with a whistle and a wave of his arm called over a band of loafing soldiers to lead the stock and wagons in one direction and the children in another.

Right there in the yard Stroud lined up his men. He placed a coin in each extended hand and when he reached the end of the line he turned and repeated the process until only his portion remained.

The formality holding the company together saw its last straw broken. Like moths into a fire the city swallowed them. Into taverns and mezcal houses and windowless shacks in whose bleak interiors they spent their money on vices long nursed along the trail and sated there veneered in foreign things strange and lending cover. Some remained in pairs or trios and others set forth alone and unattended.

Lloyd trailed them a while but kept on when they entered the bath houses. He thumbed the coins in his pocket. They were cold; they warmed at his touch. He drew his hand from them and when he touched them again they were clammy and clung to his fingers. He entered a door where drunkards lounged and sought to spend them but the drink they gave him choked his throat and he coughed and left it for another. Amongst the streets where dogs ran loose he found a woman hauling buckets of water from a well. He stopped her and pressed a coin into her palm. She set the buckets down. He knelt before them like an animal and slurped while she watched. He extracted his lips and paused to catch his breath and drank again. The woman said something and offered him back the coin, but he only pushed her hand away. When he'd had his fill he regained his feet and ambled on with the water dripping down his chin and spreading against his shirtfront.

When darkness fell he'd not quit wandering. The city fractured into endless avenues and he rambled lost within them. He wound a path through hamstrung alleys slung with echoed voices, up cobbled lanes and tracts of busted peasant shanties cut by slender trickling rivers composed of human waste. He walked until from somewhere distant rang the notes of church hymns. He let them lead him, a soldier blind and drifting. They brought him out of trash-filled backstreets, abreast a zócalo paved in stone. He stopped and stood and sought the source. Parted on the far side of the zócalo beckoned the doors of a cathedral. Light and song poured forth.

He picked his way through vendors towing steaming carts of cooked elote and children capering in the square, and ascended the chapel steps. His boots across the threshold made no sound. He placed a foot through the open doors. Two paces in, he stepped to the wall and pressed his back against it.

A choir three rows deep sang behind the altar. Parishioners filled the pews and stood along the aisles. Down the center nave a man in white linen let sway before him a burning tray of sage, its smoke curling as he walked among the brethren. Those crowded nearest looked Lloyd over and pulled their children closer. He stared unfocused at the choir and felt a bulb rise in his throat. It pressed against his lungs. His vision blurred. The taste of metal. At the hymn's completion the parish fell silent and Lloyd regained his focus. Heads of black hair floated like buoys on a calm sea before him, each fixated on the father in command at the altar.

From the side pews there arose an almost imperceptible lament. It grew in pitch and ardor-- louder, jarring, the sobs of lamentation. Heads turned to find it. Lloyd, short as he was, stood over most of the others pressed against the throng. What he saw when he looked was a dust-ridden soldier bent on his knees nearly prostrate on the parish floor. The man's sobs shook his ribs, and though Lloyd could not see the man's face, he knew it was Linus Tate.

He spun and darted through the doors and crossed again the zócalo. In a cantina he laid a coin over the bar and drank what was served. It tasted no better than the last. He shut his eyes and swallowed. The barman laid out his change and Lloyd pushed it back and the barman shrugged and poured another.

When Lloyd stepped again into the night he was drunk and had not yet rid himself of the coins jangling clammy and heavy in his pocket. He wandered into a barrio where thievery was the prime vocation, and in his careless vulnerability no one sought to rob him.

By a heap of rotting corn husks he stopped to urinate. When he finished he looked up and saw a squat woman standing across the way with a slip cut off at the knees and her arms bare. She held his gaze. He followed her into the alleyway and when she muttered something in Spanish he pulled up all the coins he had and dropped them into her hands. She tucked them away and turned and pulled the slip over her waist. With one hand braced against the wall she bent slightly and waited.

Lloyd unbuttoned his trousers. He slid them down and took the woman by her waist and pressed himself forward. His cock hung limp and flat against her. She made no sound. Her eyes fell against the wall. He took a step back and looked at her bare waist and the curve of her rear and he attempted another sad simulation of coitus that again failed in consummation.

The woman straightened. She turned around. She took hold of his penis and frowned while she jerked at it. In her hand it was lifeless and cold. She said something he couldn't understand and he pulled away from her and drew up his trousers and left her standing half naked in the alleyway.

Eight

Four days north of the Mexican presidio the company looked less a band of slavers and more a collection of jolly gamblers, for that they were; the captain had swung them in direction of Milltown. Off to prick his woman, they whispered round the fire. What bets they would have wagered if only they might spy through her window. They passed a bottle of clear liquid around and ruminated on the matter.

"I'd lay he don't strip off his uniform," said McKenny.

"And his boots?" said Clemons.

"Them neither."

They bandied about the nicknames she might call out, or if Thaddeus was her cry of passion.

"My Captain, she calls him," said one of the Virginians.

"Or do you reckon he's convinced her he's a general?" said the other.

"President Stroud," Viker mimicked a woman's pitch. He turned his backside to the fire and placed the half-empty bottle to his ass. "Polish me clean as your boots."

They squealed and giggled and shot wary looks at the captain's tent and prodded Viker for more.

Lloyd left them. He walked the outskirts of camp past the braying mules and into the detritus where he stood on rocks and gravel eroded down from fallen heights in times unwritten. The men watched him go. They joked that Viker's acting had aroused him such that he'd fled to the desert to pleasure himself. Their words carried over the blowsand. When he heard them he drifted further out. He wiggled his toes in his boots and shivered some. A carpet of stars wrapped the earth. The stench of eighty beasts hung thickly in the night, and with it the heat wafting off their hides in pillars of steam to twinkle in a fog above their heads.

Aside from the captain and his lieutenant conversing in their tent, and Gil hovering outside it, the only soldier not invested in the campfire banter was Linus Tate. He'd sat like a sullen child four days and four nights along the trail. His old face pinched. *I ain't a part of this,* his creed.

In the morning he was gone. Viker reported his absence. Stroud walked the length of the encampment from the wagons on down to the latrine gully and came back up with his eye on each soldier as though he'd find some accomplice, or perhaps Linus himself hidden there pouting between the men.

The first minutes of that search revealed he'd taken two horses. Several scoops of lard had been swiped from a barrel. Salt pork and biscuits. At every revelation of thievery the captain's face fell more placid. More serene. He convened with Lieutenant Burgess and called the men to order. They locked step against the sunrise with no one to see the straightness in their backs, and each back straight it was, stationary stone shadows, for the only eye that mattered was Captain Stroud's.

He called these names and each stepped forward in turn: Joel

Viker, Francis Price, Gil Pucker, Lloyd Reed.

"Saddle your horses," he told them. "I want each man with two canteens and a spare mount."

"What about grub?" said Price.

"Only what you can eat in the saddle. I want him found before the day is out."

While the search party readied themselves, Lieutenant Burgess harried the company into their morning duties. Before camp was broken, the four chosen had filled their canteens and sat their horses around Stroud in a half-circle at the edge of the remuda. Over the captain's pommel hung a length of coiled rope. Lloyd wondered at it. The air smelled of horse flesh and leather.

"Reed," said the captain. "Get to it."

The men parted. Lloyd walked his horse out a few steps and turned his head to ask a question but Stroud's face turned him back around.

The sun at its low angle coughed up Linus Tate's decampment, the trajectory like a trotline in a stiff current. The old man had walked the two stolen horses out a quarter mile north before taking to the saddle. In the dark he'd not ridden hard. A trot, the horses picking their own way. He'd gotten a six hour start on them, and by mid morning Lloyd had cut that in half. As the sun rose, shadows retreated beneath their sources. Lloyd slowed his horse. The sign ran up an alluvial fan and ghosted out in the foot canyons of bare and shapeless rock. A hoof scrape on stone and a dislodged pebble were all the traces left. Lloyd cast his eyes up the canyon rim and prodded his horse onward with the spare tugged along by the lead rope. Without another look at the ground he topped over and skittered the horses down the other side where straggled tufts of feather grass grew in yellow clumps.

He wove his horse like he was drunk upon it. After fruitless wending down the pediment he stopped and sat staring at the ridge of canyonlands separating one desert from the other. Stroud caught up with him shortly. Gil and the others hung back.

"Well?" said Stroud.

"He'll be on one side or the other."

"Of the ridge?"

"What I reckon," said Lloyd.

"Well?" Stroud's horse twitched beneath him. "Which side?"

"That's what I'm wondering on."

"Where do the tracks lead?"

"Tracks done petered out."

"When?"

"A ways back. Base of the fan there."

"Where we just rode up?"

"Yeah."

"I saw nothing there."

"Well," mumbled Lloyd.

"I haven't seen a single track, horse or man, in the last three hours," Stroud's voice rumbled low and he drilled the words out quickly.

Lloyd squinted. He laid a hand on his saddle horn. It was hot, he took it off.

"You understand why you're here," said Stroud.

Lloyd shied from the sun's glare.

"You understand why you're here, Lloyd?"

"Yes."

"You could be buried in La Chureca."

Lloyd nodded.

"You're not though. You're here. You're here because of me.

I gave you new life, and that life depends on your ability to track a man. If I've misjudged that ability, the error is mine and I shall correct it."

Lloyd bent his head against the sun. The sound of Gil and the others drinking from their canteens in the shade of an overhang bounced against the canyon slopes, muffled and incoherent. One of them laughed at something.

"What'll you do to him?" said Lloyd, staring at the ground.

Stroud sat rigid on his horse for a while without answering. He waited until Lloyd raised his head. "Your job is to find him."

"I know it. Then what?"

"Does the answer affect your ability to track him?"

"No."

"Because that's the only worry that should stress you. Now show me where he's gone."

Lloyd kept his head bent away from the sunlight. He raised an arm to the ridgeline.

"The ridge?"

"He rode the line."

"The ridgeline?"

"I expect."

"Explain how you know that if there are no tracks to follow."

"Tracking ain't always reading sign."

"What the devil does that mean?"

"He wasn't wanting to leave no tracks. By the time he got this far the sun was coming up. He'd have wanted to look behind him a ways. Looking for us, I reckon. So he stayed up on that ridge where there ain't no sand or dirt or pebbles or nothing and he just follered it."

"That's your guess."

"That's what he did."

"On which side of the ridge did he descend?"

"Other side."

"You're guessing again."

"That's part of tracking."

"You think your guess is as good as another's?"

"On this side there ain't nothing but more desert. On the east he'll find water. People, if he rides far enough."

Stroud gave an exhale out his nose. It sounded at first like the horse huffing. "If you're wrong I'll take you back to La Chureca."

"I ain't wrong."

"Then get moving."

Lloyd did as he was told. The horse underneath and the spare alongside and the bits and bridles and reins and saddle and tack and canteen and the Harpers, and Lloyd's new boots well-formed around his feet, all across the patch of flat earth and scrabbling back up the rock slabs, up the broken slags, onto the spine of the ridge. He rode a moment along what looked like an old indian trail and dropped over the other side. The shadows there fell east as though the ridge were the median by which the sun parted all things. The others followed. Their shadows too fell eastward.

In a straight line a quarter mile out from the canyon ridge they rode. Jouncing on leather saddles. Lloyd's head canted alongside the horse's, the others tight in a group behind him, silenced by their captain's agitation. They rode close enough Lloyd could hear the clopping of their horses' hooves strike rocks along the trail.

Stroud did not question him further. Even when Lloyd pulled up and sat for nearly a quarter of an hour drinking from his canteen and scratching at the lice squirming along the nape of his neck. Gil began to jaw, singing Lloyd's praises as the finest tracker the world had known, and praising himself for having discovered him. Stroud told him to be quiet. The four sat their horses and watched Lloyd work.

The sun dropped a might and he moved on. His head kept swinging west, fingers stacked over his brows. An hour later in a spot of nothing he reined up and pointed at more nothing. He looked back from the saddle. "That's where he come down."

They rode up and stilled their mounts beside him and followed his arm out with their eyes.

Stroud studied the ground. He looked at the ridgeline and the slope and looked around at the rocks. The focus of his eyes was misplaced but Lloyd stayed quiet.

"How far ahead is he?"

"Not far. He didn't make good time up on that ridge."

"Two hours? Three?"

"Less."

"I want him before nightfall."

"In another hour it'll get fairly easy, and an hour after that the sun'll be below the ridge and it'll be nigh impossible."

The captain scrutinized the ground again. He looked up. "Get moving then."

For the heat shimmering off the earth, his form would not appear until they were close enough they might have shouted at him. He seemed distant at first, then suddenly large and silhouetted against the sky. As it was they spread out, five men out of the swelter, eyes like dogs on the heels of some lame and helpless prey.

Linus turned at their approach. He twisted back and lifted his hands and his face was old and sad and there were tears cutting streaks through his dusted cheeks. The butt of his rifle poked out of the scabbard alongside a stirrup. He paid it no mind. He stilled his horse and showed his palms. He held them weakly with the gnarled fingers curled, falling away, and when they reached him they grabbed him and tore him from the saddle. On the ground sobbing through choked pleas of mercy he seemed no worthy prize of such grand pursuit. Stroud straddled his back and wound the rope around his wrists and tied it off. He bound his feet next, jerked the old soldier upright and turned him around.

Lloyd hadn't left his saddle. He watched Linus sway and lean over like his back was injured. The old man's jaws seemed to chew the air, he aimed to speak and they let him. "Just let me…" he started. "Just let me go, I ain't done nothing." Spittle formed on his lips. His beard was thin and spotty, his cheeks speckled with sores. He opened his eyes and looked directly at them for the first time. "I never wanted no part of this."

"Put him over his horse," said Stroud.

"I ain't a part…" he cried.

Viker took him by the arm and Gil reached down and grasped his feet, and the two together threw Linus belly-first over the saddle. His head dropped against the horse's ribs and his dusty little hat hit the dirt. Viker picked it up. He made a motion to put it back on Linus's head but realized the futility of it, and instead shoved it through his belt where it hung flapping thin and threadbare all the way back down the ridgeline that night through the cold, the silver light of stars and moon on the soldier's motley uniforms and on the floppy little hat until they reached the company some fifteen miles from where they'd left them and collapsed into their tents like bludgeoned deboned carcasses costumed up in soldier's garb.

Those days of riding that followed were marked by silence. The wagon carrying Linus, bound hand and foot like some violent beast they could scarce control, rumbled behind the team of mules like any other wagon. No sound came from it save for wheels over rocks. At midday Lieutenant Burgess would allow him a drink of water. At night he'd bring the old soldier a bowl of mush. He'd set it before Linus, and Linus would roll to his knees and sink his face into the dish and eat with his nose pressed against the slop.

One night Osmond Culkin commented on the treatment. He said it while filling a water bucket at the supply barrels. Lloyd waited behind with two empties, the surgeon forming the end of the three-man queue.

"You best keep those notions to yourself," advised the surgeon after Osmond aired his thoughts.

"It's the truth."

"Doesn't matter what the truth is. You speak it and you'll get a lashing."

Lloyd interrupted. "What'll Stroud do to him?" he asked.

The surgeon rolled his neck and looked in direction of the captain's tent. "Desertion is a dying offense."

"He gonna kill him?"

"The captain won't kill him," the surgeon answered. "It's us will do that."

Osmond backed away from the barrel. He let Lloyd take the spout, then set the buckets on the ground, water sloshing, and said to the surgeon, "Why don't he just do it now and get it over with?"

"The captain likes an audience. You know it as well as I."

"Well he ain't gonna get it," said Osmond. "We ain't going back to Fort Tackett, not for months. And Santa Fe's a long ways off. It ain't right keeping him tied up all the way, waiting to die.

Eating like a pig in a slop trough."

"He'll have his audience before then," said the surgeon.

Lloyd waited for the surgeon to say more, but it was Osmond who spoke. The man pulled the buckets from the ground and the spidered veins of his neck wiggled in response. "If that's what it takes to woo that woman, he can have her."

Lloyd's buckets topped out. He drew them away and watched Osmond stalk off toward the mules. The surgeon stepped forward. Water hit the bottom of his pail like a knock on a clapboard door.

"Why don't he just let Linus go?" said Lloyd. He stood with the two rope handles digging into his palms.

"Let him go?" said the surgeon.

"Just let him go."

"If there was any leaving do you think we'd be here?"

"I'm leaving," said Lloyd.

The surgeon exchanged pails. Water slapped the wood and gurgled as it filled. He studied Lloyd while the weight built in the bottom. "Is that what you think?"

"I don't want no part of this neither. Linus wanted me to run off with him a few weeks back and I didn't go. I should have. Stroud wanted me to do some tracking for him and I done it. I'm done now. I don't care if I got pay coming to me or not, I ain't no part of this."

The surgeon dropped the pails from his hands and took hold of Lloyd's jacket. He pulled him close and his eyes were angry and there was fear behind them. "You goddamn fool," he said. "You sound just like Linus. You don't think you're a part of this? You're every bit a part, just like Linus is a part, just like every one of us sorry bastards is a part, and you won't be leaving unless its an indian who takes you or Stroud himself who draws the mark across your grave."

"I didn't kill that trapper," answered Lloyd.

"It doesn't matter who killed him."

"Let me go. It's that damn indian got me into this--"

"It doesn't matter who killed him or who said what," the surgeon shook Lloyd hard again by his jacket, then shoved him away. "You're in this now as much as any other."

Water splattered onto Lloyd's boots. He steadied his feet beneath him and said, "I got no cause to go murdering. I never killed nobody in my life."

"Yet all you talk about is how you'll kill Black Paw."

"Him I will-- he deserves it. But I ain't one to go killing women and children and innocent folk. No," he shook his head. "That ain't in me."

"Boy," said the surgeon. He picked up his pails. "You've no idea what's in you when the gun's to your head."

Nine

A circuitous route along a chain of hogbacks liberated them from the worst of the naked lands south of Milltown. It drew them up through rocky country where the wagons stuttered and smacked, the axles screaming and the wood bending in groans that echoed off towering limestone facades. Where they met the quarry road they took it. Clear to the north of town they'd ridden, and descending on down the road they traversed a sheet of rock that stood out over the ancient quarry as thin as parchment paper. Below them in great monoliths stood the carvings of some ancient peoples. Patterns of hand-cut stone, great slabs resting at angles, others flat on the ground. The clopping of hooves on rocks tumbled into that open amphitheater and bounced against the walls in such ferocious pounding echoes that some of the mules took fright and scampered ahead to escape the reverberations.

When they came down into the flatlands the echoes had still not faded. They rung the men's ears and vibrated their lungs like tuning forks struck and held to quiver. The wagon holding Linus Tate lurched into sight of his burial ground.

In this state they closed down on the adobe huts. Down on

Molly. She held a wooden shepherd's staff and walked the fields among her goats. Grass grew all about where the waters from the town's lifespring overran its banks and trickled down through desert marshland. The captain docked the company's course and they reached her in a thunder of cavalry hooves.

Lloyd sat his horse two lengths behind Stroud. Molly shielded her eyes to them. It was the closest Lloyd had seen her. The dress she wore was faded and the body beneath it reaped the gaze of each man's eyes on down the line.

"My dear Molly," Captain Stroud boomed in a baritone worthy of the stage. "What pleasure it gives me to see you after such long days in the desert."

"Captain," she nodded. Her hand still shielded her eyes.

"Have you been well?"

"Very well, thank you."

"Allow us to accompany you back to town."

"That's quite alright, Captain; I've only just let them out."

Stroud did not let go his smile. The beauty of it so captivated Lloyd that he felt himself tipping forward over the pommel. He broke his eyes away and straightened. He looked at Gil. The boy smiled also, a horrid grimace as if the glass by which he attempted to mirror Stroud's charm had cracked and warped.

Stroud looked at the goats. "I won't have it any other way."

The company of eighteen men and four wagons and forty mules and forty horses stood in a laissez state of attention. Saddles creaking. Waiting on some inclination from the woman that she understood and accepted the order of events to which her day had now been structured. She focused instead on the goats.

"Come now," said Stroud. "The day is short and many tasks await within it."

"Yes, of course."

He dismounted and tossed the reins to Gil and walked with her across the desert meadow to where the flock roamed. All the company a witness to his courtship. A touch of her staff sent the goats moving. The two walked side by side behind them, Stroud with his hands clasped behind his back and Molly's dress hanging from her hips and swaying as it brushed over the grass. The sun at its angle lighting the bluestem and the red cliffs of the far reaches made for them a frame, the picture within its borders a piece worthy of painting.

"Hup!" the lieutenant bawled. An ordered commotion dominoed out behind him. The company leaned into its march, slow and ceremonious in its trailing of the couple. They kept it up until a hundred yards out from Molly's cabin, then veered away along the lane leading into the adobe huts. Several heads turned to watch the captain enter through her doorway and the door close behind him.

Before the company reached the sawmill, Burgess veered them out again to the corral beside the stream. For a quarter of an hour they walked the banks and threw stones into the water. They avoided the wagon and Linus Tate. He made no sound anyway.

Lloyd kept his distance. His eyes fell on Black Paw's hut and remained there a long while. The indian neither came nor went. The hut appeared empty. Lloyd walked a quarter mile down the stream and back up again. He walked the corral perimeter, hunted for sign along the edge of the huts. He found Black Paw's moccasin tracks but nothing fresh enough worth following.

Bruder came ambling up from the town to speak with Lieutenant Burgess. While the two conversed, the soldiers commented on Molly's dress. The treasures underneath.

Movement came from the cabin. The door opened, the captain emerged.

"I'd have given her more than twenty minutes," said McKenny.

"You'd not have lasted half that," said Price.

"Maybe not. All the same, I wouldn't have left. I'd have stuck around another hour and when my willy was spry enough I'd have given her another go."

The surgeon kicked a stone and walked on.

They came to order at Burgess's call, and when Captain Stroud reached them they stood at attention with their rifles and muskets laid against their shoulders, the bayonets like fence posts jabbing at the sky. Stroud called for Linus Tate to be brought out. They pulled him from the wagon, gently, like an infirmed man. He was quiet. Older. He kept his head to the ground and chose not to look another man in the eye as they marched him down the lane through the adobe huts to the sawmill. Stroud stopped him at an awning post. He stood him with his back against it and began to tie his hands behind of it.

The company formed a line at thirty paces. Lloyd stood in the middle, the surgeon to one side, Clemons on the other. He heard the whine of the batwing doors and he swiveled his head and saw Old Crazy and Bruder standing just outside the saloon. Bruder had his thumbs tucked in his suspenders. He saw Lloyd and his thumbs came out and he took a step forward, his face scrunched and puzzled. Lloyd turned back to the sawmill.

Stroud pulled tight the rope with a flourish, which squeezed Linus's arms behind his ribs. Something bird-like exuded from the old man the way he stood with his thin chest forced out and his shoulders wrenched back. In Stroud's pocket was a cloth. He drew it out.

Lloyd wondered if he'd had it there waiting all along. A pocket of sweat formed between his palm and the rifle stock. He wiggled his fingers. The muscles in his neck and along his spine felt cramped. He tensed them, tensed his legs, wiggled some more. Burgess, standing perpendicular to them at the end of the line, scowled. Lloyd licked his lips and fought to still himself.

The cloth came over Linus's eyes. Linus whimpered some but no one heard it. Lloyd switched his weight from one foot to another. The Sampson brothers came walking down the lane.

"Hold still," the surgeon whispered beside him.

The cloth ends flapped as Stroud cinched the knot. He stepped away. Linus's mouth gaped open. The man's head made little movements, little circles. Stroud took two steps out from the post and addressed those gathered. The line of soldiers, the Sampsons who'd stopped across the street, Bruder and Old Crazy beside the saloon.

"Desertion," he thundered, as if he wished his words might reach the woman not in attendance, "is not simply an abandonment of one's post; it is an abandonment of your fellow man, an abandonment of your country. The selfishness of the act affects more than the perpetrator. It imperils the very lives of those whom he has betrayed. For that is its name-- betrayal. And any man so cowardly as to betray his fellow man, his brother in arms, his very patrimony, who so callously endangers the lives of others and the future of this great nation, will have returned upon himself the full reckoning of that sin. May every man know that the punishment for desertion is death. Private Linus Tate, by virtue of the authority vested in me as Captain of the armed forces of the United States, I hereby sentence you to execution by firing squad. May God be the judge of your soul."

Stroud crossed the dust in a near goose step. Linus's mouth hung open still. He leaned forward against the ropes.

Lloyd gulped air. His body itched everywhere, everything was shifting. He looked behind him again. Bruder had his thumbs in his suspenders. Black Paw nowhere, as if he'd never existed.

Stroud stopped beside Lieutenant Burgess. He turned. Heels slapped together. His boots had somehow found a polish; they hurt Lloyd's eyes, he looked away.

"Ready," called Stroud. Hands clapped weapons.

"Aim."

The Harpers came off Lloyd's shoulder. He saw the end of it, saw the bayonet wave at Linus like a finger in accusation. Linus standing still. Clemons' gun steady, the surgeon steady. He tried to breathe, his head squealed.

"Fire."

Dust plumes popped off Linus's shirtfront. His legs buckled and he slid down the post. His chest hung, his head hung lower. The rope at his hands kept him up a moment, suspended him at an angle in the air, then his torso swung around and he fell backwards with his knees tucked in front of him and he lay still with his lips parted breathless and the sound of gunshots bouncing over the flats.

Stroud called another order. Lloyd didn't hear it. The men swung around with their backs to the sawmill and Lloyd turned with them. Stroud marched around to the front of the line. In slow, measured paces, he began an inspection of his men. Lloyd held the Harpers against his chest. His eyes hurt. He closed them against the sun. When he opened them Stroud was three men down the line. He came eventually abreast of Lloyd and jerked the rifle out of Lloyd's hands. A look at the flash pan was all he needed.

"Lieutenant Burgess," he barked. "Seize up Private Reed. Corporal Pucker, remove the deserter's body from the post and bring me the rope."

The two moved to the tune of their orders, Gil scurrying like a ferret to work the ropes free from Linus Tate's dead hands, Burgess plodding under the burden of his corpulence and the excessive heat of the day. He reached Lloyd and shoved him forward. Lloyd tripped and stumbled a few paces. Another shove slammed him up against the post.

"Remove his shirt and jacket," ordered Stroud.

Burgess obliged. He ripped the coat from Lloyd's arms. The rank-smelling shirt he flung to the ground alongside it. Lloyd shivered white-skinned and bare-chested under the desert sun. He crossed his elbows but Burgess grabbed him and spun him into place, pinned his chest against the post. The lieutenant next pulled Lloyd's arms horizontal and wrapped them around the wood now stained by Linus's blood and held him there while Stroud walked forward to tie Lloyd's wrists.

The captain's neck bulged red as he cinched the knot. He stepped back and ordered Burgess to fetch him a horse whip from the wagons. The company of soldiers stood watching. Stroud took three steps forward and halted to address them along with the few townsfolk looking on. His second speech matched neither the length nor the eloquence of the first.

"Orders are to be carried out. Any disobedience will be punished. First offense; a warning. Second offense; a dozen lashes."

Silence followed while Burgess searched for the whip. Lloyd's breath came back. It surged inside him and he pressed his forehead against the post and closed his eyes and cursed Black Paw between panicked breaths. He heard the lieutenant's footsteps crunch over the sand and he heard the silence while Burgess passed the whip to the captain and he cursed Black Paw and he screamed out in one sharp and wild blurting as the first strike cut his back. His breath left him. He choked at the second strike, his forehead hit the post. He hugged it, fleeing from the whip. It came again, a wet slap, dull and quick, a swish before the smack, the leather peeling away the flesh in thin bloody strips. The feeling of ants crawling along his back, stinging and biting, and the whip struck again. He cried out. His arms filled with splinters as he sank to his knees down the length of the post, and there on the ground he received another lash, blood splattering into the lane along the whip's path.

Stroud paused to run his fingers down the strip of leather, removing bits of clinging flesh before rearing back again, his neck thick and his back wide with muscle, arm raised, his arm a blur of movement, the swish again of leather slicing air and ending in the splat of tearing skin.

Of the first six lashes Lloyd felt every one. The last half dozen he felt when he woke, glazed and reeking with camphor oil in the darkness of a red adobe hut. He opened his eyes and closed them again and felt the ants devour his back.

"Hold still," the surgeon's voice.

"He awake?" Old Crazy.

"He's moving."

"Give him some of this."

"Put that away," Bruder this time.

"What's the harm? Help with the pain I reckon. Ain't that right, surgeon?"

"As much as anything else."

"He doesn't need grog," said Bruder, "he needs medicines."

"Chicha is a potent medicine."

"Real medicine."

"It's real alright. Takes the pain away."

"I would think a surgeon might recommend something else is all."

"I'm no surgeon."

"Isn't that what they call you?" said Bruder.

"That's what they call me."

"So?"

"They call you Sheriff don't they? And this old fellow Mayor?"

"Well…," said Bruder

Old Crazy cackled. His hands came up and he rubbed the translucent skin covering the old scalping.

"I can read my letters and I'm quick with the saw. So they call me surgeon."

"I just thought maybe there'd be something else. Yarrow or mullein or some such. Ginseng, even."

"I've got needle and thread and I've got the saw. Aside from that there's drink."

"Well," Bruder said. "At least we had the camphor."

Old Crazy scuttled closer to Lloyd. "Let him have a sip. He chewed up half a batch with me and drank hardly nothing of it."

"Wait till he can sit up," said the surgeon.

Old Crazy backed away. Lloyd could hear him sipping. The smell of chicha drifted; it warmed the air.

"It wasn't him shot Jim Crudger then?" said Bruder.

"I don't know," answered the surgeon. "He says it wasn't him."

"What did Henry say?"

"Henry?"

"In La Chureca. The man he robbed."

"We didn't ask him."

"Didn't ask him? That was the whole point of taking him up there."

"We never went."

"To see Henry?"

"To La Chureca. Captain figured otherwise."

"Otherwise? There ain't no otherwise. You was supposed to ask Henry if it was him that stole his flour. And if it was him, why, he'd have been the one shot Jim."

The surgeon dabbed up the crusted blood from Lloyd's back with a towel. He gave a final wipe and stowed it in his bag. "You know anything about this man?" he asked Bruder.

"Only that he calls himself Lloyd and that he robbed Henry and more'n likely killed Jim Crudger. And all for a damned coat."

"You know anything else?"

"He's an ornery son of a bitch, I know that much."

"Did you know he can read sign?"

"Anybody can read sign. What about it?"

"No," said the surgeon. "Not like this one."

"Why don't Stroud find someone else? Let this here man see justice."

"There's not another like him."

"Tracker?"

"Lloyd Reed could track a man through the ocean. Swear on the grave. It's more than a skill-- it's a gift. You won't find any better as long as you live, I'll tell you that much. Stroud won't give him up. He could kill a thousand men for their coats and Stroud wouldn't let you touch him. He's that good."

Lloyd heard his name and groaned. He slung a knee up underneath his chest and wobbled as they watched him. The other knee came up and he shoved off the ground with his palms. Old

Crazy pushed the jar out. Bits of chicha clung to the rim from where he'd sipped.

Lloyd turned on his palms the way a chained bear would turn. He reached for the jar and winced when the pain stabbed him. The first swallow went down as warm as it smelled. He took another. Bruder's face blank, Old Crazy grinning.

"Drink it till you go back to sleep," said the surgeon. "You'll need to be able to sit a saddle tomorrow. And pray the captain doesn't come across a mission, or you'll be turning a shovel as well."

"That's you all doing that?" said Bruder. "Digging up the mission floors?"

"Stroud has the idea there's gold buried somewhere."

Old Crazy cocked his head at Bruder, who grunted something and folded his hands.

The surgeon stood. He watched Lloyd drink. "Rest up now," he said. The advice was all the surgeon gave. He left the hut with Bruder behind him.

Old Crazy stayed. He sat across from Lloyd with his legs crossed, knees bobbing in the air. He watched Lloyd slurp, then held his hands out, his fingers wiggling. Lloyd passed the jar. It made several trips back and forth. When they'd drained it Old Crazy came to his feet. Lloyd tipped sideways.

"I'll be back," said the old man. "I got customers need attending."

He returned as he promised, some time later. An oil lamp in one hand, a jar in the other. He nudged Lloyd with his boot. "Hey," he said. "I brought ye something."

Lloyd lifted his neck as though an iron ball were fastened atop it. His back tingled. The sensation of little pins pricked at him like the ants from before had grown needles on their feet and were trampling miniature paths up and down his hide.

"Go on, take it."

Lloyd accepted the jar. He touched it to his lips.

"That'll do ye."

Warm and rich. A comfort reminiscent of times long passed. Motherly affection. His head swirled. Ants, and the old man rose and left him and he lapped at the jar, lapping and swallowing, the chicha replacing the pain, and the pain clearing and memory returning. He heard the swish of the whip and he winced and looked about but all was dark inside the hut. In the street through the doorway arch, blue moonlight glowed. His limbs procrastinated at their orders. He unwound a leg and watched it move in front of him. New boots. Good soles. He heard screaming outside, gunfire and children crying on the backs of horses. He dropped the jar and stood and wobbled through the doorway.

The soldiers had spent the afternoon tearing planks of wood from the land office walls. They stood them on their ends in the middle of the lane outside the saloon and pounded them into the ground and lit their tops aflame. Through these makeshift torch fires, in and out of the saloon, the soldiers tottered with jars of chicha and bottles of aguardiente swinging loose beside them, and into this scene of burning depravity staggered Lloyd.

Francis Price saw him coming. He raised his arm, a finger extended along the bottleneck. "That Lloyd?"

"Is he drunk?" someone asked.

"Hey, come look at this, Lloyd's drunk as a muskrat."

They tripped down the boardwalk and spread out amongst the flaming planks. Lloyd peered at the faces all shimmering in orange. His arms winged out to balance.

"What are you looking for, Lloyd?"

"He's looking for a drink."

A bottle was thrust to his chest.

"Take a drink, Lloyd, do you good."

"Take some of that sting off."

"What you looking for, Lloyd?"

Lloyd drank and spat half of it out. It burned his lips.

"He wants chicha."

"I want get," Lloyd's words ran out in front of his tongue.

"Pass him that jar."

"I get that indian," he managed.

They watched him swing around. He fell and cried out. Clemons grabbed him under the armpit and pulled him up and Lloyd screamed out again. Clemons let go.

"What's he worked up about?"

"About getting whipped. You would be too."

"Give him that jar."

Lloyd was drinking. He pulled the jar away and then it was at his lips again and he was drinking again and he pulled it away. It kept coming back. "I didn't kill none. No one. Is a lying Black Paw."

"What's he saying?"

"He's going on about the indian again."

"You done told us fifty times you're going to kill him, Lloyd. Ever time you's drunk."

"Where my rifle?"

"Hey he's looking for his rifle."

"You better watch out Gil. Maybe he'll come to his senses and turn on you. Forget about his indian ghost."

Laughing.

Lloyd stopped. His feet stopped. He raged out and his scream brought the orange glowing faces silent. "I'm gonna kill that indian!" He swung around at a sound no one else heard. "Where is he?"

Faces looked at one another. Lieutenant Burgess stood in the batwings with a mug of whiskey run off from an oak barrel.

"Hey you know what he's talking about, Lieutenant?"

"He's drunk," said Burgess. "Surgeon! Get him back in that hut. Give him something that'll put him to sleep."

"That's what I gave him chicha for."

"Well it didn't work."

Hands gripped Lloyd. He sank into them. The human touch. He saw flames whip in the orange fluorescence and the smell of dust and rock, and he thought he heard music playing.

His face hit dirt and twisted sideways. A blanket fell over him. Voices flickered overhead. They came and went and he lost them.

"I don't like him talking about me."

"He wasn't talking about you."

"He said my name."

"No he didn't," the surgeon grunted.

"Well he was talking about killing, weren't he?"

"He was talking about an indian."

"Ain't no indians here."

"There's Black Paw," said Old Crazy.

The surgeon and Gil turned to the old man hovering behind them, drunk and frothed in chicha.

"Is he even real?" the surgeon asked.

"Course he is. That's who knows about the gold."

"What gold?"

"Ain't that what ye's diggin for? You want gold, it's Black Paw knows where it's buried-- he seen it."

The surgeon stepped closer. He faced the old man and looked him up and down from his scalped head to his feet. Gil reared in between, shortest of the three.

"What did he see?" said the surgeon.

"He saw it buried. 'Fore he burned all them folks up. But that's Sheriff Bruder's story-- he likes to tell it."

"Why don't you tell it, old man?" said Gil.

"No, no, Bruder likes to tell it."

"Bruder ain't here."

The old man smiled his toothless smile and scratched his head. Gil returned one of his own, this one laden with small nubby things poking up from bleeding gums. He extended his mug of chicha. Old Crazy accepted. He sipped and surveyed his audience, Lloyd asleep on the ground.

"He seen that nigger slave run off with it. Seen him bury it."

"Who saw it?"

"Black Paw."

"Go on," said the surgeon.

"He was trailing them that killed his folks. Black Paw was. They done killed all his people-- that's why he ain't got no kin."

"What's that part about the gold?" said Gil.

"Bruder says they had gold. Or Black Paw said it, and that's what Bruder says."

"Who had gold?"

"White folks."

"And a slave buried it?"

"Black Paw seen him do it."

"Where?"

"If I knowed that I'd be a rich man." Old Crazy laughed a high-pitched gabble and rocked back on his haunches.

"Where's the indian?" said the surgeon.

"Somewhere. He comes and goes."

"And the slave?"

The old man shrugged.

"What happened to the white men?"

Old Crazy laughed. He tickled his skull and his eyes jumped around.

"You telling us stories, old man?"

"That's Black Paw's story. Bruder likes to tell it."

"This old man's crazy," said Gil.

"That's what they call him," said the surgeon.

"What?"

"Old Crazy."

The old man warbled another species of laughter. He spooned out the last of the chicha with a finger and stuck it in his mouth. It came out with a pop. "I'm the mayor," he said.

The surgeon rubbed a fresh layer of camphor across Lloyd's back and led him through the morning sunlight where Lloyd pirouetted on a single foot and landed sideways in the lane. The surgeon grabbed him up by one arm and Lieutenant Burgess took another. On the shoulders of men Lloyd floated, up and upwards and placed astride his horse. A film coated his teeth. He licked at it while an order was called out. The exact words or who gave it evaded him. The horse's ears were pricked and by its own volition the animal marched forward in line with the company, Lloyd weaving in the saddle and watching the adobe huts pass by.

Their exodus from Milltown steered them past Molly's door. Every back straight but Lloyd's. Men hungover and preening all the same. A few minutes and they'd slouch again and belch their curses in foul breath and foul words and smear their filthy hands on piss-stained uniforms unwashed in the stream that all that while had flowed in crystal currents by the border of the town without a single thread of clothing scrubbed within its waters.

They slowed and slowed and when she failed to appear the captain halted the line and dismounted. He walked his glistening boots across the yard and rapped upon her door. It opened. Her light filled its frame.

Lloyd attempted to admire along with the others but his eyes stung and he dropped his head. The ground proved gentler on his vision. He stared at it and breathed in sync with the pounding in his skull. Tracks lay in profusion. Goats. Molly's dainty feet. There were horse tracks, other boots. Bruder's he recognized. The Sampson boys. On top of these, fresh from the morning, the imprints of moccasins. Neither were these new to him. One eye shrunk, the other grew. He knew these tracks. He ran his head past the horse's ears and caught each footprint on its path, the stride length, the easy gait. The prints farther out were no more than a change in color on the sand. Lloyd's eyes plucked them up one by one. Right to where Black Paw sat crouched in the shade of a hut. Crouched in shadows. Lloyd felt a careening in his ribs. His body jerked. He slid the Harpers from its scabbard and reigned the horse around. Stock to his shoulder. The horse restless, hands wet. His lacerated back uncooperative and Black Paw sitting there unmoving and shadowed and still not moving and the barrel swirling, rifle bead hunting.

Crack.

Lead thunked adobe. Commotion on the line, reverberations of gunfire. Stroud whirled, his hand shoved Molly inside. Gil snatched level his Springfield and the men drew weapons and called out to each other, the horses turning and the empty town all quiet around them.

"What the hell are you shooting at?" Burgess shouted from the wagons.

Lloyd fell from his horse. The rifle clattered. He pulled it up and staggered over the moccasin tracks while the soldiers watched. A ways from the hut he stopped. He searched the shadows and advanced several paces more, then stumbled out to where he could see along the edge of the wall, but there was no indian, no Black Paw.

"Get that fool on his horse," said Burgess.

The Virginians were closest. They brought him back between the two of them. Stroud left Molly behind the door. He reached Lloyd's horse as the Virginians were heaving him up, Lloyd flopping and mumbling about indians and coats of mottled hides. He made the saddle. The horse balked. Its front hooves came up a touch and when they landed Lloyd spewed a torrent of yellow bile across its mane. He spasmed again and another cascade of vomit spilled down his jacket front and splattered onto the pommel and over his legs. The Virginians and Stroud fled back with arms upheld. Another last heave. Bits of corn sailed into the horse hairs. Lloyd started to fall and one of the Virginians jumped forward and steadied him with an outstretched hand.

Stroud turned from him. His face transformed as he lifted it, from rage to something quite the opposite. Like nothing amiss. His mouth in a beautiful smile of straight white teeth and confidence. He shared a word with Molly, newly emerged from the doorway, bid his farewell, and marched across the yard. On his horse he tipped his hat. The men driving the wagons clapped the reins. In a creaking trundling commencement they rolled out of Milltown, Lloyd in the middle of the train with his hands gooped in vomit and his head untethered from his body.

Ten

All that day they drove the mules and horses northward into the high plains. Days later, at the first bunches of reedgrass, the animals halted to sate their hollow bellies but the riders bullied them onward over sandy loam and through mesquite and sagebrush and through the little bluestem that clutched at the earth in parched and wilted patches. In a week's time they spotted acres of switchgrass waving on distant pasture thirty miles out. When they reached it they unhitched the teams and set the beasts free to devour the land at their leisure.

On this night Lloyd probed the depths of the bottle. Whiskey and mezcal and something traded for in the shadows of the Mexican fort that smelled of turpentine and tasted metallic on his tongue. A deliverance from carnal pain he found, though the vows he howled as he reared like a tyrant amidst the campfires gave his fellow soldiers fodder for speculation upon his deeper torment. He whirled from rage to tears. The ground rose up to trip him and he fell and clambered up again and veered from man to man besot in alcohol repeating all the while the name Black Paw the indian man who'd circumscribed his fate and whom he'd surely kill. He said it to the fires. He smashed his bottle against the rocks. He railed inchoate to the night, and when the men grew tired of his madness they took hold his squirming limbs and held him down on the canvas tent with sun-chapped fingers round his neck until the blood ran weak to his skull and he fell quiet and unconscious and off to fitful slumber.

He woke at the commotion of Lieutenant Burgess harassing the men into their morning routine and kicking the tent flaps open to usher in the light of dawn. McKenny swore. From somewhere nearby Lloyd heard a splashing stream of urine from someone too lazy to walk a dozen paces further.

The Virginians began to rustle beside him. He drew up on all fours, the movement sending pangs across his back not fully healed, and grimaced while they laced their boots and guffawed at the potency of one another's flatulence. The two crawled into the open air and began to uproot the tent stakes while Lloyd fumbled with his boots. When he reached for his feet something tore in his back. Skin raw and unhealed. One side of the tent collapsed. He shouted at the Virginians and they laughed and slapped the canvas near his head.

On his horse he felt no better. It fussed beneath him, slowing suddenly, breaking into a trot, slowing again. He pulled his spare from the remuda and swapped the saddle over, which set his back to bleeding again. The delay dropped him back from the company. The pace he needed to catch up caused a bouncing in the saddle that further aggravated the broken skin, and when he reached them where they'd stopped to water at a streambed his shirt was wet and heavy with blood.

All that day and the next they rode through switchgrass. Where it mixed with western wheatgrass the mules and horses bent their necks and not even the whips could get them moving.

Boredom rode with them. Rolling grass, the company of one another. Beards and lice, the same stories told and retold, the same bets wagered and old arguments regurgitated in tired monotony. The same food, Clemons' deck of cards. The whiskey barrels did little to assuage their apathy. They drank anyway. They spoke of Molly while Stroud and Burgess convened away from earshot.

From boredom was born discord. A seed of malcontent grew by the day. It germinated on whiskey and as it flourished the men began to brawl, the arguments each time more desperate, until one evening Francis Price stuck Osmond Culkin with a blade over a disagreement neither man could recall.

"Too long without women," was Burgess's opinion.

Stroud watched a cloud pass over the moon. He sat on a wagon bed while Gil buffed furiously at his boots. Lloyd sat in the entrance of his tent nearby. Stroud called him over.

"Have you been to Santa Fe?"

"Once," Lloyd answered.

"How far from there to the Weminuche country?"

"Depends on the weather. Couple weeks, maybe less."

"And if it snows?"

"There ain't no getting around in that country once it snows."

"How long do we have?"

Lloyd scratched his neck and looked at the moon. He looked at Burgess then at Gil, who'd paused at his polishing. "There'll be snow on the peaks by now. I reckon another month till it snows in the passes."

Stroud bowed his head and shook it.

"They don't got a month left in 'em, Captain," said Burgess. "They'll break before that."

"Give them more whiskey."

"That's half the problem."

"Give them the whip then."

"We can whip 'em," Burgess agreed. "Hard to keep 'em in fighting condition if they're whipped up though."

Stroud grunted.

"There's that town," said Burgess. "It's close."

"It's out of the way. And there's nothing there but old men and cigarettes."

"Half a day at most. McKenny swears there's women."

"McKenny."

"He's got a nose for 'em."

"They just had their fill of women."

"That was weeks ago. Besides, most of 'em got too drunk in the bathhouses to get to whorein'." Burgess ran a hand down his belly, over his buttons. "And even if there aren't, it does a man good to sit at a table-- eat a meal he hasn't cooked himself. Makes him feel human."

Stroud gave another grunt. He looked at the moon again. "Give me those boots," he said. He stamped them on. "Go on now," he waved Gil off. When the boy was gone he turned to Lloyd. "A month you say?"

Lloyd nodded.

Stroud stood from the wagon bed. "From here forward I want us marching before sunrise."

They approached the aldea from the south so jinnied up with anticipation that they'd spent the morning sneaking shots of whiskey from the trailing wagon and postulating on McKenny's theories of women hidden in the shacks and virgin whores dressed in linens awaiting the soldiers with legs spread wide and supple breasts to suckle.

Among the sober counted the surgeon. They'd drawn straws and it was him who drew luckless to guard the remuda and wagons. At Lloyd's offer to replace him, the captain only shook his head and announced that Lloyd would ride to town. There was no discussion on this point.

He choked on the rising dust and took no part in the commotion that rang across the flats a mile out in any direction, and it was no surprise when they left the remuda and wagons on the hillside with the surgeon and shuffled into town that not a living soul came out to greet them. They ambled in on legs unsteady, herding before them a scrawny packmule. To its back they'd strapped a half-empty barrel of whiskey. At the cantina door Lloyd ducked his head and entered with the rest. It reeked of smoke and vomit. They stacked their rifles against the wall while the barkeep watched from behind his wagontop. One lone anciano clothed in threadbare homespun joined in silent observance. Francis Price rolled the whiskey barrel over the dirt to the base of the bar, and with Clemons' help they heaved it over the wagonboards.

The barkeep stepped back. His jowls swayed with the movement.

"We've come to make another trade, my friend," said Stroud. He motioned to the barrel, then brought two fingers against his lips and through them drew a breath of air.

"*Sí, claro,*" the barkeep bent behind the wagon boards. When he straightened he held a box between his hands. He slid it over the planks.

Stroud flipped the lid up. Neat rows of white paper cigarettes. The sweet fragrance of tobacco. "You have food for the men?" said Stroud.

The Mexican searched for explanation. He found Viker's face and queried with his eyes.

"Comida," said Viker.

"Ask him where he's hid the women," said McKenny.

"Comida," repeated Stroud. He drew a circle over the men with a finger. *"Todos."*

"Sí, claro. En seguida." The barkeep's eyes flashed to the anciano and back to Stroud. He came out from around the bar and stepped past the men and past the stacks of rifles and out the door through which he had no need to duck his head.

In his absence the men smoked cigarillos and ashed in the dirt. From behind the bar they stole cups and filled them from the barrel and sat at the benches and stared at the tables awaiting their banquet. The old man sitting in his faded threads kept silent on his bench.

"There must be fifty houses here," said McKenny. He held both cigarette and whiskey in the one hand. "Where are they all?"

"You tell us, John," said a soldier.

"You said there was virgin whores," said another.

"Who do you think's cooking the food?" McKenny's eyes glistened red with whiskey.

The question held them up awhile until Price answered. "It's that old man's wife. She's all yours, John, he won't mind."

They swung around to the anciano staring from his bench and belittled him as he sat unsmiling in their cloud of smoke. Through the doorway the barkeep returned and again a look was shared.

Lloyd lit himself a cigarillo. He pulled at it, the smoke bit his throat. He coughed. When he withdrew it the paper stuck briefly to his lip and came away stained in blood. He dropped it and climbed off the bench. Through the door he went. Stroud watched him go.

Outside behind the cantina he loosened his trousers and urinated against the wall. It splashed onto his boots and he skirted away, leaving a crooked river of piss winding through the dirt. It reached a divot and pooled there, shimmering in the sunlight. He stepped around to the edge of the cantina and not even a dog stirred on that empty street. Dust and adobe there was in plenty, the fancier doorways shut with wooden slabs. Odd-cut hides hung as curtains for the rest.

As he stood there daydreaming, the barkeep crossed the lane. A short man, shorter yet in his hunched scurry. He stole a glance up the lane and ducked through a hanging cow hide. A minute later he elbowed back through with a cauldron wobbling between his legs and both arms straining at the iron handle curved across its top. Wisps of steam escaped the lid to flutter over the man's clenched fingers. A voice called out and he stopped and turned back. A girl leaned through the hide. One hand lifted the lid, with the other she slung a ladle into the pot. The barkeep hissed an order and the hide fell back over the doorway.

Lloyd ran along the cantina wall. Over the little river of urine and around the corner, under the doorway, back into the cloud of smoke. The barkeep appeared a minute later. He tottered across the dirt and with great effort swung the cauldron over the tabletop. He had no bowls or spoons, but with gestures and words in Spanish he indicated they might use whiskey mugs as suitable receptacles.

They ate as drunkards will; the stew dripping into their beards and the men shouting and cavorting with their mouths full of half-chewed tubers. They drank more whiskey, the box ran empty of cigarillos. They demanded the barkeep produce another.

Lloyd gulped down a mug and served himself another. He was handed a dram of whiskey that sat untouched where they left it. Beside him, Osmond Culkin teetered off the bench. He straightened and stumbled blind through smoke. Before he'd fully disappeared into the sunlight he whirled around and came plowing back through the doorway, shouting in exaltation, "There's women!"

Within the hush the statement produced, the barkeep gave a pleading look to the anciano and the anciano shook his wrinkled head.

"What?" said Price.

"A wagonful. In the street."

McKenny rose first. He knocked Osmond aside with a stiff-arm and the men ran into the street behind him.

Driving in from the canyonlands came a chuck wagon pulled by a single horse. A squat fat Mexican held the reins. Beside him sat two women. They wore rebozos around their shoulders, and over their breasts hung their hair in black braided trenzas.

McKenny tottered into the road. The driver turned the horse and McKenny sidestepped into its path and held up his arm. The rest of the company circled the wagon. Lloyd stood at the doorway watching. Gil and Stroud beside him.

McKenny proposed something to the driver or to the women, no one knew. The words swarmed drunk and garbled from his beard. When he reached his hand out and touched the rebozo nearest him, the driver slapped the reins across the horse's back. McKenny snatched the woman's arm and jerked her clear of the seat. She spilled into the lane, her dress fluttered over her calves. McKenny fell on top of her. With his good arm around her neck and the stump pressed at her shoulder he appeared a deformed jackal pitted against an adversary as well equipped as he.

The driver yanked still the horse and turned in the seat and in that moment as the soldiers shouted and crowded around him, a door opened on the far side of the lane through which appeared a man with a smoothbore musket pressed against his shoulder. He sighted down the barrel and fired into the crowd.

The ball shattered Joel Viker's femur. A soft dull thunk. His leg folded beneath him and he fell strangely lopsided beside the wagon wheel.

Like bats to a cave the soldiers swarmed back to the cantina. Gil, nearest the door, entered first. He ran straight into the pointed muzzle of an old Baker rifle the barkeep had pulled from below the wagonplanks, but the barkeep fired too quickly and the shot instead blew a jagged hole through the cantina wall, auguring in a gush of fresh air to that chamber of gloom and smoke and stench. Gil, eyes wide open, drew the Springfield from his belt in a motion well-practiced and returned fire. The shot slammed a .69 caliber ball into the barkeep's chest. It lifted his body, hurled him against the wall. The smear he left upon it as he sank to the floor glistened dark and wet above him and his eyes were open and he babbled something there on the floor as the blood ran down the wall in a viscous trek of plasma.

A body shoved Lloyd forward. An order was shouted to take up arms and the order repeated in various voices in varying levels of drunken hysteria. Men ran back out the door, bats out of the cave. Lloyd held the Harpers, no recollection of having grabbed it. He carried it against his chest and ducked his head through the doorway.

In the street, shots popped in fuzzy blasts. The first thing Lloyd saw was the wagon driver, slumped dead across the seat. Joel Viker dragging his leg behind him. From the houses came short ripping bursts of fire, gunsmoke rising. Soldiers ran crouched along the walls, sliding into alleys and posting up behind what cover there was. He saw the Virginians pull a man from a doorway and club him with a rifle butt and disappear inside.

Two shots followed.

Campesinos filed out of houses into the streets, appearing like a ragged peasant deputation armed with machetes and hoes and things grabbed up in haste. The few carrying firearms were the first shot. The Americans, drunk as they were, performed an execution of the townsfolk in exemplary militaristic fashion. Captain Stroud ambled down the center lane like a Sunday leisure stroll, casually firing his weapon, pausing to reload, firing again. Clemons caught a musket ball to the shoulder, fired point-blank from four feet behind. He twisted when it hit him. Completing his spin he came face to face with the man who'd fired it-- a campesino's face, brown and empty and suddenly beset with surprise as Clemons impaled sixteen inches of bayonet into his chest.

Two minutes it took to quell the campesino uprising, after which the only rifle cracks to accost the town were those provided by the soldiers, the screams entirely the Mexican's purveyance. As men died, women appeared. They ran from their homes, braids trailing. Some screaming, mostly silent. They held children in their arms and children ran after them, and third in line were soldiers. Footchases ended in tackled bodies. Women were jerked up by their hair or arms and dragged back into huts or down to the river bank, the final gunblasts cracking like percussion canticles to accompany their molestation as the last remaining male adults were murdered in the streets.

Lloyd hadn't moved. He stood beside the low doorway, cramps running up his hands from the fierceness of his grip on the rifle. A girl ran past him into the cantina. Stroud, strutting back down the lane the way he'd come, saw her. He pointed. Lloyd looked to the doorway and back at Stroud, but his feet took him in no direction at all. He stood frozen with the rifle barrel against his chest while the captain marched him down. Lloyd's body tensed. He anticipated a blow, but the captain only brushed by him and ducked through the doorway. Gil came running behind. He looked at Lloyd and he was grinning and there was blood smeared along his neck. The boy ducked and entered and almost immediately Stroud appeared again. Without a word the captain stretched a hand out from the doorway and yanked Lloyd inside.

In the gloom behind the wagonboards the girl knelt beside the barkeep. She held his face in her fingers. Stroud crossed the floor and grabbed her by the arm, ignoring her screams while her father in his blood-choked voice begged, *"Es mi hija, por Dios."*

Stroud pulled her away. She slapped his hand, a useless gesture.

"Captain," Burgess leaned through the doorway. "We're going to need to get Viker up to the surgeon. His leg's busted up bad."

"Then take him up there. And take this girl with you," Stroud shoved the girl across the floor.

The lieutenant took her in a bear hug. He lifted her feet clear off the ground and hauled her out of sight. The barkeep raised a bloody finger after them. He said something in Spanish no one understood.

"That son of a bitch near killed me," Gil had the Springfield out. He measured a charge of powder into the barrel, dropped a wad and ball down after, rammed them flush.

Stroud turned to Lloyd. With a raised arm he signaled to the barkeep. "Lloyd," he said. "Shoot that man."

Lloyd mouthed half a word. His unfired rifle remained tight against his chest. He looked through the haze at the captain and at the barkeep slouched against the wall.

"Shoot him," Stroud said again.

Lloyd's eyes caught the barkeep's.

"Now," said Stroud.

Lloyd shook his head. "He ain't even got a weapon."

"Corporal Pucker, if Private Reed has not shot this Mexican ingrate by the count of three, shoot him in the head."

Gil raised the pistol. He waved it vaguely between the fallen barkeep and Lloyd. "Which one you want me to shoot?"

"Reed."

"Lloyd?"

"On three."

The Springfield moved slightly. When Lloyd turned his head he could see direct down the barrel. A might beyond that stared back Gil's empty face, eyes blank, neck smeared in blood.

"One...," Stroud counted.

"No," said Lloyd.

"Two..."

"No, please. I ain't never killed nobody in my life." As he spoke he leveled the Harpers. His finger curled over the trigger.

"Three--"

He pulled the trigger. His mouth formed the word *No* once more, but the tail end of that negation was drowned out by the blast. The barkeep jerked. A stream of blood spilled from the fresh hole in his shirtfront and he sat the same as before only quiet now.

At the table in back the old man observed all this in silence. He'd not moved, and there he sat in his cloud of smoke.

"Him too," said Stroud.

Lloyd shook his head. His lips moved, nothing came out.

"Reload."

"No," he managed to say, but the rifle was already lowered and the breech broken and he was loading his shot even as he continued to plead his single-worded supplication.

"One..."

Lloyd closed the breech.

Again Gil leveled his pistol.

"Two..."

Lloyd raised the rifle. He pressed tight his lips and caught the anciano's eyes at the end of the barrel and then the second blast sounded and the eyes disappeared along with the top portion of the old man's skull. Bits of brain and gore erupted. It speckled the three Americans, and all three cringed in tardy response. Stroud wiped the side of his face where he'd been splattered. He looked at his boots and frowned. When his head came up his face was calm. He gave a nod to Lloyd, another to Gil, then left the two soldiers with their weapons still raised, and crossed through the tables and ducked out the door.

Gil lowered his pistol. The barrel of Lloyd's rifle sagged.

The two stood in the mix of gunsmoke and cigarillo smoke and the smell of blood and dirt and vomit and spilled whiskey, both freckled in cranial matter and neither possessing a word for the other though they stood face to face long enough for protracted conversation. Mugs of stew steamed on the tables. The cauldron too, its contents still warm.

The anciano's skullless cadaver toppled suddenly from the bench. Both Lloyd and Gil jumped when it hit the floor. The brief commotion gave way again to silence, and Gil broke it with a laugh.

He grinned and ran a hand down his face and neck. When he found no reciprocating look in Lloyd's morbid face, he turned and ducked out the doorway.

The smell of death drove Lloyd out shortly after. That and the barkeep's lifeless glare.

In the street lay dead campesinos. Everywhere. Children knelt beside them. They stared at Burgess who had dumped the wagon driver from the seat and, with the help of Captain Stroud, was helping Viker into the back. Gil ran to lend a hand. Francis Price came out of a doorway stumbling drunk and called out to the captain. His words carried through the town.

"You want us to round up these children?" he shouted.

Stroud looked up. "No," he answered.

"We ain't gonna sell 'em?"

"Who do you think you'll sell them to?"

Price adjusted his crotch and considered. "What'll we do with 'em then?"

Stroud dropped Viker's feet. The heels clunked the wagon boards and Viker let out a cry. Stroud stepped away from him. He circled the wagon and stood glaring at the massacred bodies and the children bawling at their sides. He looked at Price, and Price looked away and nodded his drunken head.

Lloyd ran. In his hands he bore the rifle like some precious stick extended from his body. The ground gave way beneath him. Boots slapped grass, seedheads burst in miniature detonations. His breath tore at him and he wheezed his way uphill, up to the remuda where the sound of eighty mules and horses cropping grass hovered like swarming insects. Behind him the gunshots started up again. Solitary. Precisely measured.

From the pile of saddles he pulled his own. The rifle he bobbled in the other arm. His horse sidestepped when he approached, and when he threw the saddle over its hindquarters the horse jumped away and the saddle hit the ground. He laid the Harpers down and took up the saddle and stalked after the horse. The whole time he was crying. He didn't realize it. Not till the surgeon spoke behind him did he become aware, and he dropped the saddle and wiped a sleeve across his cheek.

"Where do you think you'll go?" said the surgeon.

Lloyd stood empty-handed. Hiccups cut through his sobbing.

"You know you won't get far. Osmond ain't that bad a tracker. And Stroud won't give up-- you know that. Won't matter how long it takes him."

Lloyd hiccuped. "I killed a man. Two men."

"So you did."

"I didn't want to."

"But you did."

"I ain't no killer."

The surgeon watched him.

"He made me do it."

The surgeon stepped closer.

"I didn't want to," said Lloyd.

"You said that already."

"He would have killed me."

"Maybe."

Lloyd fell. He landed with his knees over the saddle. His palms pressed the grass and his back arched and convulsed. "It don't make it right," his head swayed.

"No," said the surgeon.

"I don't want to be here."

Below them, the wagon carrying Viker had reached the hillslope. Burgess whipped the horse up the incline, his shouts volleying up the hill.

The surgeon shaded his eyes. He turned back to Lloyd and looked down at him. "You think anyone wants to be here?"

"Gil does."

"Yeah," the surgeon granted. "I expect you're right about that."

"I ain't supposed to be here."

"Well here is where you are."

"I ain't like you all."

"What do you mean by that?"

"I ain't like you."

The surgeon lifted a foot and placed it on Lloyd's shoulder and shoved. Lloyd flopped back. He opened his eyes and the surgeon was over him with his hands on his throat. Lloyd threw up his arms in defense and the surgeon slapped them away and backhanded him across the face. He struck Lloyd again, then pulled him erect. "You think you're nothing like us?" He shook Lloyd and Lloyd squirmed. "You're no different. Look at you. You saved your hide in exchange for others. That and a new pair of boots."

"No I didn't."

"You did."

"I never killed that trapper. That damn indian…"

Another blow of knuckles struck him.

"What are you?" the surgeon growled, his eyes inches from Lloyd's.

"What?"

"You're a thief."

"I.."

"You're a liar."

"Black Paw…"

"You're a whore monger. A lover of sin, a drunkard. You're a soldier like any of us, you follow orders like any of us. You've got one gift and what have you used it for? How many times now have you lead the captain to his prey? How many lives have you tracked down? You think that's no worse?"

Lloyd panted. His head swung around. He looked for escape but the surgeon's face was all he saw, red and angry and spitting from the mouth.

"So now you've done the killing," the surgeon shook him. "So what. It was waiting there all along. You're no different than any of us-- you're just like us, right down to your bloody bollocks. Now put that saddle away before Burgess sees you. And shut your mouth about that indian. It wasn't him that got you where you are now. You're right where you were always headed."

Eleven

In the eighteen days on the trail to Santa Fe there occurred four deaths and one burial.

The surgeon elected not to amputate Joel Viker's leg. At first. The bullet had struck high on the thigh and shattered the bone clear up into the hip socket. Everything swollen and leaking puss like a big purple sea creature. They'd never stop the bleeding once they'd sawed it off, argued the surgeon. Instead he splinted it and laid Viker in the back of a supply wagon surrounded by shovels and bags of meal.

In short time gangrene set in. Anyone who came close could smell it. They moved the foodstuffs to another wagon. On the sixth night Viker passed out from a combination of sickness and whiskey, and the surgeon sawed the leg off just below the hip.

Viker died an hour later. He was buried in a torrent of rain. The hole filled with water so quickly they threw him in before any could say a word in remembrance. He landed with a splash. The shovelfuls they cast over his corpse were not dirt but mud, wet and runny.

While the company gathered at the gravesite, one of the

women they'd captured from the village worked an arm free of her ropes and found a loose bayonet in a supply wagon. She returned to where the other two sat and sawed through their bindings. Then she set the tip of the bayonet above her sternum and ran it through her throat. The second chose to stab herself in the heart. When the third pulled the bayonet free from her friend's dead body, she sat a long time in the rain rocking back and forth and staring at the puddles collecting in the grass. As the men came up from the grave one of them saw her and shouted. She looked up, rain streaming down her face. If there were any tears mixed in they were washed away unseen. She ran herself through and fell dead beside the others.

The soldiers in Santa Fe spotted them several miles out from the watchtower. Not all the spruces in the world could hide so many animals panting uphill in the cold. Their breath rose no different than steam off a warm lake.

The rains had stopped two days prior, but the Americans still looked wet. Like they'd ridden through a river, mules and wagons and all. They wore the faces of men too long in discomfort. By the time they reached the gates, the Mexicans had found their interpreter and the major was standing out front to greet them along with a deputation of some forty men.

Stroud presented himself with a formality of titles. The only formal thing the men had witnessed since Milltown. He related the Frenchman's story and the Mexicans all nodded their heads as the interpreter passed it on.

"Is true, we find him," the interpreter spoke on behalf of the major. "He almost dead."

"And the missionaries?"

"Dead."

"How far to the village?"

"Two day, maybe three."

Stroud glanced at Burgess then back at the interpreter. "Comanches?"

"*Sí*, Comanche. Name is…" the interpreter searched for the translation. He found it, then reconsidered and set to searching again.

"Just tell me what he looks like and where I can find him."

"Is very easy. He very tall and he have one ear no good from fire."

"Where is he?"

The interpreter exchanged words with his superior. Stroud waited. The men behind him looked about.

"Maybe many place," the interpreter finally said. "Winter come. Soon Comanche leave mountain."

"They're still up there?"

"*Sí.*"

"In the mountains?"

"*Sí. Creo que sí.*"

"You have a scout to accompany us?" Stroud addressed the major directly.

The major replied that he did not. He continued speaking and while he talked the interpreter spoke over him.

"He say this American problem. American missionary no have *permiso* be here, they make many trouble. Make Comanche sick, now Comanche angry, want war. Mexico no want war with Comanche; they have many gun. Many death."

"How did they acquire guns?"

"They trade."

"With who?"

Neither the major nor his interpreter offered an answer.

"You say this is an American problem," Stroud bent over the horse's mane.

"Sí," the major himself answered. *"Es un problema Americano."*

"It's an American problem when they kill Americans," said Stroud. "Though it happened in Mexican territory. Fine. I'll accept that," he straightened. "But you've traded them guns. And now you have a Mexican problem."

"Cómo?"

"Two weeks east of here. A whole village gunned down. Women raped and murdered, children dead. Mexican citizens-- your people."

"Dead?" said the interpreter.

"Dead. Might have been Kiowa, maybe Comanche. It's hard to tell. But they were killed with guns, and they were Mexicans. So I'll ask you again; do you have a scout to lend us? Now that you understand this is a Mexican problem."

The interpreter conferred with the major. The soldiers at attention behind them leaned in, their ears bent forward. The major replied, and again the interpreter spoke over him.

"This problem *es del gobierno. México gobierno* and your *gobierno.*"

Stroud turned to ask what *gobierno* meant, but Viker lay dead in a slop hole a week down the trail. He stopped halfway around and turned back. The interpreter saw the doubt and pointed to the flag sagging from the flagstaff. *"Gobierno,"* he said.

Stroud scratched his jaw, though he was clean-shaven and there was no stubble to molest him. He looked at the flag. He looked back at the major. "The government is not who solves problems. Men solve problems. And if we're the men to solve them, it is our solutions that will shape this land."

The interpreter nodded. It was unclear how much he'd understood-- he attempted no translation.

Stroud looked down on the major and the interpreter and the uniformed deputation standing at attention and he smiled his perfect smile. "In time," he said, and he allowed his arm to envelope the breadth of the country around them, "this will be our *gobierno*. First we'll clean it of the indian, then we'll clean it of your kind." He straightened. He pulled the reins around and the horse turned beneath him at the pull of the bit. "You can keep your scouts," he said. "I have my own."

They rode out without a meal or any hospitality shown them and camped that night against the wind blowing sideways off the Rio Grande.

Two days later they were walking between the burned-out cabins that lay in wet blackened piles through which blades of grass had begun to grow. Six cabins total, another larger building, a church most likely. Marking the graves were nineteen Spanish crosses etched by Mexican soldiers in quick and passionless craftsmanship. Past these flimsy markers the company drove the remuda. The wagons creaked by and the site returned to silence.

Later, when they'd stopped to water the stock, Stroud called Lloyd up from the rear. "I want you out ahead looking for sign. You so much as smell Comanche I want to know it."

"Yes sir."

"You can take Osmond with you."

"I don't need him."

"Go on then."

Lloyd walked back to where his horse drank and pulled it up from the riverbed and hauled himself into the saddle and gave it a tap with his boots. He rode past the wagons and past the mules and into a forest of aspen and black cherry. He ducked his head often. Everything smelled of pine and spruce and wet fallen leaves. The smell of winter on the wind. At times he would turn to look back at the company climbing along the path he led, leaning away from the branches and everyone shivering and breathing steam into the air. He guided them all that day through thickets of thimbleberry and over hummocks infested with chickasaw, and the day following he led them through forests of pine whose needles measured three feet deep and made no sound as they trod their beasts across them. In all these days Lloyd saw nothing of note.

At night they would build up fires in barely contained conflagrations and choke on the smoke for huddling so closely against them. Not a man there was prepared for the cold. Lloyd in his tent gripped his blanket white-knuckled and pressed his back into the sleeping Virginians.

They woke to frosted ground. Thin white needles crunched beneath their feet. When the going became too hard for the wagons, they loaded the ammunition onto the pack mules and left everything else in a cove of gambler's oak. The wagon tongues pointed after them, unhitched and abandoned. Sitting there in the cove they appeared the small and battered carts of peasants.

In the shallows of an alpine lake they came upon a bloated deer. The wake of the company's tramplings sent water sloshing into its mouth and over the one eye staring dead and glassy into the sunless sky. Lloyd paused when he reached it. It smelled of rotten flesh. Flies swarmed along the length of the carcass and it was tinged in blood from nose to tail. He counted the points on the antlers sticking up from the water and he guessed at those submerged beneath. Then he rode on.

At midday he switched horses and ate a quarter ration of stale biscuit while in the saddle. His mouth was full and dry with flour and the only sound was the mastication of his jaw when suddenly the horse's ear twitched, and there up ahead he saw four women passing through the trees like apparitions in a frozen fog. He walked the horse closer and one of them raised her eyes to his. She was young. Younger than Lloyd. To her back was strapped an infant in a cradleboard. These eyes watched him too.

Behind him Stroud's horse came running. Lloyd turned. The captain held his rifle in one hand, reins in the other. His face was hot.

Lloyd held a palm up. "These ain't Comanche," he called out.

Stroud reached him in a trot and jerked the horse still. The women continued on by. Stroud scowled. "What are they then?" he said, staring at their backs, at the cradleboards and the heavy hide dresses embroidered in geometric patterns and their black hair shining long across their shoulders.

"Utes," said Lloyd. "Weminuche."

"How do you know they aren't Comanche?"

"Cause they're Utes."

Stroud snorted. The rest of the company came trotting up through the ponderosas, the mules braying at the sting of whips on their backsides. Clemons and McKenny took off after one of the women and Stroud shouted at them and they stopped and turned back.

"We'd be warmer with 'em in the tents," said McKenny.

"You want another mouth to feed?" said Stroud.

"I didn't say feed 'em."

Stroud looked at McKenny awhile. "Find yourself a Comanche squaw."

"What's wrong with these 'uns?"

"Nothing. And there was nothing wrong with the Mexicans. If you wanted a woman to keep you warm at night you should have tied the ropes better."

"With me one arm?" McKenny blurted. He raised up both arms and the sleeve of the amputated limb caved over. He slapped it with his hand. "It was Osmond tied 'em."

"I don't care who tied them. We're not here to chase women through the forest. It's Comanches we're after. The more Comanches you kill the more of their women you can have. You can do whatever you like with them. Until then you ride sharp with your rifle out."

"If we ain't starved dead by then," Clemons mumbled.

"Where are you taking us, Lloyd?" McKenny said beside him.

Eyes turned on Lloyd. All seventeen men on down the line, noses red with cold.

"How far, Lloyd?" said Stroud.

Lloyd rubbed his neck. "Not far."

"How far?"

"We're close. Either we see 'em or we cut their sign. Won't be long."

"Get moving then. Find them."

Lloyd turned his horse and prodded it through the ponderosas and the men fell in line behind him.

That night Stroud ordered one of the mules slaughtered. The

surgeon cut the liver into strips and set them in a pan over the fire. Only a slight cooking did he give them before passing the pan of half raw offal to the men. They set the mule's ribs over the fire and they cut slabs of meat from the backstrap and roasted them in cubes pierced through the whittled ends of birch switches. After they'd eaten, Stroud and Burgess took to their tents. Gil followed to shine their boots.

The rest sat about grumbling. Bellies full and still they carped and coughed in the woodsmoke. A few bottles of liquor had remained in the wagons and they'd taken them despite the captain's order of sobriety. Just one bottle, Price suggested. No objections stopped him. He pulled the cork and tilted it back and passed it on.

John McKenny sat shaking his head, waiting his turn. He looked at Lloyd. "How do you know the difference between a Ute and a Comanche anyway?"

"Everything about 'em," said Lloyd.

"Like what?"

"Their clothes, their hair. Their faces."

"I reckon the women are just as warm," said McKenny. When Lloyd didn't respond he added, "Stroud ain't gonna let us leave till we kill somebody."

The bottle came to Lloyd and he took it and drank.

"Captain don't know the difference," said Clemons. "Does he, John?"

"He don't know one from the other."

"Hey surgeon, how long will the food last?" said Price.

"Depends how many mules the captain'll butcher," said the surgeon.

"We keep killing mules and who'll carry the supplies?"

The question was not a question and no one answered it. They drank from the bottle.

"What happens if it snows while we're up here?" said Price. This was put to Lloyd, and the men's faces turned to him all lit by fire and bathed in smoke.

"Depends how bad it is," said Lloyd. "Sometimes it comes in slow."

"And other times?"

"Other times it comes in fast."

"How fast?"

Lloyd blinked at the smoke in his eyes. "You'll see the clouds get dark. They'll get to churning and rolling. You'll see one flake come down before the rest, then you won't see nothing but white. An hour later there'll be drifts blown eight feet high."

"What then?"

"Then we're stuck."

McKenny swore.

"How long?" said Price.

"A good while."

"A week?"

"Maybe. Maybe all winter."

"All winter?"

Lloyd cocked his head and shrugged.

"Hell, it could snow tonight," said Price.

McKenny swore again.

The liquor made another loop around the fire. Price took the last swallow. He wiped his mouth and corked the empty bottle and set it between his feet. "You better find those goddamned Comanches, Lloyd."

By daybreak the men's boots had frozen. They beat them against the ground and shoved their feet inside and went crunching across the grass to their horses.

In a mounted procession they descended one slope and climbed another, and for a while the sun came out. All tranquil and still. Somewhere a woodpecker hammered at a tree, the sound strangely peaceful. Clouds drifted in again, and as the men rode they lifted their chins and watched the passing skyshapes and sniffed the wind for snow.

It didn't come. Instead the clouds relented and the paltry warmth the day had given surrendered up to night. The soldiers woke half frozen in an astral winter starscape with awkward bluish fingers and knuckles slow to bend. They crawled from their tents and struck their knives to flint. When the fires took they bowed before them wrapped in blankets, and before the day had broken they were on their horses herding pack mules before them like war-torn shepherds lost and frozen on the windswept cordillera.

So numb they were with cold they rode head down, beards buried into necks. Cold everywhere. On their tongues they could taste it. It dried their eyes and chapped their mouths and set their lips to bleeding. Their thoughts were frozen, hypnotized within the rhythm of hoofbeats on frosted grass, and even Lloyd half forgot the purpose of his vanguarded position-- head lolling side to side over stacks of fallen needles frozen to a solid matt. He'd wrapped a piece of cloth about his head and he pressed a hand against one ear and then the other as he rode.

When the shot clapped out not a hundred yards away it seemed to drive right through them. They stopped as one entity, mules and horses and men, wrenched from mindless reverie and back to a forest shadowed in white fir canopies. In one motion they turned to the echo's last impression. Lloyd closest. His horse took a step and he stilled it. Two Comanches sifted between the trunks. Appearing and disappearing. Rifles hip level. Lloyd slid the Harpers from the scabbard. Soundless motion. He looked back and saw Stroud's mouth form a silent one-worded question. Lloyd nodded. He turned his head back around.

The wounded deer lay panting and bloodied on its side-- the sole focus of the two Comanche hunters. They paid no attention to the white-breasted nuthatch chirping on a spruce limb, or the squirrels digging amongst the fallen leaves. They failed to notice completely the company of American soldiers watching from up the slope, their mules and horses coated in a varnish of frozen sweat, their rifles and muskets sliding out from scabbards and taking aim beneath a row of filthy beards. An oversight produced by a mix of adrenaline and youth. They didn't see the captain raise his rifle to his shoulder, nor the seventeen men behind him do the same. They didn't hear the shots. Their bodies jerked and spun and tore in butchered flesh, and when the delay of gunblasts reached them they were already dead and falling to the forest floor.

As one body, the cavalry advanced. The deer lay gurgling blood from a hole in its neck, and its eye rolled over the soldiers and settled on Lloyd. Gil dropped from his horse and snuck the Springfield from his belt and fired a ball into the animal's skull and the eye disappeared in a gusher of blood and mucus. Gil stepped back. He raised his eyebrows to his fellow soldiers. He stepped to the two dead Comanches and leaned over them and straightened back up and he let a one-syllable laugh plummet out his throat. He looked at Lloyd.

"These is Comanches, Lloyd?"

Lloyd confirmed they were.

Gil set his boot against a temple and turned the head. He did the same with the other. "Both of 'em got their ears."

"Where they came from there'll be more," said Burgess.

The dead Comanches' tracks stood out against the frost as clear as if they'd been set there on purpose. Dark green on silver-white. Lloyd rode over them. Stroud trotted his horse ahead, the men pushed forward. They trampled down the slope over the deadmen's tracks across a flattened scrawl of underbrush and through rays of rising sunlight sifting between the cedar boughs, and when the land dropped away again and they came abreast of a second precipice they yanked the horses hard enough to rear them up in startled whinnies, for trekking through the valley below was a village entire, their tipis broken down and packed on horses, two-hundred souls in number, an army of well-fed men, muscled and rifle-armed and close enough Lloyd could see the expressions on their faces as they looked up the slope and saw the cavalry of Americans bare and dumbstruck upon the stretch of open ground.

A warble of cries went up more sickening than the bay of wolves at night. Stroud spun, he shouted something. Whatever it was vanished in a percussion of gunfire. Lead balls laced through the branches. They slammed into trunks with smacks and splintered wood that sprayed the soldiers and horses and sent them careening back up the slope. The men flattened themselves across the horses' backs and drove them with their heels, and were it not for the mules gathered round as cannon fodder they'd have fallen slaughtered no differently than the two dead youths over which they trampled their horses as they fled.

Lloyd slammed his rifle back into its scabbard and held the

reins in both hands. Pine boughs whipped above him. Lead balls cut through the needles. Beside him a mule stumbled and fell and he turned his cheek and saw it crushed beneath a flurry of manic hooves.

He pointed his horse nowhere; it ran caught in the stampede. He turned again on the saddle and saw behind him a line of mules sprawled dead and dying across the forest floor, their packs strewn and busted open in the grass. Beyond that Comanches, some on foot, others mounted. Small apparitions of fire burst from their barrels, all booming discordant from the whistles searing past.

His horse swung left, he lost balance, clutched the pommel. The cavalry in their panic maintained a loose grouping. He'd no idea who led them. They rounded a bend and those in front wavered, unsure which way to flee. Stroud shouted at them to stand ground and they regrouped, made assessments.

Half the mules were dead. Osmond Culkin was bleeding from the head, and even as they leveled their weapons at the pursuing horde, Burgess's horse collapsed beneath him dead. The soldiers fired a volley that thundered briefly and gave way to silence as quickly as it sounded. Lloyd felt the rifle buck against his shoulder. He didn't know he'd drawn it from the scabbard. Didn't know he'd fired it until it kicked. He cracked the breech and rammed in ball and powder and snapped it closed and fired again having barley taken sight. He reloaded, fingers fat with cold. His shoulder jerked again at the recoil. He wasn't breathing. Stroud was shouting. A gasp of air seared over his tongue. It stabbed his lungs and suddenly he was moving again and the horse was running and the mules wild-eyed with the stakes and poles and rations careening off their backs.

At a rock ledge in the mountainside they stopped and gathered. They pulled tight what mules were left and lined them up in a living wall between themselves and the advancing Comanches. Two of their company were gone. Vanished. Clemons had seen them shot dead and he relayed it matter-of-factly.

Lloyd dropped from his horse as did the others. He laid his rifle over a mule's back and waited. His heart battered against his ears. Like it was running at him. He looked around as if to figure where he was, where in all that wilderness of crag and slope. The rock ledge where they'd regrouped rose up taller than the treetops, sheer dirt and rock and bits of ivy clinging on where it could hold. Moss on all of it. Beside the wall the ground dropped off in a mass of broken trees where an avalanche had swept them clean a winter prior.

The surgeon beside him caught Lloyd gawking. "Keep your eye on the bead of your rifle," he said.

"We're gonna die up here," said Lloyd.

"Not in the daylight."

The first few Comanches visible through the trees took a round of rifle fire. Their bodies jerked and the horses reared beneath them. After that no one showed. Over one-hundred warriors armed with muskets and rifles disappeared into the forest. Nothing to betray them save the occasional war cry. High-pitched and far-reaching. It gave Lloyd a start each time he heard it.

While they stood there leaned against the mules, the captain rallied them. He walked the line at the soldiers' backs with words that held no purpose but to calm the shaking rifles. When he reached the surgeon he stopped. "You see Osmond?"

"I saw him," the surgeon answered.

"You have your kit with you?"

"It's gone with the mules."

"How bad is he?"

The surgeon looked back to where Osmond slouched against the rock ledge with blood spooling out of his skull. He shook his head.

Stroud called for Burgess. The Lieutenant came in a crouch.

"Put a rifle in Osmond's hands and get him on the line."

"Can he even see?"

"I don't care if he can see or not. He can pull a trigger. Now put him up there."

Burgess kept himself hunched as he ran to the wall. Stroud moved on.

Near dusk the Comanches broke from where they'd lain all day and rushed the hill. They made twenty yards before any shots were fired, and before the echos died they were gone again. Gone behind the trees and bushes. Hidden in the shadows of the day's close.

"They're coming," Price said aloud.

"They're still sixty yards out," said McKenny.

From the ground a Comanche rose. Not from sixty yards, but under twenty. He was running when they saw him, and they'd no time to fire a shot before he'd hopped the mules and came sailing over the backs with a hatchet swinging down as he landed. It caught Clemons in his arm and severed it to the bone. Clemons, rifle in his good arm, simply swung the end around and impaled the bayonet through the warrior's skull. It drove clear through the Comanche's head, and if his body wasn't dead when he hit the ground his soul was.

They turned all of them to stare at the body twitching under Clemons' hacked up shoulder, and as they did there came another Comanche over the mules' backs armed with a jawbone club. He brained Lieutenant Burgess and was back over the mules and into cover of undergrowth and still the Lieutenant stood there with the side of his head caved inward and the pulp of his skull smeared white and red throughout his hair. He took a full step and his mouth opened and he seemed to speak, but he said nothing and instead crumpled dead with the hat still adorning his bludgeoned head.

The men fired into the trees and into the grass and they reloaded and let loose another round. Phantoms shifted everywhere. Elusive in the eventide. From the soldiers' guns were hurtled balls of lead on trajectories bereft of targets. The captain shouted at them to hold their fire and another bout of silence followed while the sky converted from blue to crimson purple. Lloyd opened his eyes wider, but the forest blurred to gray.

Murmurings assailed them like froth on water. They'd die before the sun rose. They should run. No, they'd find no better place to make a stand. Quiet on the line you fools.

Stroud's voice rose behind them smooth and measured, and all ears grabbed upon it. The order quick and simple. They left the mules where they stood. Each man took his horse, no spare, and walked them out along the ledge and down the slope beyond. Lloyd looked back once. Osmond Culkin sat with his back propped against the ledge. He thought he saw the man raise a hand, whether in some plea of mercy or a strange goodbye he couldn't tell. He wasn't even sure he'd seen it; night was quickly falling.

The grade was steep. Men slipped in their hurry, falling and flailing and stumbling on. Lloyd strained his eyelids wider and followed the shadows with a hand held out before him. Shapes of men fore and aft. Dark and faceless splotches. Darkness everywhere. He recognized no one, no one addressed him, the men were whittled down to harried fleeing prey. He cursed Black Paw and looked again. The mountain twisted upside down in blackness.

Night had fallen.

He let go the reins. The horse kept on. A silent train of man and beast passed by. He stepped away. He stepped back further. He crouched and turned and fled between the trees, sliding and righting himself, the rifle lurching violently above him at each blind stumble. A branch caught him square across the nose and drew a wheeze from his throat. He spun and faltered. Warm goo ran over his lip and turned cool. He licked it. Viscous iron.

A hand out of the darkness grabbed him and he jerked and pulled back, but the figure stepped closer and he could smell Gil in the space against him.

"Where you going, Lloyd?"

"Huh?"

"You runnin' off?"

"No."

"You runnin' off like Linus?"

"I ain't. I can't see nothing."

Gil's breath rolled out in a silver mist. Smell of rotten gums.

"This way," Gil shoved him.

When the clouds came in some hours later they found themselves on a dead end slag of rock and bramble on which the horses would catch no footing, and the spill-- should they fall-- would deal them certain death. Their hooves sent rocks tumbling down an endless cliff. A cascade of sound that fell away in fading clatters, stone on stone. A hand before the soldiers' eyes they couldn't see. They pressed their backs against the ledge while the wind curled around the mountain, and in such positions they endured the night.

Lloyd thought he wouldn't sleep but he did. He dreamt of a mission and in it a man half-deer with antlers sprouted from his head and antlers for hands and his mouth the snout of a deer with its small square teeth bared angry-like and its eyes dead and glassy. He woke several times and each time he thought his toes had frozen. He would wiggle them and stomp his boots and when he slipped he would flatten himself breathless against the cliff face while pebbles skittered down the sightless slope below.

The dawning along the eastern horizon showed them to be staked out on a precipice bare of trees and the men flattened vulnerable against it. It also showed Clemons to be frozen solid. The mangled arm had bled all night and in the pale light of morning they could see his final posture; the frostbitten fingers of his good arm clutched to his shoulder and a look of pained reverence stretched along his frost-blackened face. They left him stuck against the rocks and filed down the way they'd come, back into the trees and expecting Comanche war cries on the turn of every heel.

Lloyd on his horse could hear the whispers of warriors plotting in the aspen. He heard their powder measured out of buffalo horns and tapped down rifle barrels. He heard the rattle of musketballs, metallic and oddly hollow. Clouds the color of wasted charcoal funneled through the passes and over the peaks, the tops of which sat white-capped in snow, and these he also heard, though he smelled nothing on the air but his horse's rancid breath. He let it scrabble after the others; he knew not who led them or where they supposed might lie some refuge. He simply clutched the rifle and twitched in the saddle and felt the itch of frozen urine rashing up his thigh.

The way out was down. The only way out. They kept at it,

descending in lopes, each stretch of hillside a boost of morale that fertilized their hopes until they came to the draw leading out of the range like a fabled path of exodus and found it crammed with Comanche villagers.

Francis Price saw them first. He rode in the lead and pulled up and called the captain from the rear. Some hundred yards below, the indians marched their horses and travois, and among them walked their children bundled in buffalo robes. Close enough to call out were there any reason.

The company hugged the edge of the trees and looked down upon their failed escape without a moment to wallow in despair, for at their backs the warriors had caught them. From a hundred separate rifle barrels came the whistling sail of musket balls. They cracked with the sound that hollowed branches make when filled with water and frozen till they pop.

Lloyd's horse turned and threw him. He scrambled up and made to remount it, but its legs buckled and slipped edgewise. Lloyd cradled the animal's neck and thought he'd heave it up by an act of will until he saw the stream of blood gurgling out from the hole between its ribs. He let the neck fall.

Upslope, running free-legged through the pines, the most brazen warriors came. Lloyd raised his rifle and took sight and felt a barren waste inside him.

The flint dropped, struck the frizzen. A spark flashed, and in that same buck and blast an indian lurched and flipped face-forward into the pine carpet. The man behind him hurdled the body, stride unbroken.

Lloyd spun around.

The soldiers were fleeing back into the treeline and crashing through the undergrowth and firing shots wildly at their backsides.

Lloyd ran on foot behind them. He heard a bullet whip past as he ran to catch them, saw a horse fall, a rider fall with it. No idea who. Men were dropping from their horses. The pitch of the hillside stove the animals' hooves, and the soldiers jumped to the ground and pulled their beasts behind them as shields from rifle fire.

Below them in the valley, the migrating throngs of women and children and old men and beasts had stopped their pilgrimage and even these peoples were armed with rifle and musket. They turned in the draw, a tribe of untroubled spectators to take witness of that certain and looming massacre awaiting the Americans.

In the grove of pines where Stroud finally dropped and laid his rifle over the saddle, the men stopped also and parroted his actions. Lloyd came running. Shots whistled past his head. He reached the grove where the sting of gunpowder bit his nostrils and obeyed the shouted commands-- a well-trained soldier, the breech opening, the breech closing, firing. The nine-shots-a-minute capability of the Harpers he outdid. He fired at bodies and when the bodies disappeared he fired in the bushes where bodies might be. He'd have fired more if Stroud hadn't grabbed his arm to quell him.

That piecemeal attack that no man led disappeared back into the forest as silent as though swept away by the divine hand of providence. Still there seemed a commotion in Lloyd's ears. His breath came apart from his body and his body moved with motions he'd not ordered.

"They're coming up our backside," he heard Price say.

"Hold your ground," Stroud ordered.

A hush followed. Death impending, cinching tight.

The Virginians cursed, the one to the other. The surgeon like a statued sentry with his musket steady at his shoulder. McKenny one-armed on his weapon.

Lloyd's own chest heaving caught his eye. He saw the bullet hole in his jacket and a pain hit him and he realized everything was the same as it had ever been. He was the next dead fool to wear it. He looked about the grove and saw those half-uniformed mercenaries, saw Gil reloading behind a horse's flank, and then he smelled it suddenly parched and dry and he looked up into the peaks where the charcoaled plumes rolled in seething angry surfs and even while he watched he saw the first flake wander down like one lost wanderer before the tide and he knew.

He knew.

Twelve

He bounded past the Virginians' whispered blasphemies and ran.

A command clapped out from the captain's throat.

He heard it rise and rattle and break apart behind him but he did not pause or turn his head. Instead he clutched the Harpers rifle one-handed at his waist and tore down the grade on nimble feet through a veil of blizzard that plucked the company's woeful stand from the eyes of the world, though not-- for a moment-- from its ears, for their shouts and exclamations and thunderous explosions of gunfire chased Lloyd down the mountainside as Captain Stroud and his men shot blindly into a falling albino curtain.

Those audible clues that might have hinted as to the outcome of that battle-- pops of gunfire, shouted orders-- were brief and quickly muffled. They sunk soundlessly into the blizzard with such swiftness it was as though nature had snuffed them out by a blanketed hand.

Lloyd didn't know. He only ran.

Flakes stung his cheeks and nose. They drifted down and fluttered up and turned sideways and melted in his eyes.

He ran.

He saw nothing through the white until it was upon him; a branch, a pine bough, a Comanche warrior swinging a ball club.

The Harpers jutted upwards. The bayonet leaned beyond the barrel, stretching forward to impale its point through the soft brown neck just above the adam's apple. It ripped the young indian's throat open by the shear force of Lloyd's forward momentum. He didn't stop. He pulled the spearpoint from the gore and ran on, downslope in near silence save for his own breath rasping before him, his feet tearing through leaves and twigs and briars, snow-covered branches thwacking his upheld arm.

Somewhere off to his right were Comanche villagers. Behind him warriors. He hit a spot of flat ground glistening in fresh fallen flakes, broke through the treeline and sprinted across a clearing free of anything at all, and fell suddenly, his lungs cut rife and raw and bleeding. He crawled several choking paces forward and leapt up at the sight of a gaping cavemouth dark and looming against the falling snow and, without a faltered step, he dove inside.

He stood upright. An odor touched him, not quite odorless but faint. A smell he'd never smelled before. Black dome before him, behind him a curtain of white.

Something moved.

War club. The man came swinging.

Lloyd yelled *No.* Yelled it even as his left hand slapped the barrel and aimed without so much a wobble. His finger pulled the trigger and the man's chest flared open and the Comanche thumped hard and certain and lifeless on the cave floor, the war club clattering in the chamberspace and the woman waddling to it, picking it up, the newborn glistening half expelled between her thighs. Again Lloyd shouted *No.* He worded it. He meant to shout but his lungs were bleeding. She came swinging into the bayonet, straight into the spearpoint, Lloyd braced statuesque at the opposite end with his arms straining to keep the weight of her at bay and his face contorted in the darkness. The war club dropped again, another clatter. Lloyd shoved the rifle. She slid off the bayonet and landed on her back beside her man. From her legs bent open like a grasshopper, the infant parted its tiny lips. It shook on the cave floor and uttered its first cry to the world as the cold bit into its lungs.

Lloyd stood in the afterbirth.

Warriors ran in the blizzard. Comanche voices.

Plaintive came the newborn's cry.

Hush now.

He heard them running, heard their language dipping and swelling and the newborn crying and he hushed it and it cried and he hushed it now his hand over the small anguished mouth it cried and he hushed it the footsteps running and the snow falling and building and the wind and Lloyd breathless and hushing and it cried on the snow blown on the cave floor now closer the voices closer he pressed the mouth and hushed the cries and they stopped and the voices faded and the snow in a white cascading blanket cascading and mounting and the baby stilled and silent in the echo of the chamber of the cave.

Thirteen

By layers the snowdrift built. Lloyd watched it from his hidden refuge, crouched in the last gray fading light as each flake built upon the last, climbing in a masoned wall devoid of color, one foot, two feet, a waist-level barricade of snow over which the imprecise illumination of the outer world shone still too brightly, its brightness an act of judgment over three dead bodies ringed in blood.

His focus turned from them to the mounting snow and back. He had nowhere else to look but the blackness of the cave depths.

He heard the baby howl and he reared back and knocked his head against the wall. He rose, dazed, crept forward. The shriek came again, but the baby's lips were dead and parted, the color no different from its cheeks. Soft and plump and cold.

Again the wind screamed. He spun to it. The rifle came up, he'd not known he held it. Another sound, this one too of undetermined provenance, and Lloyd answered in his own appalling howl and cowered back from the father's outstretched hand. A chill not of the winter tacked along his spine. His skin, dry and flaky, itched in every fold. He turned to the dying light outside and crunched toward it through snow blown onto the cave floor until it reached his thighs. Then he dropped to hands and knees and crawled to the cave lip where the drift had piled chest-high and continued building even as he stared out through the last remaining space between the snowdrift and the cave roof.

A long time he knelt there on all fours, staring through that closing space at the low-hung sky beyond. Listening. A thick sludge in his throat.

The sailing snow.

Flat sky.

Comanches, Stroud, and things unknown. All out there. All waiting.

Until it finally closed. The last hint of light glowing through the fluff. Disappearing. Gray to silver to sooty faded black.

For a while he remained on hands and knees. His vision gone. At some point he turned and crawled back to the cave wall and sat breathing and blinking and listening to a belly of blackness.

To measure the passage of time he counted. Up as high as he could go and then back down again, his fingers keeping solemn track. His eyes were useless. Everywhere was an oily black. He turned out his pockets and caressed their contents and by their feel he knew their names. Powder horn. Cartridge box. Flint he'd stolen from a supply wagon. An army knife-- the blade secured on a wooden handle. Pieces of leaf and dirt. Trash. A wet tangle of lichen. He tucked it in his belt to dry. He fondled the sewing kit that held no more than a single needle and half a spool of thread. One by one he returned the items to his pockets. Then he rested his head against the stone wall and slept.

When he woke he counted again his numbers and finally he stood from his huddle and heard the snow crunch underfoot, his hands held blindly out to meet the drift. He stumbled into it and sunk them in and pulled out a handful of ice cold wetness. He tore out another. He shoveled until the sting pierced his fingers, forcing him to tuck them a moment in his underarms before lunging back again, scraping, clawing, the rash of searing frozen skin advancing. He judged his progress by the length of tunnel he bored to the outer world. At three feet deep he crawled into its circumference, legs hanging in space. The snow he burrowed out he cast behind him. By this too he judged his progress, turning every so often with a wave of his arm to thwack the growing pile. By the obstinance of its size he knew the world was closer.

Back into his tunnel. Back out, back in.

His arms tired. He stopped, disoriented. Against the numbness of his skull he puzzled on directions. Which way was up. Or down. How the tunnel could measure his entire body length and still not liberate him to the outer world. He repositioned and continued digging.

When he broke through he broke into a gust of air that carved a line through his lungs and turned him gasping and choking from it. He swallowed and pulled a breath through his nose and squinted through the hole he'd made. It measured as large as an apple and opened onto starlight. Snow landed on his eyelids. It fell against his cheeks and melted there in droplets.

From his nostrils he sent a curling mass of vapor into the night. His shirt and trousers hung heavy and soaking on his frame, his arms and legs wet and frozen and cut with cold. He wiggled backward through the tunnel and dropped once more into the chamberspace.

It took a while to locate the rifle. In all his searching the dead Comanches watched him. They whispered to each other. The baby whimpered. A family in the darkness.

When he found the Harpers he patted down his person for something by which to wrap the barrel but his stiffened fingers turned out dirt-filled pockets nothing more. Through the tunnel streamed a woeful gloom, barely visible and sacredly precious against the blackout of the cave. He bent into it, rifle first. No more had he fit his torso in when far away a rumble stopped him. Far up the mountain. The sound of shaking. Vibration all about him. At its core a groaning rupture of the world collapsing, a hurtling angry army pounding, a thousand Comanches painted red with feet of lead and in their jawbone clubs the glow of newborn retribution brimming.

Whump, the tunnel flattened. It expelled Lloyd, spit him back onto the snow-laden cave floor, back into darkness, back to the company of the dead Comanche family lying side by side in their open sepulcher, and in that earthly tremor Lloyd covered his ears and felt hope take flight, leaving nothing but a bare forsaken space within him.

In the wake of the avalanche all was silent. A silence and a blackness and a palisade of rock and tree and bramble all tangled and packed solid in the entrance of the cave. It left Lloyd back against the wall with his arms drawn around his ribcage and his knees bent up with his nose between them. He aimed to trap his breath against his face but the blackness stole it every time.

He heard all manner of noises; rushes and drops and strange quartets of sound. Then they would stop and he would sit in the dark with his head aching against his knees and silence all around him.

He shivered.

When he came out of his huddle with an arm stretched out before him it was not of his own conscious decision but of some sickly thing within him that would not die and which he knew he had no means of stopping. It had him crawl like an eyeless worm over the frozen ground, his hands grasping out at emptiness, another shuffle forward, in his head the anticipation of what awaited.

But it was not as he expected. The indian remained still at his touch. He did not fight Lloyd's tug at his leggings. Not in any form of combat. He fought instead with a frozen recalcitrance, his legs unbending and uncooperative, and as Lloyd's deferential undressing came to nothing, he tugged harder, ripped and pulled harder, huffing in the darkness, standing and pulling and finally toppling backwards when the leggings did snap free. In a bound he was up again, working the buffalo robe off the man like a skinner works the hide from a carcass. Swift brutal strokes. Rips. The robe he let fall over the leggings, then hands out before him he reached for the woman. She wore nothing below the waist, but around her chest Lloyd remembered a tunic. He found her, grabbed her by the neck and pulled her up and stood her like a squat fencepost against which he proceeded to wrench the clothing from her chest in jerks and grunts, his own small frame over the woman like some blinded butcher hacking at the rigor mortis and making sounds he didn't hear nor would he recognize if he did.

Blackness. No recession of its completeness despite the march of time. It hung in every corner and expanded the confines of the chamber into infinite onyxed apertures into which Lloyd would stare for long stretches with his eyes wide open, clothed in translucent flesh and cursed to writhe in solace deaf and blind and sniffing about with his nose for an exit perpetually out of reach.

He would sleep and wake and watch the streaking bands of lightning play behind his lids. Touch a grimy finger to his eye to check if it was closed. With a hand to guide him down the wall, he'd tiptoe blindly to the rear and squat and shit and tiptoe back, the other hand his escort back.

On one of these trips he met the antlerman. The same as in his dreams; same glassy eyes, same hooves clattering over stone. He shouted, the apparition vanished.

With no clear borders he slipped from dream to hallucination. Slumber to wakefulness. Voices accosted him. Once he clamped his hands over his ears and felt movement in his jaw. He reached his fingers around and found his mouth in motion, his throat vibrating beneath it, all of it matching up in perfect timing with the loathsome babbling that seemed never to desist, a constant persecution that ambushed him from each dark hollow of the cave. He cupped both hands over his mouth and the torment halted. For a while.

It returned in forms beyond sight or smell or touch, more jarring than audible affliction. It came in waves of internal upheaval, a twisting of proprioception, time suspended, his sense of self-determination crushed and burned, the ashes scattered over the cave floor.

His will left him. He shivered. He let his limbs flail out and lay where they may. The antlerman gnawed at his head, but Lloyd made no attempt to save himself. He felt his chest rise and fall and waited for death to take him.

Fourteen

The halo of sunlight against the melting snowdrift began as a single pinprick and multiplied by twos and threes as its color grew from grayish blue to a promenade of orange. Lloyd first saw it as he lay on his back sucking a ball of snow. He stared hypnotized. When his mouthful melted he swallowed and asked the antlerman for clarity. He heard his question voiced in the darkness, and in the silence that followed he sat with his fingers pinched under his armpits while the halo widened. A ledge of slush shifted as he watched. It made a scraping sound and broke free, and a shaft of light shot into the cave and hit Lloyd in the face. He reeled backward and turned from it with an arm crooked over his eyes and his body jerking in quivers.

A tide of air strange only for its freshness whittled through the cavern. It carried scents of pine and alder and the smell of fallen leaves long trapped beneath the winter. To its source Lloyd turned. He rose and tottered, hands still braced before him. He stood a moment against the drift bewildered by its presence, then launched his body forward and tore his milk-white hands into the hole.

Sludge and ice and snow and brambled briars, sticks, leaves, twigs and rocks and all of it frozen and cutting into his hands and his hands bleeding and smarting and the blood red and shining on the snow in the blue light of day. He spun around and pulled the Harpers from the dark and returned to the snowdrift with the weapon turned backward and rammed the butt against the ice. It thudded and knocked loose a jumble of rocks. He drew it back and heaved again. It broke through and he lost it, heard it skid down the drift. He clawed after it, worming through the hole and squirming out the other side like a maggot hatching from an egg, and so did he return to the world, breathless and limp and hacking lungs of bloody spittle onto the melting mountainside.

A quarter mile down he sat on a rock with his face bathed in sunlight. His breath came gargled in phlegm. Below him stretched the swath of valley through which the Comanches had made their exodus. Snow melted in strips of white and green, and along the shadowed edges of the woods it sat in mournful piles.

He stood and gained another hundred yards and sat again. Face in the sun. He listened to the calls of snow quails and an argument of finches, and when he felt he could, he rose again and dragged the Harpers with him another hundred yards.

That night he crawled beneath a coralberry bush. A sheath of snow was held suspended in its briars and from this snowcave Lloyd observed the turning constellations. He watched the slivered shrapnel of a waxing gibbous moon float by, the same cycle on which he'd last surveyed it. He considered what this meant in terms of days. Then he wrapped his fingers around his arm and felt the bones move loose beneath the flesh, felt his anorexic shanks beneath the leggings, and finally traced the outline of his skull from which his face was hung. The feel of it thin and limp turned his stomach. He curled his arms beneath the robe and shut his eyes and slept.

The following day he found the cast off bones of mules, scattered by wolves on down the valley. Their teeth marks lay impressed upon the white cartilage, and below these the knife lines of Comanche butchers.

He set to gathering them up, and when he'd collected a number of larger femurs he laid them in a pile at the woodline. Then he drew his knife. At a black poplar long dead he scraped a load of inner bark and shoved it in his pocket. For the coarser kindling he snapped dry spruce twigs from a deadfall and carried this armload back to the mule bones where he dropped them and dropped himself, chest heaving and dizzy. He sat there a long while, then drank a mouthful of snow and pushed back into the trees.

By dusk there sat an unlit pyre of twigs and logs and branches hauled out from the woods and piled up in a manner that was not haphazard but looked it. Into this mound Lloyd set the poplar shavings. He pulled the dried lichen from his pocket and inspected it and tossed it over top. The spruce snappings he gathered into a bundle with the finer twig ends on the bottom. He held these in the palm of one hand and placed the flint between his thumb and forefinger and gripped the knife in the other. Then he bent into the pyre. It took two scrapes for the shavings to catch. They burst in a frantic aura of red, and Lloyd steadied the spruce an inch overtop and blew a stream of air across it. Twigs, then sticks, and finally logs. He built the fire out to body length and laid the bones within it, then fell before the flaming wood and smelled it as it burned.

After a while he sat up and pulled his boots off. A stink wafted up that made him gag and turn his head away. He sucked in air and held it and turned back. His feet were white and shriveled and there were blisters everywhere and the skin red and blotchy and falling off in chunks. The nails curled like soft wet paper over the toes. He ran a hand along a sole and took a gob of skin with it. He felt only a tingle. He flipped his boots over and rested his heels on them with his feet facing the fire and waited for the mule bones to cook.

For three full days he roasted them in batches. He cracked them open and sucked the marrow and left his perch only to drag more wood from the underbrush and haul up femurs from the valley floor. He spent hours drying his feet at the fire and watching the color creep back into them. When he set out down the valley chute he did so dragging behind him in one hand a collection of roasted mule bones tied in bindcraft, the Harpers rifle in the other.

The snow each day was less and then it was gone. Melted into the earth. The nights grew warmer, though not by much. In the peaks of the mountains gaping up on either side of the chute it stormed again, wind squalling on the rocks and the sky a massive whiteout. Lloyd turned his sunken eyes upon the furor and watched it churn. Far away it seemed.

For days he walked. He didn't think to count them. In time the valley turned and narrowed and spilled him at the shore of the Rio Grande. One last mule bone he carried with him. He set it in a patch of moss before a wind break and dropped the rifle beside it. He listened to the birds fluttering in the bushes and he laid his face in the moss and stared at small flowers that all throughout the winter had clung to life. He fought the urge to sleep. Instead he pulled his body up and towed a load of deadwood to the moss patch.

When he'd built the fire into a conflagration six feet wide and popping madly, he tossed in the mule femur and took his rifle to the river. He set it on a rock and took off his boots and socks. He slid out of the Comanche buffalo robe, out of the woman's tunic. He took off the army jacket with the bullet hole in its breast. He stepped out of the leggings, pulled down his trousers, peeled his shirt and undergarments from his body and laid them all out beside the water.

Naked and bearded he stood in the sun. The sun was warm, the air cool. He bent his head and examined himself. Where his skin was not covered in rash it was white. Diaphanous. It was thin and tight and through it poked his skeleton; elbows and shoulder blades, the long flat bones of his ribs circling out from his sternum. Two hip bones stuck up from his pelvis and the skin folded over these and around a patch of matted pubic hair and down over cords of emaciated thigh muscles to sit in wrinkled folds above his kneecaps. Over all this field of rashy limpid skin roamed lice. Nits in his hairline, crabs in his genitals. He lifted his arms to the sun and they resembled the clear-veined wings of albino bats.

He peeled his eyes from his sorry frame and waded in. Snow-melted river water slapped his calves and stole his breath away. Pain swam up his neck. He stepped in further and forced an inhale while the water climbed over his testicles. It snuck into his naval and numbed the vertebrae along his spine. Using his hands as blades he flayed the grime from off his skin in swaths of filth that shone like oil spilled in water, pooled and floating, reflecting in their greasy film the colors of the rainbow. He scoured with his nails his raw and stinging shell. Clawing, shivering. Wincing in a grimace while the river chortled by.

His garments he rinsed and wrung out and rinsed again. He tossed them back to the shore and noticed that through his knees swam schools of minnows. They would dart and pause and bolt again, and like a madman he splashed up to the bank and retrieved his shirt.

He caught a half a dozen-- two inch fatheads-- and threw them onto the bank where they flapped and glistened in the sun. When his fingers numbed to where he lost control he sloshed out and stood naked on the shore and used the edges of his hands to sluice the water from his skin. When he was dry he clapped them together and rubbed them nimble enough to pick the fish up and drop them in his shirt. The rest of the clothing he laid out on the rocks. He picked up the rifle and slung the buffalo robe across his shoulders and walked barefoot back to the fire with the shirtfull of minnows dripping along beside him.

The first thing he noticed was the mule bone missing. Sticks and embers lay smoldering in the moss where it had been rolled free. Imprints of feet beyond it. Lloyd's eyes picked them out to where they folded into the trees. He dropped the fish and swung the Harpers up. The barrel smacked into his free palm and he walked hunched over beside the tracks and into the treeline.

His feet made no sound on the floor. What he followed were bent blades of grass and intertwined branches through which the thief had snuck. Injured vegetation trampled in haste.

The tracks swung back to the river. As Lloyd came through the trees into the open stretch before the shore he caught the man climbing into a dugout canoe. Lloyd slammed the stock against his shoulder and shouted and the man whipped around with one leg already into the canoe and the stolen mule bone in his hand.

He wore a white gnarled beard and the outfit of a trapper, and beneath his coat he looked no better fed than Lloyd. He stared down the barrel and scowled at Lloyd's naked skeleton standing bare beneath the open indian robe.

"Throw that bone up here," said Lloyd.

The man eyed his escape route downriver and looked back at the gun. "I ain't et nothing in a long while," he said.

"Me neither. Throw it up here."

"If'n I don't eat, I'll die."

"You'll die if I shoot you."

The man's eyes narrowed. "You'd shoot me?"

"Yes."

"I'm just an old man."

"Throw that bone up."

"I ain't even got a weapon."

"Throw it up here."

"You'd kill an old man?"

Lloyd closed the distance a few paces. He kept the barrel on the man's chest. "I don't want to," he said, "but I will. I've done far worse."

The man held his position; one hand on the edge of the dugout, the other tight on the bone. His lips quivered some. "You would," he said. "Wouldn't you."

Lloyd said nothing in return.

With a lurch of his arm the old man chucked the bone out. It rolled in the dirt between them. They stood the two of them staring at it until finally the old man swung his leg into the dugout and took up his oar. He made to push off with the blade against the muck and Lloyd called out again.

"I got fish up by the fire."

The old man stilled the oar.

"I got a whole passel of 'em," Lloyd fetched up the bone. He held it same as the Harpers; waist high, balanced in his hand. "I'll split the marrow with you too. I do that and you give me a ride downriver."

The old trapper looked at the bone and he looked into Lloyd's eyes. Then he towed the dugout to the shore and pulled his wasted figure out.

Four days they shared each other's company with hardly a word between them. They listened instead to oar strokes. To geese honking and to the long sustained screeches of cicadas. They sat in reverence to the spit and pop of the campfires at night, to the crickets and bullfrogs and the owls hooting lonely in the treetops. Morning birds. Water on rocks. Coyotes howling at their clans. They roasted wild onions and trawled for fish, and on the third day floating downriver Lloyd saw a pig-like hoofed animal with its snout submerged in water. The Harpers cracked. The beast laid over.

They shored the dugout and pulled the carcass up the bank. Lloyd stared at it a while. He thought he'd shot a pig but it didn't quite look it, and he said as much.

"Peccary," said the trapper. "Some folks call it skunk pig." It was the first he'd spoken in three days.

They skinned and gutted and butchered it, and right there they built a fire and ate in silence. The rest they divvied up between them. The following day when they came within sight of the presidio of Santa Fe, Lloyd took his half and had the trapper drop him on the western shore. He hiked into the grass and turned to wave goodbye but the man was already bent at his oar with his back hunched over and his eyes downriver.

Westward he struck. Behind him sunk the river into old

horizons. He ate the butchered peccary and from wilted grass he made his bedding. At night the winds would cut beneath the indian robe to remind him that winter had not fully retreated. He turned south in hopes of finding warmer weather. The trees thinned out. They gave way to dry and browning grass, back to rocks and sand and parched and thirsty land. The days were warmer, the nights no less frigid than before. He kept on. South, west, under flocks of crows and raven pairs. What vegetation he found growing he would eat. Pigweed and dandelions, wild plums he found growing in a stretch of boulder clay. He shot a hare and missed a shot at several more. The powder in his horn shrank to nearly nothing. He counted out his balls of shot on a flat rock, lining them up and staring at them and wondering vaguely how he'd feed himself, or where he'd find his next drink as the land continued drying up. He wondered what he was doing-- doing in the most basic sense, and he found no answer.

The thought that he might die struck him. It came once, then came again at all hours day and night. A thought to which he believed himself indifferent, though every time it rose he found himself pushing harder, his eyes searching for clues in the landscape that might harbor water or wildlife or anything at all that might give purpose to his wandering.

The moon completed another phase. He walked under it; a plodding figure cloaked in the dead Comanche's buffalo robe and heeled in army-issue boots that left impressions of intact soles upon the land behind him. He wore no hat, no horse followed him, no single item did he possess that had not been given him or stolen.

In the sear of a midday sun he blundered upon a creek sloshing along the flat edge of a cuesta. He followed it all that day and drank until his belly hurt. In the night he dreamt of cattle lowing in green pastures and the braying of donkeys and chickens cackling and squawking with their tiny heads pecking and jerking, and in the morning when he woke he heard all these things still. He grabbed up his rifle and stumbled down the creekline into a field of harvested corn where livestock gnawed at the last dead hanging stalks. Beyond this a field of wheat. Further on a fallow hectare of tilled-up earth and further yet were horses corralled by sycamore beams, and all around this were the old broken remnants of a Spanish mission, the storerooms and stable and grain mill, a cemetery of faded tombstones, tanning vats and ovens, and against the creek a damn to redistribute water to the fields.

The mission itself bore a litany of arches at whose end stood great stone columns, bells in the towers hanging motionless from massive wooden vigas. All across its facade the plaster had sheared away in jagged swaths and crumbled into piles of rubble above which the exposed sections of quarried stone and red ladrillo brick flared like open wounds. The four mission walls formed four right angles and guarded within them an open courtyard. From the entryway men and women drifted in and out in lithe and graceful motions, brown-skinned and all but naked. Some paused at their chores to look him over, then continued on, keeping him all the while in the corners of their eyes.

There seemed to Lloyd in all that movement of indians and cows and chickens and donkeys an odd stillness. A quiet within the bustle. In his buffalo robe he felt suddenly hot. He slid from under it and dragged it along with his rifle up through the fields where the indians parted for him and murmured suppositions on this gaunt and washed-out whiteman trudging hollow-eyed into their midst. The same looks he received from the women weaving baskets in the courtyard. Against a fountain brimmed in lilies they reclined, long-haired children in their care, infants nursing at their breasts. Their hands stilled when Lloyd appeared beneath the keystone. He averted his eyes from their bodies and turned down the open archway lining the courtyard walls.

In each doorless entryway he poked his head. Down past the living quarters and guest quarters, the kitchen and the padre's office. He sniffed in the granary, heard the echoes of his boots in an empty classroom. He took only a peek inside the chapel before reaching the cathedral towering high above the outer walls.

The smell of stone inside. He stood in the center aisle between two rows of pews and stared open-mouthed at the tapestries and paintings hung upon the walls. The bust of a crucified man leaned against a corner. Everything silent and covered in dust.

For a long time he resisted the urge to look up. And then he did. The compulsion was unassailable; he would have raised his eyes even had he not possessed the knowledge of what might be tucked away up high. But even before he cocked his head he knew this was not the place. There was no thatched ceiling, no vigas or boards or reeds, but instead an awesome dome of fitted stones, covered in lime-based whitewash, painted cornices topping the walls, and all of it stunning in its vast pageantry of cavernous grandeur.

A noise from the choir brought Lloyd's head down. He stepped forward. Laid out on an altar table in the chancel was a man. He wore a vestment embroidered in gilded flowers flowing down to his knees, below which were soiled calf-high boots bound in rawhide lacing. He wore a stole around his neck. The man's beard scrunched against it, and from his wrist there dangled a tasseled maniple.

Lloyd eased another foot forward. The man looked dead.

Lloyd's fingers on the Harpers tightened. He swallowed and waited, saw the man's chest move. On the balls of his feet Lloyd backed himself down the aisle and out the cathedral doors.

He found himself a sun-drenched wall outside and put his back against it. He grew sleepy watching the fieldworkers labor. Soon he sank down cross-legged on the buffalo robe and laid the rifle across his knees. The indians forgot about him. They tended to the livestock and threw grain to chickens. They wheeled carts about and carried hand tools and bent their backs across their plows.

A voice beside him jarred him. He'd nearly fallen asleep. He looked up and saw the boots and the ornate robes and the man staring down at him from two furrowed brows.

"I said are you indian or are you army?" the man said again.

Lloyd looked at the face haloed against the sky. "I ain't neither one."

"That's a injun robe you got there. Cavalry boots. You got you a Comanche woman's tunic on, and I'm looking at a army jacket beneath it. So which are you?"

"I said I ain't neither."

"You're wearing the clothes."

"They's just clothes."

"Uh huh," the man shifted his weight from one foot to the other and lodged his fingers on his hips. "Where'd you come from?"

"From the mountains."

"They ain't got no food in the mountains?"

Lloyd only stared back.

"You look like a goddamn skeleton. I can see your skull settin' there in your face."

"I know it," said Lloyd.

"Well?"

"Well what?" said Lloyd.

"What do you want?"

"Food," Lloyd said.

"Yeah," the man nodded. "I expect you do." He ran his eyes over Lloyd and looked out over the fields where the indians toiled. "It won't come free. You understand?"

Lloyd nodded.

"There's shovels in the storerooms. Go find yourself one and get your ass into that field where those fellas is trenching water. You do that and you'll earn yourself a supper."

Lloyd stood. He turned in direction of the storeroom and the man called him back.

"You ain't doing no digging with that rifle in your hands."

Lloyd looked at it like he'd forgotten it was there. "Where'll I put it?"

"Set it right here."

"I don't want no one taking it."

"Ain't nobody gonna steal your damn rifle. Lay it up against the wall there."

Lloyd set the butt on the ground and eased the barrel against the stonework.

"And another thing. Listen here. One who runs things here is me. You hear that?"

"I hear you."

"Me."

"Alright."

"Don't get you no ideas."

"All I want is a meal."

"You get ideas and you'll end up same as the preacher."

Lloyd didn't ask how the preacher ended up. He marched off to the storerooms and found a shovel and took it out to the field where the men were trenching and he bent his back the same as them. From the mission walls the man watched him. The indians made space. After a few words exchanged between them in a tongue Lloyd had never heard before, they sunk their shovels in the dirt and returned to digging like he wasn't even there.

He dug the line and paused to rest and dug again. The turn of the shovel an old familiar thing. Its weight familiar. His hands were soft from lack of use and blistered quickly. He wiped sweat from his eyes. When he grew thirsty he walked to the stream and drank from a cupped hand, and when his back cramped he straightened and rolled his shoulders, then bent again to his task. He lost track of the day. When the men climbed out from the trench he looked out at the mission and saw woodsmoke rising from the kitchen chimney.

The women had made a soup of tubers and they served it to him in a clay bowl in the courtyard. While he ate, the man attired in the padre's vestment walked among them wetting his thumb from a chalice and placing it against the indians' foreheads. They'd lower their bowls and close their eyes and mutter something taught to them in Spanish. When he reached Lloyd he set the chalice down and sat on the fountain a few feet away.

"You moving on?" he said.

"I got nowhere to go," Lloyd answered.

The man watched him eat.

Lloyd chewed. He swallowed. He sucked a drop of broth from his lip and pulled the bowl away. "It alright if I stay?"

"It don't matter to me what you do. Long as you work."

"I'll work."

"Don't be putting no ideas into these people's heads."

"I don't speak none of their language."

"Still," said the man.

Lloyd slurped the last of the broth and placed the bowl in his lap. "I'm Lloyd."

"Alright."

"What'll I call you?"

The man stroked the stole down to the tassels and stared hard at Lloyd. "You ain't army?"

"I was for a little while. I ain't no more."

"Uh huh," he let the stole go and held the edge of the fountain. His fingers sunk into the water, his knuckles knocked against the lilies. "You can just call me padre."

"You ain't no padre," said Lloyd.

"And your story don't add up."

"I ain't give you no story."

"Still," said the padre. "It don't add up."

They sat in the truth of these accusations, neither offering to share more about themselves nor pry into the other. In this accord the man calling himself padre retired to his chambers and Lloyd to an empty bed in the old soldiers' quarters. He slept beneath the buffalo robe and woke the following morning with the hope of a breakfast loose in his mind. There was none. The native men and women he found at their chores, the kitchen empty. He took up his shovel and joined the same men trenching the same trench, and worked all that day till supper.

It took a full week to trench out to the new field on the far side of the grounds. Lloyd's hands calloused over but he dug anyway, and in the evenings he'd eat whatever was served without asking anyone for more, no matter the growls in his belly. It ached and gassed and gave him pains, and after a while it settled. He put on weight. Each day for nine days he rode out on a wagon with the same men he'd trenched with, an hour's ride to a stand of velvet mesquite and thirty-foot tall ironwoods where he'd take turns splitting wood and turning up logs on their ends, and at the day's completion they'd load the firewood onto the wagon and steer the donkeys homeward.

Occasionally he'd see the padre taking long walks in the fields, inspecting the work. Some days he would share a meal with Lloyd, their conversation marked by sparseness. He led no service in the church, no hymns or baptisms or anything aside from carrying the chalice around at night and marking each forehead present with his thumb. Always in his robes. It seemed to satisfy the native population. Or perhaps they simply endured him, Lloyd couldn't tell. They seemed to endure Lloyd well enough. Enough to feed him.

One day in early spring the indians hitched the wagons and drove them to a washed-out playa where they were loaded down with salt until the axles whined and the donkeys trembled against the weight. Nearly every able-bodied soul took part. The following day when they struck out again, Lloyd stayed behind. He walked the empty mission, stepped inside each doorway. He knocked at the padre's quarters and poked his head inside. He let his eyes cross the ceilings of each room, one side to the other, blinking at the reed-covered beams with no expression on his face.

He found the padre napping in the chancel where he'd first seen him. Robes immaculate. Dirt on his boots. Lloyd's own boots made soft patters down the aisle way. He stopped at the altar table where the padre slept and stood listening to the echoes of silence swirling off the domes, and he looked back the way he'd come, began to turn around, when the padre spoke.

"What do you want?"

Lloyd pivoted back around. "I thought you was sleeping."

"I was. What do you want?"

"Why do you sleep in here?"

"Where do you want me to sleep?"

"You got a bed in your quarters."

"I do."

Lloyd turned his thumbs up slightly. He cocked his head, lifted his shoulders.

"I sleep there at night," the padre rolled to an elbow. The table below him didn't move or creak. "I like the sound the cathedral makes in the daytime. It relaxes me."

"It don't make no sound," said Lloyd.

"No," said the padre. "It doesn't." He swung his legs over and sat up. He straightened the stole. "You're supposed to be getting salt."

"What's it for?"

"Tanning."

"Ain't no hides around."

"There will be. They'll trade for 'em."

Lloyd nodded.

"Now what do you want?"

"I just came to talk."

"About what?"

Lloyd swallowed and looked around. He looked at the tapestries hanging and he studied the floor a moment, then faced the padre. "What happened to the priest? The padre."

"What happened?"

"I mean there must have been one. All these indians living here and working and all, there must've been somebody running it."

"Uh huh."

"You kill him?" said Lloyd.

The padre pushed down on the table with his hands and stretched his back out. His chest flared beneath the vestment. "That what you come to talk about?"

"No. I don't know."

"Well?"

Lloyd tucked a thumb in his waistband and wiped his nose. "How long you been here?"

"A year. A bit longer."

"You come looking for gold?"

The padre shifted some and finally settled into a comfortable perch with his hands clasped over the table edge, much like he sat at the fountain while the indians ate their evening suppers. He took a long draw through his nose. "I come here for the quiet," he said. "I don't know about no gold."

"You ain't heard that story? About the slave hiding it in a mission?"

"No. Sounds like a story."

"It ain't."

"How's it go?"

Lloyd told it. The padre kept his mouth shut, breathing through his nose with a slight frown over his brow. When Lloyd finished, the frown remained. "I never heard that one," he said.

"That's why you see all them mission floors dug up."

The padre's eyes shifted up and back. "Yeah. I seen that."

"Thing is, it ain't buried. It's hid in the ceiling."

"How do you know that?"

"Cause I met the man who put it there."

The padre stretched his fingers and repositioned them. "Is that why you're here?"

"No."

"You been hunting up in the ceilings?"

"No. This ain't the mission."

"No?"

"The one with the gold in it ain't got no people."

"So what are you doing here?"

Lloyd's mouth opened but nothing came out. His eyes glazed over.

The padre waited. When Lloyd still had formed no answer he said, "You come here hoping to find the padre? Ask him about it?"

"No," Lloyd said.

"Seems you got something on your mind. Something gnawing at you."

"Well is he alive or dead?"

"He's dead."

"I reckoned as much."

"Then why are you asking about him?"

"I'm just asking."

"You think I killed him?"

"I don't know. I was just wondering."

"I didn't. I never heard no such story as what you just told. He died the day I got here. Saw me come through the cathedral and just fell over dead like he was waiting for someone to relieve him. He had a good thing going, so I took his robes. Now I'm the padre. Folks here seem to like it. They keep me fed. It suits me." He stuck a fingernail between his teeth and picked something out and studied Lloyd. "Seems you'd like to talk to him."

"You said he's dead."

"That's right. He's dead and I ain't no preacherman." He picked out another piece of crud from his teeth and scowled at it, then flicked it on the stones. "That's what you're here for? You want to talk to a preacher? You got that look on you."

Lloyd thought about this. "I'd talk to him if he were alive."

"Why did you think I killed him?"

"I don't know," said Lloyd.

"It wasn't about the gold. You'd have seen the floors all dug up, the ceilings busted open. They ain't. Still you thought I might've killed him."

"I thought maybe."

"Why?"

The palm that wasn't tucked against Lloyd's waistband he turned over to the cathedral. A gesture that raised the padre's eyebrows.

"You thought maybe I killed some old man so I could steal his robes and take his place. Eat his food, sleep in his bed," the padre waited for Lloyd to answer but there came no answer. "That's a hell of a thing to think."

"That ain't all of it."

"What is it, then?"

"I don't know."

"Yes you do."

"I just thought..." Lloyd's voice scratched like it had gone a long time unused.

"Go on."

"Seems like that's all there is in this world."

"What."

"Killing."

"Killing?"

"That's all. It's just people killing people, and it don't matter who does the killing or who does the dying."

"You think that?"

"Yes."

"That it doesn't matter?"

"I don't know. Seems like it don't matter to the world much. People die. They get shot with a bullet or an arrow or a hatchet kills 'em. They get run through with bayonets. Kids get sold off as slaves and their mothers is killed and their fathers and everyone else, and those that's doing the killing just go to sleep and wake up the next day same as before."

The padre finished cleaning his teeth. He ran his tongue over them. "You ever kill anyone?"

"I have," Lloyd's words reflected off the dome and came back, and he heard them as though they'd been spoken again from some other version of himself in some distant place. "Have you?"

"No. I've never found anyone deserving of it."

"I have."

"Then maybe it's not so bad you killed them."

"Them ain't the ones I killed."

The padre's fingers found the stole and caressed it down to the tassels while he considered this. "Who'd you kill?"

"Others."

"Why?"

"So's I could stay alive."

"Was that not worth it?"

"Not to the ones that's dead."

"No," said the padre. "I suppose not. You're alive though."

"I am."

"Are you the same as before?"

"Before what?"

"You said about those that kill-- when they go to sleep they wake up the same as before. Are you the same as you were before?"

"Yeah. I'm the same. There's only one thing different."

"What?"

"Somebody told me one time, he said, 'Within each man there lies a monster.' I didn't pay no mind when he said it. Thought he was just talking. Trying to sound smart. But it's true-- it's there. I seen it. So yeah, I wake up and I'm the same as before, same as I ever was, only now I know what that is. I know what I am, what's inside me. That's all that's different."

The padre passed his tongue over his teeth again. His beard moved with the motion. "That's got to weigh heavy on a man."

Lloyd's vision wandered. "Yeah," his voice hardly a whisper.

"Will you kill again?" asked the padre.

"I ain't hunting nobody."

"But if you have to."

"I can't say I won't."

"You'll kill to stay alive."

"It's what I done."

"Even those that don't deserve it?"

Lloyd shook his head. "I guess that's another thing that's different. I know who deserves it. I guess I knowed that all along."

That evening Lloyd followed the trench he'd dug out to where the creekwater pooled against the damn and took his boots off. He held them a while, looking neither at them nor at anything else, his socks wrinkled in the mud and the mud squishing cool and sandy up through his toes. In one hand he pinched the boots together by their pull straps. As he swung his arm back his torso turned, and he saw some ways up from the creekbed one of the indians who'd trenched beside him standing on that very ground. When Lloyd's arm came through with the swing his fingers kept tight on the boots. They rocked out over the creek and for a moment were suspended in the air, his fingers pinching the leather, then came back to sway by his side until they stilled.

The indian watched him. Lloyd shifted his feet in the mud. He held the boots out and the man came forward. Slowly. He was old. Lloyd had seen him work a shovel, swing an ax, till soil. He did everything the younger men did, only slower, as if possessing some well of patience that had no bottom.

When the man reached him, Lloyd raised the boots. "You want these?" he said.

The indian's cheeks drew down in deep-cut lines. Liver spots dotted the ridges under his eyes, and when he spoke they moved slightly.

"I don't know what you're saying," said Lloyd. He gave the boots a shake. "You want them? Here."

The man made a bowing motion that continued on downward until his hands reached his sandals; two flat brown pads of woven tule fiber. He slid them of first one then the other and extended this meagre offering with open palms.

"I wasn't meaning to make a trade," said Lloyd. "I'll just give them to you."

The old man closed his eyes and made another statement. The spots along his cheekbones moved again. He opened his eyes.

"Alright," said Lloyd.

When the hide traders arrived in early spring, Lloyd was in the corn fields planting seed in a swath of fresh-tilled earth. He could see they were plains indians. Not only because the hides were all buffalo, but by their clothing. Pawnee or Cheyenne. They gave him only a passing glance and when their trading reached its end they rode out with bags of salt and baskets and woven sandals and ammunition cast from Spanish molds, and still other things, all of it strapped to their backs and loaded onto horses and driven back out into the wild northern emptiness.

The work that followed spanned the course of months. The hides were scraped of clinging membranes and staked by their corners to dry in the sun. Flies lit upon them by the thousands. They buzzed in swarms of angry clouds that kept Lloyd up all through the night as he lay swaddled in his bunk, the tule sandals lined neatly underneath. He fought through them days later when they ripped the stakes up and submerged the hides in vats of saltwater, and again as he pounded the stakes back into the sopping stretched-out pelts. Only when they'd rinsed them and soaked them four days in lime and scraped the hair with chiseled stone did the flies renounce their siege. To replace them came the stench of oakbark water rising from the tanning vats. It crept across the mission grounds into the courtyard and the indian barracks and the soldiers' quarters where Lloyd choked on it as it settled into the dry bones of his nostrils.

It let up not a fraction in all those months, and Lloyd's nose would not accustom to it. Even with his face buried in a sheep's neck, all around him the commotion of women gathering up the wool that fell in matts from rusted shears and hauling it out of the courtyard where the men held down the bleating animals, the sun cooking them all together in a swollen summer heat. Even then the smell would not disperse. He closed his eyes against it, and in that state, kneeling in the courtyard with a sheep embraced against him, he took no notice when the shears fell silent and the women dispersed into the shadows. Not until he heard his name.

Fifteen

He opened his eyes.

The first thing he noticed was not Gil Pucker, who had spoken, but the boots beside him shining bright in their stirrups and, above these, the flat white beautiful teeth of Captain Thaddeus Stroud.

"Is that Lloyd?" Gil said again.

Lloyd let the sheep go. It landed ungainly, waddled to its feet and skittered off.

Soldiers rode through the archway. Francis Price, John McKenny. The Virginians side by side. The surgeon. A dozen new recruits. Some reached up to touch the keystone, dazes on their faces. They stared at the fountain and leveled their rifles in confusion at the half naked indians pressed against the walls, and they regarded Lloyd sitting there in a pile of shearings, wearing tule fibre sandals and covered in dust and sweat and wool, and some of those whom Lloyd didn't recognize began to laugh.

"He don't got his boots," said Gil.

"Sergeant Pucker," called Stroud. "Price. Take Private Reed out and bind his hands and feet with rope. Put him in a supply wagon. And stay by him. He'll be coming back to Fort Tackett with us."

They dragged him from the courtyard, a man on either side, out to fields of head-high corn where forty mules and even more horses nibbled at the shoots. Mules no different than the ones shot dead and torn apart by wolves in the Weminuche. Same strong femurs thick with marrow. Just as these had been replaced, so had the wagons.

They bound his feet and hands and sat him up with his back against the sideboards. The two soldiers stepped back when it was done and looked around. Price averted his eyes. Everywhere but on Lloyd.

"What's he want us to do with the children?" he said after a while. "He want us to round them up?"

"He ain't said nothing about it," said Gil.

"They'd fetch a good price."

"He can't sell no kids in Santa Fe, he done burnt his bridges there. And I don't expect he wants to take 'em clear down south."

"Lot of money running around."

"Still," said Gil. "He's itching to get to his woman."

Price snorted. "Surgeon's gonna lose his bet once they're married."

"Ain't nobody even taken that bet."

Price paced through the corn. He kicked it. He shielded his eyes from the sun and craned his neck out to the mission. His eyes ran down the length of arches and over the bell tower and up the great round mass of the cathedral dome. "Biggest one I seen yet," he muttered. "We'll be here a week digging."

Gil squinted. He opened his mouth as he did so, baring the ground-down stumps of his teeth to the world.

Price turned to him. "I'll lay you a bet right now, Gil."

"What."

"A mug of chicha says Stroud's got our men digging. Indians just sitting around watching."

Gil kept his squint up. He brought his hand down and fingered the chevrons on his chest, then laid his palm on the handle of the Springfield.

"It's what he done on the Clearwater," said Price. "Remember? I had to tell him to put the damn kids to work. I bet it ain't no different now." Price paced some more. He kept his back to Lloyd. "We'll be here a week in this stink."

"Hey what's that smell, Lloyd?" asked Gil.

"I'm gonna tell him," said Price.

"Go tell him then."

"I will," said Price, and left without looking back.

Gil stepped to the wagon. He looked at Lloyd's feet. He shook his head. "What's that smell?" He waited for Lloyd to respond. "We figured you was dead," he said. "You must've reckoned we was dead too."

Lloyd stared out at the remuda.

"Ain't you curious how we made it out?"

"No," said Lloyd.

"That snow come just in time," Gil looked again at Lloyd's feet. He fingered the chevrons. "I'm a sergeant now. You hear that? Sergeant Pucker."

"I heard it."

"You make rank, you make pay. You didn't believe me, did you? I told you and you didn't believe me. It's true though."

"Sergeant don't make no pay," Lloyd said after a while.

"Lieutenant does. That's next. I make lieutenant and after that I'll be a captain just like Stroud."

Lloyd sat watching the mules rip corn up by the mouthful.

"You know he's gonna shoot you," said Gil. "You know that?"

They could hear the animals masticating, the stalks breaking apart in their jaws.

"He got himself a new tracker. West Point man. He's good too; I've seen him at it." Gil came closer. He rested a hand on the sideboard. "I can't save you this time, Lloyd."

"I ain't asking you to."

"You want me to though."

"I don't want nothing from you."

"They're gonna shoot you, Lloyd."

"I know it."

"Ain't no way out," Gil's eyes ran from the tunic to the leggings and down to the sandals. "What's that smell, anyhow?"

Lloyd didn't answer.

"Lloyd?"

"Let me be."

Gil took his hand off the sideboard. He gave the sandals a final inspection and walked off to a rock where he sat with his chin cupped in his hand.

It took two days to dig up the courtyard. Two more for the floors of each room. Even with a shovel in every indian's hand. In the cathedral the soldiers walked the aisle and tapped the stones and finally gave up and hitched the teams to the wagons.

The cloud of dust they raised on leaving hung over the decimated corn field in a thick brown fog that churned and hovered like some prophesied plague of desert lore. From the wagonbed

Lloyd peered through it. He thought he might see the padre or the old indian with the spotted cheeks, but he saw nothing. Still he looked. In time, when the dust settled, there was nothing left to see, and Lloyd reclined over the boards and felt them lurch and rattle beneath him as the company marched eastward into the sprawling sun-baked desert.

Their routine differed in not one aspect save for the new faces clamped to the bottles in the flicker of the nighttime fires. The same empty wagers, boasts of women conquered. Their conversation drifted in the still of the desert twilight. Once Lloyd heard a soldier ask the others what the deserter's fate would be; imprisonment or hanging, or would he be reissued boots and a jacket and another rifle and shoved upon another horse to ride again under Captain Stroud's command. Wasn't he supposed to be a tracker? When the answer came it was spoken quietly enough to be snuffed out in the crackle of the fire. The men disbanded for the comfort of their tents and in the morning woke sore-eyed and sullen to sweat the day beneath their piecemeal uniforms while the animals swayed their bleary eyes across the desert floor for grass that never grew.

Lloyd's mind veered often to Linus Tate. He wondered what thoughts the old soldier had nursed as he'd ridden the same as Lloyd, tied in the back of a supply wagon with the soldiers cavorting around the fires and attempting by elaborate measures not to look at him or speak to him or pass so close that he might call their names. Only Gil addressed him. A daily bowl of gruel. A sentry to stand guard as he emptied his bladder or shat precariously while balanced on his heels with his hands tied behind him and the Springfield stupidly pointed in his face.

One evening while the soldiers lugged buckets of barrel-drawn water to the remuda, Stroud approached the wagon. He greeted

Lloyd with a practiced cordiality. No one around to hear them. "Once we reach Fort Tackett," he said, "you'll be executed by firing squad. You understand this?"

"I know it," said Lloyd.

"It is the sentence."

"Yeah."

"Desertion is a wretched thing."

"I've heard you say it before."

"It's true. A wretched thing."

The sounds of animals jostling reached them. From where they spoke, Lloyd and the captain could see them quarreling, the mules shouldering in between the larger horses and pushing back the soldiers, the soldiers backtracking with the buckets raised and sloshing.

"You see that man there?" Stroud pointed to a blond-bearded man between two packmules. "Sergeant Eggars. West Point graduate," he nodded as he said it. "A good soldier. A good tracker too. That's what West Point will do for a man; give him an education, a skill. He's as good as the Paiute was, maybe better."

The sergeant looked up at them as though he'd heard them, but he was far away and the horses were kicking and snapping all around him.

"Even so," said Stroud, "training is one thing. A gift is another. You have a gift, Lloyd. Do you understand that? A gift."

Lloyd shifted against the sideboards.

"It's a shame to lose that. A shame for the country. These savages leave almost no trace upon the world, and even a man like Eggars, trained as he is, can come up short. A gift like yours," Stroud leaned over the wagon, "it's strong enough to keep at bay a sentence of desertion. It can bring new life, Lloyd. A new uniform, your rifle back," he glanced at Lloyd's feet and back up his curious attire. "New boots."

Lloyd stopped shifting. He met the captain's eyes.

"That or a firing squad, Lloyd,"

"I ain't gonna track down no one else for you. That's done."

Stroud's smile flattened. He traced his thumb along the wagon boards. The soldiers were trudging up through the tent stakes swinging empty buckets at their knees. Stroud held Lloyd's stare a moment then turned and filtered into the mix of soldiers. Lloyd, his wrists bleeding from the ropes, laid his head over a bag of munition balls and closed his eyes against the world.

They were still over a week from Milltown when Sergeant Eggars riding out front saw a lone indian stand from a fresh-killed antelope and shield his eyes to the sun. It was clear to the sergeant that the savage could see the company's dust billowing miles in the distance and had taken fright. He had abandoned his kill and whipped his horse in a dead run east. Left the meat just sitting there. When the soldiers reached the site they crowded around the carcass and laughed. Captain Stroud's reputation, they agreed. The barbarians are running scared. They feasted on antelope steaks and berated the fool who'd left it.

Only Lloyd took interest in the indian's tracks. Gil parked the wagon by the kill site, and when Lloyd leaned over the edge to read what story they might tell, he had to blink his eyes and weigh the notion that this might be some anguished dream from which he'd wake to find himself in the peace of the mission where he'd go on shearing sheep in the company of peaceful men. Yet there they lay by the wagon wheels. Unmistakable. He said the name Black Paw out loud but no one heard him. When Gil set a scrap of meat in the wagon bed, Lloyd tore at it like a dog, his face in the plate and his hands tied at the small of his back. He made no mention of the tracks, and no one thought to ask him.

Eight days later they entered Milltown by the quarry road. The new recruits dawdled on the ledge to gawk at the gaping hole of earth and the monolithic stones within it. Stroud barked an order that Gil was quick to mimic, and harried the company on down the road and into the abandoned sprawl of huts below.

No delegation met them in those deserted streets aside from a pair of crows haranguing them clear to the stream. The men unhitched the teams and led them down to water. They refilled the barrels, sent the livestock out to graze, all the while waiting for the captain to make himself presentable. He lathered up a bowl of soap and shaved himself with a two inch piece of mirror. He combed his hair, removed his jacket, swatted the dust from it. He had Gil work a rag over his boots until the toes sparkled like black pearls hued in ocean water. Before he made his march to Molly's door he drew the handkerchief from his breast pocket and unfolded the corners and touched a finger to the ring that lay inside as if to verify its reality, then folded each corner back into a square and with two fingers eased it back into his pocket. Then he walked up through the huts and turned onto the lane.

When the captain reached the sawmill the men quickly drew cards from a deck one of the new recruits carried, and it fell to a runted boy with the face of an imbecile to stay behind with Lloyd. The cards having set their fates, the soldiers set course for the saloon.

From the wagonbed Lloyd watched Stroud walk the path to

Molly's cabin. He saw him pause at the door, knock, wait. Knock again. He saw him step back and adjust his collar. He looked up. After a minute he reached out and knocked again. Down the road the men were stepping out of the batwings with mugs of chicha in hand. The tailings of their laughter reached Lloyd. He swung his focus back to where the captain was stomping through the grass on an angle for the barn where the goats were kept. He ducked his head inside and came out and walked a full circle around the barn and stopped again to bang on Molly's door. He hit it hard enough that Lloyd could hear the thumping.

By the time the captain had walked all the way back down the street past the mill and the land office and to the bar, some of the men had already imbibed two mugs of chicha and were on their third. He pushed through the batwings. The men lazing in the street became serious and followed him inside.

Lloyd looked at the imbecile guarding him. The boy sat on a rock with a finger twisted deep inside his ear. His lip hung open some. Lloyd looked away from him and directed his eyes into town.

When the batwings opened they spit out a ball of men, Stroud and Gil in front. They pushed Old Crazy before them, the man making strange gestures and pointing and clutching his scalped head in his hands. They marched up the lane and turned in between the adobe huts and pulled up in a mob outside the Sampson brother's place. They didn't knock. They ripped aside the hide that hung in place of a door and pulled them into the street.

The Sampson's knelt as told, boys scarcely men, homespun shirts and patched elbows. Their arms came up in obedience to another order, and from a distance they looked like beggarly zealots genuflecting at the captain's boots .

The imbecile tasked with guarding Lloyd took notice. He rose from his rock and waddled dumbfounded several feet forward and turned back to Lloyd with his mouth drooling as if Lloyd might elucidate him on the inquisition taking place in the streets of Milltown.

"What's going on?" said the imbecile.

Lloyd hushed him. The fool swung his hanging jaw back around. As they watched, Stroud swung his fist into the side of a Sampson boy's head. The boy went sprawling. The other cried out for him. He hushed when Gil snatched the Springfield from his waistband and set the end of the barrel against his forehead. Old Crazy clutched his skull. He ran several steps back and forth like a gopher caught between two fires.

Lloyd waited for the sound of gunfire. To see the boy fall limp beside his brother. Instead he saw Bruder running down the lane with his hands waving above him. Several soldiers swung their guns on him and Bruder skidded to a stop on his knees beside the Sampsons, another penitent groveling before the captain. He motioned to Molly's cabin and flung his arms this way and that, and suddenly in one motion the three men came to their feet and like a swarm of bees the entire assembly herded themselves up the lane, past Molly's cabin, and out to the quarry road where all four men of Milltown made wild imploring gestures, this time at the ground and out to the northern horizon.

The soldiers returned in a straight line, nearly running, cutting through the adobe huts to where Lloyd and the imbecile and all the mules and horses and wagons waited by the stream. What orders were given were followed through without discussion. Teams were hitched to wagons, packmules loaded up. Saddles slapped the backs of horses. Some of the men still held empty mugs of chicha. They threw them to the ground and trampled them to pieces as they rode up from the streambed, past Molly's cabin, past Old Crazy and Bruder and the two Sampson boys who stood in the wake of their dust and watched the army thunder out of view of Milltown.

Where the quarry road dissolved back into sand, Stroud called the company to a halt. Sergeant Eggars walked his horse into the swath of desert. Stroud and two others accompanied him. They sat their saddles while the West Point tracker criss-crossed the ground in great swinging arches, his head bending at times alongside the horse's as he cut for sign.

Gil held the team reins in his hands and watched them from a distance. From the driving bench he shouted orders to the men to check their weapons, to fill their powder horns and cartridge bags. After a while he climbed down and stepped back to the wagon and folded his arms over the sideboards. He smiled. He waited for Lloyd to ask, but Lloyd didn't ask, and finally Gil told him what had happened. "She been stole," he said.

"Molly?"

"Supposed to be in a wagon going north. That's what them townsfolk is saying."

"Who took her?"

"Injun."

"Where?"

"Went north is all they said. Just took her. Eggars is looking for tracks; it wasn't a week ago he stole her."

Lloyd could see the West Point tracker plodding over the ground with his eyes straight down.

"Something else," said Gil. "It ain't just any indian. It's that one you been going on about." He waited for Lloyd's reaction. His lips curled in the beginnings of a smile, and soon the teeth appeared. "Looks like you'll get some satisfaction 'fore you die."

A mile up the road Sergeant Eggars found where the wagon had turned off. Sand had blown over the tracks but they still showed through in spots. Stroud led the company over them, and when they'd passed there were only the tracks of soldiers left and the droppings of the animals steaming in brown shapeless piles.

The trail led them into dull empty country bare of waterholes and devoid of any sign of man or beast save for the indian's wagon tracks and the hooves between them. Country no man present had ever trod. They marched until the last bit of daylight faded out, then made camp in a dry wash. After they'd eaten, Stroud retired to his tent. The men stayed up around the fires to speculate, and Lloyd had no choice but to hear their postulations.

In the morning they broke camp and rode all day without pause. Twice Lloyd had to shout for Gil to stop the wagon in order to relieve himself. At night the company dined on stale biscuits and salt pork, and such was their routine for five days straight until they came upon the wagon. It sat empty in a gravel bed with the reach split down the center and the whole underpinning caved in upon itself. What goods it had carried had been unloaded. The canvas cover had been detached from the braces, leaving them pointing skyward like naked iron lances to cut the passing wind.

Price crawled beneath it. He came up shaking his head. "There's no repairing that," he said.

Stroud called Sergeant Eggars from the front of the patrol. "How far out are they?"

"Less than when we started," said the sergeant. "We've done some catching up."

"Can you pick up their sign?"

"I already did. Only one horse, but he's using it to carry the supplies. They're on foot, both of them."

Stroud examined his men. "Be smart with your weapons. Anyone so much as attempts a foolish shot and I'll line you up along with Reed when we reach Fort Tackett."

It was all the direction he gave.

Before raising the tents that night Sergeant Eggars apprised Stroud of their progress. Two days he estimated. Two and a half. The captain only snorted and vanished into the solace of his tent.

At the fire McKenny brought out a bottle of whiskey snuck from a supply wagon. He clasped it between his knees and twisted out the cork. After he'd taken a swallow he wiped his sleeve across his mouth and put a question to the men. "I don't see no point in following," he said. "What's he gonna want with her after the savage has had his fill?"

The soldiers considered this.

Lloyd, his head on the munitions bag, considered it.

"You think he's treating her like a lady?" McKenny kept on. "Treating her like a dog, more like. Probably worse. You say he's making her carry supplies?"

"It shows in her tracks," said Eggars. "He's got her carrying a heavy load. You can see it in the way her toes dig in more than they should. She's carrying it out front."

"What's the savage carrying?"

"Not as much as her, far as I can tell."

"See that?" McKenny pointed the bottle at them. "And what do you figure he's doing with her right now?"

"Lower your voice, John," Price warned. "You don't want the captain hearing."

"You think he don't know?"

"He knows."

"Then why follow? For all we know he's leading us into a band of savages waiting to cut us down like they did in the Weminuche. Or one night he'll sneak into camp and knife us in our sleep. This ain't no army work-- this is Stroud's campaign. It ain't ours."

"He's in love," said Price. "Probably convinced himself the savage ain't touched her."

"Revenge is what it is."

"Either way, John, you got no say in it. None of us do. He'll keep on till we find them."

"All for one goddamned indian?"

For a while it seemed there was no more to it. Until Gil spoke. "That indian knows where there's gold buried."

McKenny pointed with the bottle. He meant to say something but he was drunk, and his tongue labored fruitlessly until Francis Price cut him off.

"What do you know, Gil?"

"I know what Old Crazy told me."

"Say it then."

Gil preened while the men edged closer around him. "He said that indian we're following knows where there's gold buried."

"He said that?"

"He did."

"What does he know?" said Price. "He's just a crazy old man with no teeth. Drunk all the time."

"It's true," said Gil. "Surgeon was there, he heard it."

"That true, Surgeon?"

"Aye. He said it."

"Don't make it true," blurted McKenny.

"No," said the surgeon. "It doesn't."

"What did he say?" asked Price.

"What Gil just said-- the indian knows where it's buried."

"You mean which mission?"

The surgeon shook his head. "He didn't say anything about a mission. This is some other story. Says it was a slave that buried it."

Lloyd's head came off the munitions bag. He wormed along the wagonbed until his head hung off the end. Ears pricked, he filled his lungs in soundless breaths.

McKenny slashed the air with the bottle. "It's goddamn fairy tales like this that's got us running all over the country with a wagonload of shovels."

"You sure this isn't the mission story?" said Price.

"He didn't say anything about a mission," said the surgeon. "Or soldiers-- Spanish or American. It was all about a slave burying it. It's a different story altogether."

"Remember that little mission with the desert willows growing out front?" said Price. "Couple years back we dug it up."

"I remember it."

"It's only a few days from here. We're heading straight for it."

"We dug it up already."

"Maybe we missed it."

McKenny slashed the air again with the bottle. He stood and flapped his armless sleeve at them and shouted, "You're a bunch of goddamn dreamers. If he'd known all along where gold was buried, why would he wait all these years to go get it? And why bring a damn woman with him?" The question brought a chorus of mumbled agreement from the men. Drunkenness did not belie his point. He aimed the bottle at every last one, drunken and swaying in the firelight, and answered his own question. "I'll tell you why," he said. "He uses her as packmule by day and pincushion by night, and if any of you's thinking there's gold to be found, you're more a fool than the captain himself."

The sun rose that morning with beams like forged iron on their skin. It cooked the saddlery, metal bits of harnesses burned at the touch. Before noon the heat forced them twice to stop and water the animals. They poured it from the barrels; they knew not where in all that waste might run a stream or pool or any trickle with which they might wash the staleness from their mouths.

Black Paw knew. His tracks dipped into a crumbling bajada where for a while Sergeant Eggars stroked his beard and scrambled over boulders and razored stone outcroppings until he found where the indian had crawled under a shelf in the lowest fold and scooped sand away into a pile. Beside it the hole had refilled. Enough for two humans and a horse. Not much left over. The woman had stayed up above, her tracks showed she'd sat beside the horse a while, and in this same area the soldiers took rest.

Lloyd turned his face from the sun. He ran a tongue over his lips-- they'd begun to crack. When Gil finished watering the team, Lloyd asked to be let down.

"I got to piss," he said.

Gil reached over the sideboards and pulled the rope at Lloyd's ankles. It was too hot to say anything, and the routine was well-rehearsed. He drew the Springfield, held it vaguely at his prisoner's back, and with the other hand he worked the ropes binding Lloyd's wrists. When they dropped, Lloyd crawled off the wagon in awkward stiff-limbed stumbles. After several paces Gil called out for him to stop.

"Let me walk a bit," said Lloyd.

"Stroud don't want you walking around."

291

"Just a bit."

"You're supposed to be pissing."

"Let me walk up and see them tracks."

"What for?"

"Just let me."

Gil searched out the captain and saw him convening with Eggars on the bajada. He flicked the pistol. "Get on then."

The impressions Black Paw's feet left in the ground were the same Lloyd had seen before. Same moccasins. Same weight, same stride, same balance. The horse tracks he recognized also. He saw where Molly had sat. She'd made use of the horse's shadow while Black Paw went for water. His return tracks showed he'd made two trips, one to give the woman a drink, another for the horse. They'd left the spot fully hydrated.

Lloyd walked another ten yards out. He picked up Molly's prints and stopped and squatted beside them. Small, even for a woman. He traced a finger around the track entire and held his fingertip as a crude measuring stick against the ridge her toes had left. "Gil," he said to the dirt. "When's the last time you all was in Milltown?"

"We was just there."

"Before that."

Gil frowned. His bottom lip twitched while he sifted through old memories. "When we was there with Linus," he said.

"With Linus?"

"Yeah."

"Stroud ain't seen Molly since?"

"No."

"He didn't go after the Weminuche?"

"No. We went straight to Fort Tackett."

Lloyd sat a long time with his finger in the impression. He counted the months. His eyes glazed over.

"Hey," Gil said behind him. "You seen the tracks. Now you got to piss or don't you?"

"No," said Lloyd, and slogged past Gil to the wagon.

Sleep evaded him that night. Long after the soldiers found their tents he lay staring into the cosmos, and when the fires shrunk to waning embers and died in smothered unsung glory, still his eyes were fixed upon the starried vault of heaven. He said nothing in the morning when Gil untied his ropes and led him out to clear his bladder. He sat upright in the wagon with his eyes on Eggars' backside all that morning, and when conversation passed nearby he strained his ears to hear it. When the company pulled up in a flat dry stretch of desert pavement, Lloyd wiggled to the front of the wagon and stretched his neck out.

Sergeant Eggars dismounted at the vanguard. On his fourth loop over the same ground Stroud rode out to meet him. The sergeant signaled downward with his hand and brought it up in a sweeping line westward. Stroud set his knuckles in his hips. He flung an arm out. Eggars turned his palms up and pointed at the ground again, and the two walked with their heads down for a quartermile, the soldiers finally dismounting and joining in.

Gil stood on the driving bench. He uncapped a canteen and took a swallow.

"What are they doing up there?" Lloyd asked.

Gil shrugged

"Go find out."

Gil finished the water. He made a show of indifference. He brushed the chevrons on his chest, then set the empty canteen under the bench and climbed down and sauntered out to the head of the convoy. When he came back he uncapped the canteen again and scowled at it when no water came forth.

"What'd you see?" said Lloyd.

"Caravan of Mexicans came through here," said Gil. "Got their tracks everywhere." He walked around to a barrel and twisted the spout. "That indian of yours ain't no dummy. He stepped in with 'em. Can't see nothing."

"Eggars lose it?"

"For a while. He picked it up again though. They's just walking in them tracks the Mexes left." Gil climbed aboard the bench and took up the reins. The company started moving again, and before Gil lashed the reins over the mules he swiveled around and smiled at Lloyd. "I told you that West Point man was good."

Over that troop of man and beast not a cloud nor intimation of one passed. Pure blue sky, the swelter hanging from it in a fog through which they trampled. Lloyd hung his head over the sideboard and studied the confusion of sign below. A muddle of cavalry hooves composed the trail. It held no sense within it.

One more stop they made before pitching camp. The barrels were well past half-drawn. Gil filled a bucket and held it to his chest, first one mule then the other. When he was done Lloyd was quick to ask for his release.

"You done shat already," said Gil. "And I know you ain't got no piss left in you."

"Take me up to look at them tracks."

"You already looked."

"Let me look again."

"What for?"

"So I can see 'em."

"I can't do that."

"You're sergeant."

"So?"

"You do what you want."

"That ain't something I want to do."

"Ain't you curious as to what's going on?"

"Ain't nothing going on."

Lloyd worked himself to his knees and crawled over the bags and boxes closer to the driving bench. "Captain's taking a shining to Sergeant Eggars," he said. "Spends all his time with him. Got you back here playing teamster."

"That's my job," said Gil. "Burgess did the same."

"Burgess was lieutenant. And that's where Eggars is heading. Gonna beat you to it. You make rank you make pay." Lloyd could see the boy working this over; his eyes pulling together, his lips twisted. "Lieutenant Eggars," Lloyd said aloud.

Gil twisted his head away from the name. "What do you want to see them tracks for?"

"Just to see them. You can leave my hands tied."

Gil turned his back to Lloyd. In doing so his eyes landed on Captain Stroud walking side by side with Eggars, and after a minute watching the two in private congregation he turned back around. "Alright," he said. "But your hands is gonna stay tied."

Lloyd walked up past the shovel wagon, past the spare horses, hands bound behind him, the Springfield trained on his back. The Virginians drew to a halt when they saw him pass. McKenny and Price lifted their heads from their huddle of gossip. Half the company took notice. The runted imbecile among them gave voice to his confusion, and mid-sentence the surgeon cut him short.

By the time Lloyd reached the Mexican's caravan trail, Sergeant Eggars had seen what was happening and had set his bucket by his horse's feet and taken off after. He arrived as Lloyd was finishing up his second pass over the ground. Before the sergeant could fully formulate his objections, Lloyd asked him straightaway what tracks he was following.

Eggars pursed his lips. He stood a full head taller than Lloyd. He shot a look at Gil, then cast his eyes down Lloyd's frontside to the tule sandals. When he'd finished this appraisal he met Lloyd's eyes with a noticeable swell of confidence. He smiled and invited Lloyd to follow. "Look here," he said. "I'll show you."

The sergeant chose his footsteps carefully to not disturb the sign. He swiveled his head to and fro and stroked his blond beard and pointed suddenly like a gundog honed on its quarry. "There's the man," he gave a flicking motion to a heel mark, then curled his finger back and swayed his hand until he stopped suddenly and shot the finger out again. "And there's the woman. Clear as Sunday morning," he straightened up and smiled at Lloyd.

"Gil," said Lloyd. He had hardly glanced at Eggars' performance. "Bring Stroud over."

Eggars said nothing in Gil's absence. He walked off a few paces and took a sideways glance at the sign he himself had pointed out, then waited with his chest pumped out and his arms crossed over his buttons.

Half the company followed Stroud. They sauntered in behind him feigning useless excuses that even had the captain noticed he would not have bothered to rebuke, for his attention was fixed wholly on Lloyd, his face a confluence of suspicion tinged in curiosity. He stopped at the edge of the caravan trail and ordered Lloyd to explain himself.

"You're following the wrong tracks," was all he said.

Sergeant Eggars made a sort of harrumph and shook his head.

"Unless you're hunting Mexican peasants," said Lloyd. "But you ain't."

"Sergeant?" said Stroud.

"He's wrong. These are their tracks right here," Eggars pointed near his feet. "Both the indian's and the woman's."

Stroud turned back to Lloyd. The soldiers fanned out along the jumble of footprints and began their whispering.

"Untie my hands and I'll show you."

Stroud nodded to Gil. "Untie him."

When the ropes came off, Lloyd asked Francis Price to pass his rifle over. "I ain't gonna shoot nobody," he said. "Just pass it over."

Price waited for the captain's approval.

"Unload it," said Stroud.

Price went about unloading his rifle, then extended it out over the jumble of tracks.

Lloyd took it by the stock. "Look here," he said. "Eggars is saying these tracks is Black Paw's." He squatted with the rifle held lengthwise and set the tip of the barrel alongside the heel print. "From his left heel to his right we got a stride so long," he addressed the assembly, marking the length of stride with his thumb along the barrel. "Gil, take a few steps over there in that sand for me."

Sergeant Eggars hugged his arms over his chest but anyone there could see the doubt creep into his face. He snorted while Gil carried out the request. When Lloyd walked over to Gil's fresh tracks and laid the rifle barrel out beside them, Eggars uncrossed his arms and began to stroke his beard like a fire had taken to it.

"Here's Gil's stride," Lloyd ran his thumb down the barrel and stopped at the following heel print. "A good four inches longer, and Gil ain't none too tall. That means the man that left those tracks yonder is about yay high," he stood up and held his hand out flat at shoulder height.

"A man's stride can vary," said Eggars.

"Not by that much. Ain't none of you seen Black Paw? He's as tall as you are, Captain."

In the arguing that followed, it emerged that not a single man had ever before laid eyes on the indian. Opinions were drawn down lines of seniority. The new recruits sided with Eggars, the rest placed their bets on Lloyd, for bets were surely made. Only the captain wavered. His doubt unveiled itself at Eggars' mention of the woman.

"There's no difference in stride there," bragged the sergeant. "Same size foot and she walks right beside the man. So tell me how we're on the wrong trail now."

And so Lloyd replied with what had gone unspoken. He said it matter-of-factly, his voice flat, and on those words the full weight of their assignment was thrust upon them.

"Them tracks ain't Molly's," he said. "The woman who left those ain't pregnant."

Back up the same ground they'd previously covered Lloyd led them. A horse was lent him. Arms free, feet easy in the stirrups. Eggars followed mutely behind, and when Lloyd veered off the Mexican path the sergeant offered no comment. The tracks were there, hard to see but clear enough when pointed out. All down the line of soldiers there droned the fervor of speculation. Their theories carried all manner of foolishness, and for each one they would eye the surgeon for his response but his face revealed no inkling to the thoughts composed behind it.

At night they staked their tents and bound up Lloyd and set him in the wagon. Stroud stood watch to check the ropes. He nodded in approval and sent the men away. When they reached the fires he leaned over the sideboards and the two faced each other, though in the moonless night it was more each other's presence they sensed than anything else.

"All men come around to what is reasonable in the end," said Stroud. "Despite what they say."

Somewhere far off a buzzard screeched.

"Why you got to tie me if I'm helping you?" Lloyd said finally.

"Freedom is not earned in one day alone."

"I'm tracking him down. Ain't I?"

"After you swore you wouldn't," the captain shifted his weight. The sideboard creaked. "But you know what you're made of, Lloyd. You've made the right decision. And so have I. When you've tracked them down and the indian and the woman and the child are dead, you'll have earned your freedom. Until then you'll sleep as you are."

The sideboard creaked again. Lloyd felt the wagon move as Stroud relieved his weight. The only sounds that followed were the captain's receding footsteps.

Lloyd closed his eyes but soon reopened them. He sat up and watched the campfires play against the night. Before the soldiers kicked them out, McKenny hiked up to the wagon. Lloyd knew him by his voice.

"Lloyd," he whispered.

"I'm here."

"How far away is that indian?"

"Not far."

"He knows we're after him. Don't he."

"He knows."

"Is he close enough to sneak back and knife us in our sleep?"

Lloyd considered. The smell of whiskey glided over the wagon. "He's close."

"Goddamnit," McKenny spat. "Goddamnit."

Lloyd heard him turn away and he called him back. "John. That mission you was talking about the other night. The one ya'll dug up. How far off is it?"

"You think he's headed there?"

"No. He probably don't know about it. I just thought if he sees it he might take shelter there."

The smell of whiskey augmented. McKenny's figuring set him to breathing hard. "A day's ride. I don't rightly know." He took a drink. Lloyd heard the liquid slosh in the bottle. Heard McKenny's lips smack. "You hear him creeping in at night you call out. You hear me, Lloyd? You call out."

"Alright."

"I say we're walking into a trap. Goddamn indian'll slit our throats while we sleep."

The morning after, not a few hours into their march, Lloyd found where Molly had given birth in the shade of a desert willow. The tree was in bloom and its flowers lay garnished on the scene; the petals stamped into the ground where she'd lain, fallen onto the bloodstained sand after she'd departed. Everything dressed in pink.

A small mound of earth revealed where Black Paw had buried the afterbirth. The company stopped in a half-circle around it like funeral mourners, and with a barked command Stroud harried them on.

Before the day was truly out Lloyd suggested they make camp.

"It's early yet," said Stroud. "There's plenty of daylight."

"Hard to track over this ground," said Lloyd. "If we wander off trail we might lose them for good. All it would take is a strong wind to wipe out their sign. Best to stop now and start early."

"I disagree," Eggars had ridden into the discussion and he shoved his horse between the captain and Lloyd. "We're not but two hours behind. The tracks are clear. If we ride hard we can catch them before sundown."

"You want to trust his judgment again, Captain?"

"We're almost close enough to hear the infant cry!" Eggars raised his voice. "Two hours. Perhaps less."

"Half a day is what I reckon," said Lloyd. "You push now and you risk losing them."

Stroud looked from one tracker to the other. His face tight. The smile nowhere. "Make camp," he said. "We'll leave at first light."

Again Lloyd's arms and legs were bound. Moonless night. Fires stoked on broken willow boughs. He watched the stars appear and multiply. He saw Gil shuffle from the cookfire silhouetted bug-like against the flames to deliver Lloyd his bowl of gruel, and when he set it steaming on the wagonboards Lloyd lured him closer with a whisper.

Gil set his hands over the boards. Eyes wide against the dark, he leaned in.

"I know where he's going," said Lloyd.

"Where?" said Gil.

"You do to."

The boy pushed on the boards. "The mission?" he whispered.

"That's right. The mission. The gold."

"McKenny said they dug it up."

"They did."

"So it ain't there."

"It is," said Lloyd. "But it ain't buried. It's hid where nobody's thought to look."

Gil swallowed. He smacked his lips. "Goddamnit, Lloyd," his voice rasped. "I knew you knew. Ever since you was asking that son of a bitch trapper about them missions. I knew you knew something."

"It's a lot of gold."

"How much?"

"A whole lot. Enough to be rich the rest of your life."

"That much?"

"All the women you want."

"I knew you knew."

"All the drink."

"Goddamnit."

"You'll live in a castle like them kings they talk about."

"Is it that much?"

"It is. Setting there waiting to be found," he said over Gil's breathing. "And it's yours."

"Mine?"

"It can be."

"How?"

Lloyd scooted himself over the munitions bags. He hooked an elbow on the sideboard and pulled himself close enough he could smell the rot on Gil's teeth. "We go get it."

"Go get it?"

"McKenny says it ain't but a few miles yonder."

Gil drew back. He paced off a circle and came back to the

wagon. "You asking me to untie you?"

"When the fires are out. After they's gone to the tents."

"I ain't untying you, Lloyd."

"Ain't no other way."

"What about the captain?"

"Ain't nothing about him."

"He'll shoot me."

"You'll be long gone."

"No," Gil said. "No."

"Think of all that gold."

"I'm about to make lieutenant."

"You ain't gonna be no lieutenant, Gil."

"Yes I am."

"You think you gonna pass over a West Point man? You can't even read."

"Stroud likes me."

"Are you still shining his boots?"

Gil didn't answer.

"Eggars ain't shining no boots." Lloyd could smell the rotted gumline, smell the boy's unwashed body while he mulled this over. "There's only so far you're gonna get, Gil. And you done got there."

At the fires the men had risen and were kicking sand into the coals. Gil turned at the noise. He rubbed his jaw and ran his fingers to his forehead and pressed them there against his temples. He turned back suddenly to Lloyd. "What about the indian?"

"He don't want nothing with us. And we'll have our guns. You ain't scared of him are you, Gil?"

"No."

"You don't want him getting that gold, do you?"

"No."

"That's our gold, Gil. You and me. Fifty-fifty. We're partners."

"We ain't partners. You said so."

"Yes we are. We always been."

Gil stood silent at the edge of the wagon a long time. Were it not for the stench of him Lloyd might have thought the boy had disappeared back into the dark.

"I don't know," he said finally. "I like it here."

"Where?"

"In the cavalry. I'm doing good."

"You still think you'll make rank."

"Maybe."

Lloyd looked out past the coals where their dying light wiggled over the pale white tents. "I'll tell you something," said Lloyd. "Go to Stroud's tent. See who's in there with him."

"Who?"

"You know who. And when you see the two of them together you think about that gold just a'waitin'. Think about your life. And when everybody's asleep you come back here and untie me. Get my Harpers out of the other wagon. Bring a knife. We'll be partners again, Gil. And the rest of your life you'll live like a goddamn king."

Gil returned an hour later. He said nothing as he worked the ropes free. Neither did Lloyd. Only when the ropes had fallen and the Harpers exchanged hands did Gil employ his voice, alerting Lloyd that the Virginians had been assigned to night watch and were out circling the remuda.

The wagon moaned slightly when Lloyd stepped off. In the sand his sandals made only soft whispers. He reached behind him and pulled Gil along and together they circled wide around the encampment to where the horses stood like otherworldly creatures against the starlit sky. The space of a quarter hour they waited. Ears against the night. They heard the Virginians walk their loop around the herd, and when they'd reached the far end Lloyd stalked forward whispering to the horses with his hand stretched out until it found a mane, which he pulled gently out and away. The horse stepped with him. Gil's horse alongside.

They had no saddles. No bridles or reins. They walked the horses out a mile into the desert, hands gentle on the horses' crests, then stopped. Before they mounted up, Lloyd asked Gil to see the knife. Gil stepped around the front of the horse and drew the knife from his belt and offered it handle-out. He said nothing. No questions. He simply stretched his arm out and Lloyd took it.

The grip was leather-bound. Smooth in Lloyd's hand. For a moment the steel caught the dimmest glimmer of starlight, then lost it, the blade moving fast, stabbing forward and disappearing into Gil's throat. A gusher hot and black spewed over Lloyd's arm. He pulled the blade free and stabbed again, his other hand gripping a tuft of Gil's hair and jerking it forward against the knife. A gurgle choked out of the open wound and Gil's arms flew up and slapped against Lloyd's shoulders and still Lloyd plunged in with the knife, sluicing open the throat and lungs and stabbing even as Gil sank to the desert floor with Lloyd on top working the blade in and out, in and out, hacking like a mad butcher until the width of the boy's neck lay completely open and the head nearly amputated from the body. Only then he released his hold. He stepped back. Gil's leg twitched and died. Lloyd bent at the waist and ran the blade into the earth up to its handle. He did this twice, then pulled the Springfield from Gil's belt, retrieved the fallen Harpers, and walked to where his frightened horse had scampered. In a leap he took to its back. He tapped his sandals to its ribs and the horse bound forward. Gil's horse, alone in the dark, stood a moment in the smell of death and blood, then turned and trotted after.

The path Lloyd followed was neither visible nor certain. Instead he steered his horse's ears along the general direction of Black Paw's trajectory, picking out a star sitting low against the skyline and following it. He stopped often to listen. He heard many sounds, all soft and distant and none the ones for which his ears were fixed. Mostly he watched the skyline. He raked his eyes across the stars in hopes he'd see them twinkle through the willow branches. More than once he dismounted and flattened his cheek against the earth to dilate the angle.

The night turned cold and through this chill he rode a slow hour's march until direct before him the mission blotted out the low-slung stars and all around it danced the shadows of blooming purple flowers.

It measured not fifty feet by thirty. More a peasant's chapel than a stately Spanish mission. The shoveled floor had long since hardened back to solid mounds. On one of these Lloyd stood and swung his rifle. The reeds from where they sat across the sycamore beams fell in bunches at his feet. He swirled the weapon back and forth, smacking the barrel against the beams and leaping from mound to mound with his head bowed against the falling reeds until he heard the bag drop with them and the jangle of coins clink like windchimes in the dark.

His hands went scouring across the dirt. He found the bag and worked the drawstring open and dipped his fist into the coins. A long while he sat touching them. Cold and hard against his fingers. He picked them up and listened to them fall. Little golden symbols clashing in the bag. He drew tight the string and carried the treasure to an empty window and stared out at the stars gliding over the earth. He stood there a long time. Then he tucked the bag inside his shirt and exited the mission and mounted his horse and rode back in the direction he'd come.

He stopped the horse as frequently as before. He saw nothing. Nothing much there was to see. Instead he closed his eyes and held his ears against the night and waited for sounds not belonging to the desert. He sniffed the air. The horses fussed and he swung down and walked a hundred yards away and stood with the pouch of gold resting against his belly while a chill worked its way along his spine.

Back on the horse, riding with his eyes closed, he caught the smell of woodsmoke. He pulled at the animal's neck to stop it, and he took long pulls through his nostrils until he caught it again. He turned the horse. The other followed. The coterie of three trod another hundred yards across the desert, and when Lloyd held the party up to stop and listen again he heard finally the pure and candid sound of the infant crying.

He dropped to the ground. The Harpers in his right hand weighed eleven pounds. He hefted it, touched the handle of the Springfield with his left. He stepped forward. The horses fell in line behind him and he turned and pushed them back. Then he fixed his ears once more on the crying of the newborn and set his route upon it.

Some minutes later he found the camp. He circled and approached from downwind. Black Paw had hung the wagon canvas over sticks of desert willow, and from these same trees he'd broken wood and built a fire against a ledge. Its light played on the makeshift tent.

Lloyd crawled to the fire's edge and crouched and listened and stared at the canvas as though he might see through it. Inside the baby whimpered. Lloyd waited. He looked out onto the desert but nothing moved, nothing breathed. He rose suddenly. With the Harpers pointed forward he burst through the canvas flap.

The two sat side-by-side cross-legged in the dirt. The entire front of Molly's dress was unbuttoned and slung aside and her breasts were exposed and naked and covered only where she clutched the baby tight against them. She made no move at Lloyd's appearance, and even in that pale glow of firelight Lloyd could see that the baby suckling at her breast was Black Paw's child. Her bosom rose with her breath. With a free hand she lifted up the flap of her dress and covered herself.

The father made no motion save for his eyes. They drifted to the gun laying at his feet. Lloyd took notice. With one hand he pulled the weapon out of the indian's reach, then pointed the barrel of the Harpers squarely at his chest.

"A long time I been looking for you," said Lloyd. "You're a hard man to find."

Black Paw's eyes moved gently in their sockets. Lloyd could read no emotion in them.

"I never killed that trapper."

Black Paw didn't answer.

"I had his coat but I didn't kill him."

The baby squirmed. Molly made a shushing noise and readjusted her arms. Lloyd stole a glance but kept the barrel aimed where it was. "You was headed for that mission," he said. "Weren't you."

Like black like coals his eyes were, and not even the whites could Lloyd could see around them.

"You can tell me. That where you was going?"

"Yes," said Black Paw.

"You seen that slave all them years ago. That was you that seen him, wasn't it?"

"Yes."

"And now you're going back for it. All these years later."

"Yes."

"You thought you'd dig it up?"

"Yes."

"You know where he buried it?"

"No."

"Then how you reckon you was gonna find it?"

"I'll dig until I find it."

"Dig until you find it," Lloyd sniffed. "You know Captain Stroud already done it? He dug up the whole damn floor a couple years back. He didn't find no gold."

Black Paw gave no answer.

"But you reckon you'll dig anyway."

The indian looked at Molly and his newborn child and nodded. "I'll dig."

Lloyd held the barrel in his palm. His hand was warm. The finger of his right hand sat against the trigger. He could hear the baby nursing. Firelight danced on Molly's naked chest.

"Hell," said Lloyd. "You weren't never gonna find it."

Sixteen

The hold of darkness had not yet relented from the night when Lloyd swung off his horse at the edge of the cavalry's encampment. He laid the Harpers in the sand and drew the Springfield by the handle. He checked the load and tucked it back again.

Through snores of sleeping soldiers he walked. From canvas to canvas, over stakes and ropes. He used the balls of his feet, placing each one delicately in the sand until he reached the captain's tent. Outside he took a breath. He dipped into the flap. He held his breath and fought to establish, against the drumming in his ears, the exact spot of the captain's bedplace. He tucked the Harpers in his shoulder. He heard a rasp of breath.

He heard it again and he fired.

The explosion came with a flash of light, gone as quickly as it flared. He dropped the rifle and ripped the Springfield from his waist, and as he did he heard the crashing of the captain scrambling from his blankets. Lloyd's free hand clawed in an empty grasp, his arm swinging, fingers clutching out at nothing. The captain bellowed. Lloyd surged forward. He felt suddenly a nap of fabric in his hand. His fingers clutched it tight, yanked the garment closer.

He rammed the pistol forward, felt the barrel slam into resistance, and squeezed his trigger finger.

The blaze of light from off the pan lit Stroud's face an instant only, and in that light Lloyd saw the barrel thrust between the flawless teeth. He saw the captain's eyes, wide and fraught with horror. He saw all that in the space of a flash in the pan, an instant before the ball of lead tore through the captain's skull and painted its contents in a grimy swath across the sheet of canvas tent.

Lloyd let Stroud's body fall. He turned to the tent flap and ducked through.

Three lead balls caught him coming out; one from each Virginian's rifle, the last from John McKenny's. The man balanced his weapon in his one arm while shouting in a drunken panic his warning of indians attacking in the night, come to slit their throats. Slumped before the captain's tent Lloyd's body jerked and jerked again. Bullets came from nearly every soldier present, half-asleep and bursting from their tents to fire blindly on the shadowed unnamed intruder.

A wagonful of shovels made the digging quick. The surgeon broke planks from the sideboards and etched into them the names of Captain Thaddeus Stroud and Lloyd Raymond Reed, and these brittle tombstones were set deep into the ground at graves dug far apart from one another, for each man there knew the value of a closing favor for the dead.

Before they threw each man in the ground they emptied out their pockets. Stroud's valuables they divided among themselves. They planned to do the same with Lloyd, but on finding nothing more than a section of flint, a sewing kit consisting of one needle and half a spool of thread, and a knife they all recognized to be Gil's, they instead buried his meagre possessions with him.

They stood a moment at the graves after the last shovelful of dirt was cast. No word spoken or further ceremony given. The runted boy with the face of an imbecile asked aloud where Sergeant Pucker had gone to, and no answer did anyone put forth. Within the hour Sergeant Eggars hitched a wagon and climbed into the driving seat. The new recruits followed him. They rounded up the packmules and spare horses and drove them east into the rising sun where Fort Tackett sat a long way off beyond the Texan border.

The Virginians took with them a tent and a bag of rations and rode west. Francis Price and John McKenny loaded a barrel of whiskey to a packmule and took their two-man outfit south.

The surgeon was slow to lash his possessions to the mule he'd chosen. When at last his load was readied he stood beside his horse and gave a final glance at the wooden tombstones throwing shadows long behind them, then hiked a boot into the stirrup and rode into the desert.

He'd ridden not but a few miles when he came upon the imprints of Gil's horse walking alongside another. Moccasin tracks close by. He followed them up a rise, and when he crested it he saw down on the desert valley the woman riding bareback with the infant tight against her bosom, the black-haired indian walking along beside.

He sat his horse and watched until the family faded into the shimmering haze of the morning, then tugged at the mule's leadrope and turned his horse northward and disappeared into the wild.